TALES OF THE DJINN

THE LADY DETECTIVE

Emma Holly

Tales of the Djinn: The Lady Detective
Emma Holly

Discover other exciting Emma Holly titles at www.emmaholly.com

This story is a work of fiction and should be treated as such. It includes sexually explicit content that is only appropriate for adults—and not every adult at that. Those who are offended by more adventurous depictions of sexuality or frank language possibly shouldn't read it. Literary license has been taken in this book. It is not intended to be a sexual manual. Any resemblance to actual places, events, or persons living or dead is either fictitious or coincidental. That said, the author hopes you enjoy this tale!

ISBN-13: 9781731087348

Cover photos: bigstock—coka

THE LADY DETECTIVE

Beautiful genie Yasmin has many talents—the best of which might be changing into a cat!

Her crush on Joseph the Magician is less delightful. Forbidden to her when she was the sultan's wife, now that the harem has been disbanded, the handsome sorcerer seems further out of reach than ever. Better to pretend she never won her freedom than to risk him rejecting her.

Yasmin will have to get over that in short order. Her very first investigation has uncovered a deadly plot—and maybe more threats besides. When Joseph turns up at the same house party, she suspects he's on a mission too. If they hope to escape with their skins intact, Yasmin needs the genie of her dreams to supply backup!

A NOVEL OF THE DJINN

"Emma Holly transports you into a fantastic world of magic, mystery, and erotic delights . . . absolutely wonderful."—**In My Humble Opinion**

"Addictive. . . should not be missed!"
—**Long and Short Reviews**

OTHER TITLES BY EMMA HOLLY

The Prince with No Heart

The Assassins' Lover

Steaming Up Your Love Scenes (how-to)

Tales of the Djinn

The Guardian

The Double (sequel to *The Guardian)*

The Angel

The City of Endless Night (sequel to *The Angel)*

Sultan's Choice (sequel to *The City of Endless Night)*

The Lady Detective

The Billionaires

The Billionaire Bad Boys Club

Beck & Call

Lord & Master (sequel to *Beck & Call)*

The Billionaire's Bodyguard (formerly *Star Crossed)*

Hidden Series

Hidden Talents

Hidden Depths

Date Night

Move Me

The Faerie's Honeymoon

Hidden Crimes

Winter's Tale

Hidden Dragons

Hidden Passions

CHAPTER ONE

The Lady Detective

Once you'd lived the pampered life of a royal concubine, hanging out a shingle as a 'gumshoe' might be considered a step down. Yasmin Baykal disagreed. She couldn't have been readier for her third official day as a detective.

Her first had consisted of rearranging file cabinets. Her second involved finding a young girl's lost parakeet, for which she'd accepted payment in doll money. Though she didn't regret this, she wasn't exactly speeding up the heights of accomplishment.

That was yesterday, however. Every morning was a fresh start. In the name of preparing for what she hoped, today she'd pre-charged a stylus and laid a fresh blank scroll to the right of her red blotter. Her low wood desk, a lucky find at an estate sale, shone from a brisk polish. She'd plumped the floor cushion opposite in anticipation of visiting bottoms. She *believed* her clothes projected professionalism. Though it pained her to constrain one of her better features, she'd spelled her long glossy hair into a braided bun. Her navy satin tunic and black trousers couldn't have been more different than the filmy jeweled seductions she'd worn as a harem girl.

The cost to her vanity didn't matter. The only enhancements her new job called for were practical.

Honoring practicality, the wall of shelves behind her held well-thumbed books on spellcraft, plus the Glorious City's yawn-inducing ordinance manuals. A pull-down shade hid a whiteboard in a niche to her left. The board was enchanted, designed not just for organizing cases but also for accessing the city's information network. Having splurged on these tools, frugality necessitated leasing her second-floor office in a less salubrious neighborhood. Because the harbor was a mere block away, on the ledge of the single window a stick of incense burned. The slowly rising coil of sweetness *almost* masked the smell of brine.

On the bright side, the scented smoke created a homey atmosphere—suited toward confidences between strangers. Yasmin was good at eliciting those. People tended to trust her, even when maybe they shouldn't.

Now all she needed was a client.

On cue, her teenage brother Balu tapped on the office's inner door. He'd convinced Yasmin to hire him as her secretary, claiming he'd die of boredom stuck at home. Living with their parents felt flat compared to the time he'd recently spent in the human world. For him, what started as a frightening abduction at the hands of their older brother had turned into an adventure. Balu was obsessed with humans—like many djinn his age. To them, the younger race was the epitome of 'coolness.' Given Balu's enthusiasms, Yasmin hoped hiring him hadn't been a mistake. Nepotism was frowned on for a reason.

"Yasmin," her brother called impatiently through the frosted glass. "Shake a leg. A gentlewoman is here to consult you."

A real gentlewoman? Here in her humble establishment? Yasmin glanced around with her pulse jumping in her throat. She didn't have time to fancy up anything.

"Show her in," she said, taking a moment to smooth her tunic front.

Her jaw dropped quite unprofessionally when she saw her visitor. The elegant female was indeed a gentlewoman, daughter to one their city's most illustrious families. She was also personally familiar.

"Safiye," Yasmin gasped unthinkingly.

Like Yasmin, Safiye had been a concubine. Sultan Iksander's dissolution of the harem had cut her loose as well. Unlike Yasmin, Safiye hadn't welcomed her liberation. Clever and beautiful, she'd thought her prospects for winning their master's affections all to herself were better than even. Iksander choosing a human as his exclusive wife had dashed those ambitions.

Yasmin prayed Safiye didn't suspect her role in nudging that unusual match into being. The former courtesan wasn't just ambitious. She was formidable.

Yasmin cleared her suddenly scratchy throat. "Forgive me," she said, rising from her cushion to incline her head politely. "Lady Toraman, I should have said. I didn't mean to be familiar. Seeing you surprised me."

"We've soaked naked in the same hammam," Safiye tossed off dryly. "If that doesn't put us on a first name basis, I don't know what would."

The djinniya looked around, dropping her stylish headscarf to straight shoulders. Decorated with swirling pearls, the silk was saffron, its drape luxuriant. Diamonds dotted her peacock blue bodice all the way to her curled slippers. Suppressing a pang of envy for these splendors, Yasmin hoped her visitor had come by closed palanquin. Displaying so much wealth in this neighborhood practically begged thieves to attack her.

Her survey of the office finished, Safiye turned dark, shining eyes to Yasmin. Her painted mouth glistened the color of pomegranates, her lashes so thick they too could have been augmented. If they were, they pointed up the beauty she'd been born with. Her expression showed very little. Safiye never had been emotional.

The comment she uttered next was cool. "I'd have thought Iksander's settlement would cover more impressive furnishings."

"Yes," Yasmin agreed, ordering herself not to look insulted. The sultan *had* been generous when divorcing his former wives. "I've economized to ensure the sum will last."

"I was under the impression your family was made of money. Isn't your father an exporter?"

A smile tugged the corners of Yasmin's lips. Calling her father a mere exporter was disingenuous. He'd pioneered a process for shipping goods across the misty In-Betweens that separated djinn territories. As a result, his firm had prospered enormously. Naturally, old-money aristocrats like the Toramans couldn't help but find his success offensive.

"The Goddess blessed him," she conceded. "I, however, prefer to stand on my own two feet."

Safiye pressed her lips together. "That's very modern of you, I'm sure."

Yasmin doubted Safiye valued being modern even a little bit. Ignoring this, she went on. "I assume you didn't come here just to renew our acquaintance."

Safiye's look of prim disapproval intensified. "I believe your secretary is bringing tea."

She was correct to scold. No respectable djinniya engaged in business without the niceties. Luckily, before she had to apologize for her lapse, Balu bustled in with the tray. Despite being skinny as a rail—much the same as Yasmin at his age—he had no trouble maneuvering gracefully. He set the laden platter on the desk, pouring two steaming glasses as the women took cushions. Though polite, he didn't seem overawed by their visitor.

Probably he'd have been more dazzled by a human female in torn blue jeans.

"Ladies," he said, including Yasmin in the term. "I'll be in the outer office if you need anything."

Yasmin had to admit he'd performed neatly.

"Well," Safiye said once she'd sipped. "I won't keep you in suspense. I'm here because a gentleman has requested my hand in marriage. His name is Stefan. He's the sole living heir to the Dimitriou estate."

"Congratulations," Yasmin murmured politely.

"Stefan is well regarded. Many djinniya have vied for his attention."

"I'm not surprised you accomplished what they failed to."

The compliment—which was true enough—didn't soften Safiye's stiff posture. "I'm not certain I ought to accept his offer."

"You doubt his honesty?"

Interestingly, considering how self-controlled she normally was, Safiye squirmed on her cushion. "I don't know what I doubt. Stefan is intelligent and charming. Handsome enough, even when compared to Iksander. My family adores him. As for myself, I feel . . . an affection I can't deny."

"But?" Yasmin prompted.

Safiye winced. "After being so mistaken about Iksander, I hesitate to trust my judgment. I can't afford to be that wrong twice. The restoration of my status depends on this union succeeding."

"Forgive me for being indelicate, but do you fear he'll be unfaithful?"

"I'm sure he will," Safiye surprised her by saying. "He's a man, and I'm a realist. He's promised to take no wife but me. That is sufficient for my pride. What concerns me are the things I do not know that I do not know. Unfortunate habits or sketchy associations. Does he gamble or secretly dress up like a dinosaur? Something in me thinks he's too good to be true. If I know his skeletons, I can decide if I'm willing to risk them embarrassing me."

"I can do some digging," Yasmin offered. "The city has rules about how much snooping I can do magically, but I can certainly research his background and finances."

"I'd be happy to commission that report, but what I wish to ask of you involves a . . . more personal approach."

"Yes?" Yasmin asked, unnerved by the woman's sudden intensity.

Safiye blew out her breath. "I haven't officially given Stefan my answer. I promised I would this weekend. He has invited me and other of his associates to a gathering at his country house. If I accept, he plans to announce our engagement then."

"He is confident."

Safiye waved off the observation. "His confidence isn't unattractive. Not to me anyway. I know some in the harem overlooked you, but I always sensed your cleverness. I'd like you to accompany me this weekend, Friday to Monday, to take Stefan's measure in person."

Yasmin didn't bother tugging her eyebrows down. "You do know I don't have much experience. I can't swear I'd pull off going undercover."

"You won't be undercover. As long as you don't mention your current job, you're free to come as yourself. No one will blink if I invite a friend from my days at court." She had enough sensitivity to read Yasmin's reaction. 'Friends' weren't what they'd been by a long shot. "If you prefer, I can call you an acquaintance. What matters is that you be there with your eyes open. You're respectable enough for this party, if that's what concerns you."

Yasmin suspected it concerned Safiye more than her. "You're sure you don't want to hire a more seasoned investigator?"

"You mean a man? Because that would be my only choice. You're this city's only female detective." Safiye shook her head. "How could I trust a male to keep faith with me, to even understand my interests? Whether I like it or not, you've cornered the market on djinniya detecting."

This was less flattering than Safiye's claim to respect her cleverness. "May I have time to think?"

"I hope you're not this timid about everything!"

Her exclamation inspired a smile. Though Safiye didn't know it, there'd been more than one occasion when Yasmin had been reckless. "You needn't doubt my courage. I simply wish to make the correct decision for both of us."

"Fine." Safiye pushed huffily to her feet. "Consult the tea leaves or whatever you need to do. I have to know by tomorrow. If you agree, contact me via scroll. We can discuss your payment then."

Yasmin barely had time to curtsey before Safiye puffed into her smoke form and streaked out the window. Yasmin guessed this answered the question of how the richly dressed female arrived safely.

"All right," she called to her brother. "Lady Toraman is gone. You can stop hovering at the door."

"Didn't hear a thing," Balu assured her as he strolled in. "Your privacy spell was tight."

"You're not supposed to try to crack it. Client-detective privilege is sacrosanct."

"I'm your assistant. I'm in the bubble too. Anyway, how can you know the shield is working if I don't push?"

"*Balu.*"

"*Yasmin.*"

"Don't make me sorry for hiring you."

"Ha." He tossed his dark walnut locks and grinned. "Me being here to watch your back is the reason Father consented to let you go into this business."

"I'm a grown woman," she grumbled, though his statement was true. "Perfectly capable of watching my own back. Has Father forgotten I was instrumental in rescuing you from those traffickers?"

"I don't need convincing. I think djinniya should be allowed to run their lives."

"Don't let Mother hear you say that." Their female parent was very conservative.

Undaunted by the reminder, Balu punched her shoulder. "So, sis. Do we have a client or not?"

"Maybe. I expected to ease into being a detective with simpler jobs. More missing pets or employee background checks. Safiye wants to throw me in the deep end."

"You can swim. And she certainly can pay."

She could. And that was a strong incentive. For her pride as much as anything.

"I'll do a quick look-see into the man she wants me to observe. Make sure this weekend doesn't catch me unprepared."

"This weekend?"

Before Yasmin could explain, the sound of footfalls in the outer office caused her and Balu to straighten.

"Hello?" called a polite male voice. "Is anyone about?"

Yasmin's palms broke into an instant sweat. What was Joseph the Magician doing here? Before she could control the self-betrayal, her hands flew up to tidy her perfectly ordered hair. She hadn't seen Joseph since his return from the human realm. Maybe she shouldn't have expected to while the harem remained in force. The rules of seclusion forbade outside male contact. After, though, Joseph could have sent her a scroll message. At the minimum, simple politeness allowed for that.

Not surprisingly, considering her inner turmoil, Balu was quicker than she to greet their visitor.

"Sir!" he exclaimed from the outer room. "How gracious of you to honor us!"

"I told you to call me Joseph," the sorcerer said. His kind, smooth voice set Yasmin's spine tingling. "When two have faced enemies together, too much formality is an insult."

"Of course, sir," Balu agreed, still awed by his idol. Though her brother was no slouch at magic, the royal magician occupied his own rarefied level. "I mean Joseph. What are you doing here?"

Joseph laughed, and that did tingly things to her insides too. "I have brought a good will gift. And well wishes for your business. I wonder, is your sister available?"

Joseph's question made her realize she was hiding in her office as if *she* were a teenager.

"Yasmin!" Balu called. "Get your rear into Reception."

Face flaming with annoyance, she yanked the thumbnail she'd been biting out from between her teeth. Balu chose a fine time to forget civil speech! But she'd have to rebuke him later. For now, she flipped her plain white scarf to her ears, clenched her teeth, and went out.

Though she'd braced, Joseph's looks hit her as forcefully as she'd feared. Narrow of face with precision-cut, sharp features, the famous magician was strikingly handsome. Tall but not towering, lean but still muscular, his skin was an appealing toasty brown. His naturally ruddy lips—which he had the habit of pressing into a line—were too thin to count as classically beautiful, though they appealed to her. His hair was darker than hers and gleamed like mahogany. Set off by the contrast, his honey-gold irises glowed within thick lashes.

"Miss Baykal," he said, bowing deeply from the waist. Apparently, his rules concerning formality didn't apply to her. She'd faced more enemies at his side than her brother; had risked actual death, if it came to that. Maybe she'd been presumptuous to think of him as her friend, but they'd certainly been allies.

"Joseph," she said coolly in return. "How nice to see you again."

He straightened and cleared his throat. "I hope I'm not intruding. I brought you—and Balu, of course—an 'office warming' gift." He held out an ugly green spiky plant in a round silver pot. "Georgie . . . that is to say, the kadin laid a blessing on it. To promote good fortune in your endeavors."

Georgie was the sultan's new human wife. The gesture was a kind one. Among the djinn, human blessings had special potency. On the other hand, the kadin's contribution meant the gift wasn't Joseph's idea alone. Maybe, in truth, he'd been pushed into bringing it.

Refusing to let that sting, Yasmin accepted the pot from him.

"The plant is called dragon's tongue," he said. "I'm told they are hard to kill even if you neglect them. I added a tiny spell of my own, so the leaves will snap at anyone but you or Balu. You could hide keys in it if you wish."

"That was thoughtful," she responded.

Perhaps she sounded stiff. A flush of color rose into his smooth lean cheeks. "Well. Please enjoy it in good health. I'll let you return to your business."

Without more ado, he turned and exited down the stairs. If Yasmin had been paying more attention to what she did, she wouldn't have drifted to the front window to watch him reemerge on the street below. When he did, the famous magician seemed to be muttering exasperatedly to himself.

What, she wondered, did *he* have to be annoyed about?

Balu thought he knew. He smacked her arm sharply. "You don't have to be rude. Just because Joseph isn't a whole man, you shouldn't look down on him."

For a moment she couldn't speak. The last thing Yasmin did was look down on Joseph. Or think of him as anything but whole. Like most everyone in the Glorious City, Balu believed Joseph was a eunuch. The story of his teenage maiming was infamous.

As far as Yasmin knew, only she and Joseph were aware the condition no longer applied to him.

Some months ago, a vengeful empress laid a curse on their fair city. Filled with hatred for Iksander, Luna turned every resident into a stone statue. Only at the last moment had Joseph, the sultan, and two other trusted officials escaped the enchantment. Thanks to a spell that doubled their bodies, they'd projected copies of themselves through special portals into the human world. There they'd regrouped, returning as soon as they were able to free the populace. Yasmin had been among the first citizens to wake. With the capital still in shambles, she'd worked with Joseph to foil a plot her older brother had been mixed in. Along the way, she'd discovered the doubling process had healed his body. Joseph the so-called Eunuch could be with women any way he—or they—desired.

Yasmin reminded herself it wasn't her place to reveal that.

"I assure you," she told her brother, finding her tongue at last. "I have the utmost regard for him."

Balu seemed unconvinced. He faced her with one gangly shoulder propped on the front window. "Sometimes I think you and I forget our good fortune. No matter if our brother Ramis turned evil, we grew up with parents who cared for us. We were never homeless. Never hungry. Never desperate or in danger with no one to rescue us. Joseph knew all those hardships and more besides. You should consider offering him an apology."

"An apology! Balu, I appreciate how much you look up to Joseph. In truth, I think well of you for it. Apologizing, however, would only embarrass him. Joseph knows I don't consider him . . . incomplete."

She willed her cheeks not to heat. Balu scowled at her skeptically.

"I'm telling the truth," she insisted. "In any case, if I take this assignment, I won't have time for groveling."

Balu folded his arms.

"Do you want to hear what Lady Toraman asked or not?"

"Fine," he said, his desire to be in-the-know as strong as hers would have been. "We can discuss what you owe the best protector our city has later."

~

To Yasmin's relief, learning about Lady Toraman's case distracted Balu from lecturing her. He left her in peace, returning to his desk in the outer office while she fired up the spelled whiteboard. A glance at its formula manual enabled her to access the larger municipal information pools. As it turned out, her look-see at Safiye's would-be fiancé wasn't a quick process. Stefan Dimitriou was a press darling. The Glorious City's newspapers were a rich if not completely trustworthy source of material.

As Safiye claimed, Stefan was well regarded. Every other article Yasmin found described him as 'dashing' or 'princely.' Tragically, when he was fifteen, his parents died in a train derailment. Too much magic accumulated on the tracks, and their car jumped free. The local authorities ruled it an accident, and new safety measures were put in place.

The changes came too late for Stefan's parents, but the estate they left to their son was large. Originally a banking family, the Dimitrious funded previous sultans' wars. Since most of the wars were won, land and titles were their reward. Stefan's current seat was the bucolic town of Milion in Edgeward Province, where he seemed to enjoy playing Lord Bountiful. Yasmin pulled up pictures of him cutting ribbons for public parks, soaring down grassy fields on polo carpets, and—most laudable of all—opening an institution for poor orphans.

"No one's that saintly," she murmured to herself. Then again, if a djinni had sufficient wealth and influence, he could control his narratives.

She considered the latest picture she'd summoned onto the board, then enlarged it with two fingers. Dimitriou was good looking. Not an earth shaker like Iksander or even Joseph but worth a second glance. The polo pictures displayed his athleticism and the fire with which he competed. He had the sort of grin men and women would be drawn to: cocky but not bad-natured. He wore his caramel brown hair tousled, the twinkle in his eye unmistakable. The average well-brought-up djinniya might be wary of such a man, but she'd be interested.

As for the orphans whose school he'd built, to a one they turned adoring faces toward their benefactor. Their expressions made Balu's hero worship of Joseph seem mild by comparison.

Yasmin sighed and shifted on her slippers. She'd been standing in front of the board for an hour, during which time she'd discovered nothing Safiye couldn't and probably had found out for herself.

A snapping noise behind her caused her to jump. The ugly plant she'd set on the desk had killed a wandering fly. That was useful, she supposed.

"Going for lunch," Balu called through the door. "I'll bring you back something."

She murmured a vague response, still absorbed in gazing at the board. Despite her fears, her brother was a good secretary. Taking this job would help her pay him. She pinched her lower lip. Maybe Safiye was right about the need to observe Dimitriou in person. If Yasmin were in his house with permission, she could scan him magically. According to city ordinances, expectations of privacy didn't apply the same to guests.

Yasmin also had other talents she could bring into play. One in particular Safiye didn't suspect she had. All those years confined to the harem with so few visits from Iksander, she'd had little to do that interested her. She'd staved off boredom by honing her magic. Though trans-animorphism wasn't a common gift, she'd learned to shift form into a cat. Too many times to count, she'd snuck out of the palace through a drainpipe. That had been *quite* the violation of harem rules. Iksander could have thrown her in prison or banished her. He'd forgiven her because her nightly wanderings had uncovered an awful crime.

If she accompanied Safiye to Edgeward Province, her cat might prove equally useful there.

I'll do it, she decided with a surge of adrenaline. If she'd wanted to play it safe, she shouldn't have chosen detecting as a career.

A moment later, she had a more daunting thought. Stefan Dimitriou represented the tippy-top of the social ladder. Even if his weekend guests were a few rungs down, Yasmin's current working-class attire wasn't appropriate. She needed the sort of wardrobe she'd worn before—not simply in the harem but as the pampered daughter of a rich exporter.

To her dismay, she knew just where to obtain it.

CHAPTER TWO

Prodigal Daughter

"I knew your luck would return," Yasmin's mother Vinca crowed happily. "I've been praying and lighting candles ever since the sultan abandoned you."

They were in the family villa, in what Vinca still referred to as Yasmin's room. For the last ten minutes, she'd been going through Yasmin's closet, pulling out old garments she'd thought could be rescued. Those she clucked over less were tossed onto the bed. Those she deemed irredeemable she returned to the shameful depths.

Resigned to letting her take charge, Yasmin perched on an empty corner of the mattress. "Iksander didn't abandon me."

"He practically tossed you into the street. And for what? To take a human as his kadin! Don't get me started on that male he and she share as their consort. What sort of name is Connor for a djinni? He might as well be foreign too."

"I believe he *is* foreign. I met him briefly. He struck me as very kind. His heart chakra was immense."

"His heart chakra," Vinca repeated dismissively. "When I was your age, males didn't carry on with males."

"I'm sure they did," Yasmin said. "You just didn't hear about it."

"I'd rather not hear about it now!"

In spite of her own feelings on the matter, Yasmin laughed. "Don't pack that," she objected, tugging a gown from her mother's hands.

"But you look beautiful in pink. And the gold embroidery is fantastic."

"Pink is girlish. I'd rather be taken for the adult I am."

"I suppose," her mother said then recovered her brighter mood. "It was nice of Lady Toraman to invite you as her companion. You're sure to meet important people. Maybe even a nice djinni. If this weekend works out, you can quit that ridiculous career you've insisted on."

Yasmin rubbed her temple. Her mother assumed the invitation to the party was genuine. Yasmin didn't disabuse her. For one thing, she took client confidentiality seriously. If she told the truth, her mother might guess what the job concerned. For another thing, Vinca always made her feel a little cowardly.

"I know," her mother said, noting her discomfort if not its precise cause. "You think I'm getting ahead of myself. If I am, I don't see how you can blame me. You're a wonderful girl—smart and gifted and lovely inside and out. You deserve a husband you can be proud of every bit as much as your old harem mate."

"Safiye *wants* a husband," Yasmin said. "I want my own future."

"There's no reason your future can't include a worthy male. Your friend obviously knows that. Stefan Dimitriou is an up-and-comer. Last year he was elected Speaker for his province. Admittedly, it's only Edgeward, and that's the back of beyond. The position, however, is responsible."

Her knowledge surprised Yasmin. "You've followed Dimitriou's career?"

"Certainly. Your father likes to read up on politics. Lots of people in our circle find Dimitriou interesting."

Her parents' circle included fellow area merchants, most of them prosperous.

"What else do they say about him?"

"You're really curious?"

"I'd like to know who I'm going to meet."

Her mother laid down the rose red tunic she'd been folding. "Well, they say he's very intelligent. A bit of a lady's man but willing to settle down—as I expect Lady Toraman means to prove. Quite a few believe Dimitriou wouldn't have gotten us into the awful trouble Iksander did. They claim he'd have found a way to prevent Empress Luna from cursing our poor city."

Yasmin felt as if the breath had been stolen from her lungs. She couldn't say exactly why her mother's words disturbed her, only that the reaction was powerful.

"Really?" she said once she'd recovered. "They talk about Dimitriou in those terms?"

Her mother shrugged. "No sultanate lasts forever."

This statement shocked her anew. "Mother, Iksander is good man. He cares about his people. He and his friends risked their lives for ours many times over. He's devoted to everyone's well-being."

"I'm just repeating what I've heard people say." Her mother could tell Yasmin disapproved. Her expression turned stubborn. "It's possible to have too much progressiveness. Honestly, Yasmin I don't know why you're defending him."

"Because I know Iksander. I've seen up close what he's made of." She took her mother's hand and squeezed. "You know I'm clever, right? You've said yourself I'm lovely inside and out. Please be careful around djinn who talk like that. I don't think they're as light of spirit as you and Father are."

She'd chosen words designed to get through to her. When her older brother Ramis was seventeen, before he embarked on his life of crime, he'd killed a friend out of jealousy. Though the family disowned him as soon as he necessarily turned ifrit, the shame of his fall still burned. Yasmin's mother wouldn't take talk of dark spirits casually.

A single family member turning demon was sufficient.

"You're being dramatic," Vinca said, though she didn't sound confident.

"Perhaps. Just don't mistake a longing for the past as an actual good idea. Who knows if things really were as picture-perfect as your friends remember."

Vinca laughed. "You sound like your father." She imitated his deeper voice. "'Vinca, sometimes young folk are worth listening to.'"

"Father's a wise man," Yasmin said with exaggerated solemnity.

"You only say that when he agrees with you." Her mood restored, Vinca shook her head at the colorful heap of silk she'd piled up. "I should get these clothes to the servants. Make sure they have sufficient time to magick them into resembling this year's fashions."

"Don't push them to overdo it. It's only one weekend."

"You know Aysa. She'll consider it a personal affront if you aren't dressed to equal any djinniya there." Vinca patted Yasmin's shoulder before she could say more. "Change into something nice for dinner. Your father's so excited to have you and Balu home. Tonight will be like old times for him."

Knowing this was probably true, Yasmin rose to give her mother a little hug. "Thank you, Mama. You and Papa teach me what good marriages ought to be."

"Well." Her mother blinked in bright-eyed surprise. "I wish you one as happy, sweetie. That goes for your father too."

~

Dinner *was* like old times, warm and jovial and silly with family jokes. Yasmin enjoyed it more than she expected. Yes, her parents—especially her mother—wanted her to be a person she no longer was. Nonetheless, that they loved her she couldn't doubt. Unlike some harem member's families, the Baykals wouldn't reject her just because the sultan withdrew his favor. Perhaps her parents *did* feel the loss of honor, but Yasmin was their treasured daughter. They'd always welcome her.

It was late before they walked out to the villa's garden to say goodbye. The night was clear and starry, the temperature a kiss cooler than djinn skin. Because she now had a trunk full of clothes to carry, her father pressed her to accept the loan of a rug and driver to fly her home.

"I won't refuse," she said. "I'm too full of good food to smoke."

Her father smiled and clasped her face fondly. "You could sleep here tonight."

"Lady Toraman wants to leave early in the morning. I'd rather not have to rush."

"I worry about you living by yourself in that neighborhood."

Yasmin had a small apartment above her office, which her father had visited. "You know my knack for security spells. I'm as safe in my little nest as I'd be anywhere."

"But—"

"No, Papa. I like being on my own."

"At least let Balu go with you tomorrow. Edgeward Province is so close to the In-Betweens. Things go funny out there sometimes."

"We talked about this," she said as patiently as she could. "Balu wasn't invited. And Lady Toraman will have guards."

"I could pretend to be your guard," Balu said, wanting to go for different reasons than protecting her. "No one has to know I'm your brother."

Though Yasmin understood his yen to join the detecting mission, she was wound tight enough on her own account. She didn't want to risk him doing something impulsive and blowing their cover.

"It's just a house party. Nothing bad is going to happen."

"Goddess grant something good will." For once, Yasmin's mother was on her side of an argument. She patted her daughter's shoulders and kissed her cheeks. "Don't be nervous, sweetie," Vinca said for her ears alone. "You're as good as anyone. Be yourself and you're sure to shine."

Yasmin hugged her in thanks for the encouragement.

"I'm ready, miss," the driver announced politely from a flat stretch of grass. "Whenever you'd like to leave."

Her trunk was loaded in the center of the family's best antique: a silk-wool Persian with a large blue and cream pattern. The edges were already folded up for the flight. Taking her father's hand for balance, Yasmin stepped over the box's side. The cushions were new, she noticed, and cushy to sit on.

"Take care," her father said as the carpet began to lift.

"Good luck," Balu added with a wave.

"I packed *one* pink outfit," her mother called. "It's not too girly. You'll thank me, I promise."

Yasmin laughed. Of course she'd packed something pink. Yasmin's stubborn streak hadn't come from nowhere.

CHAPTER THREE

Traveling Companions

Yasmin agreed to meet Safiye in the Glorious City's main railway terminal, a building that had always been a personal favorite. Swimming inside with sun, thick silver arches supported the sparkling glass that roofed the long concourse. Her father's company, Baykal Shipping, ran a busy kiosk there. Thanks to an adaptation of his secret method, ordinary people could send small packages to far-flung points in the dimension. Though Yasmin didn't have time to stop at the booth this morning, she enjoyed knowing her family was part of the beautiful station's traditions.

Fortunately, Safiye had already messaged her the number for their train. By the time Yasmin tipped a porter to take her trunk, the shiny blue line of cars waited at Platform B. Less common than carpet travel, trains were still popular. The rails they rolled on reduced the magic required to run, which meant more than the very rich could afford tickets. That consideration wouldn't weigh with Lady Toraman. Hastening her steps, Yasmin bypassed the third- and second-class carriages.

Only first-class concerned her now.

Slightly breathless, she found Safiye already settled in a plush private compartment. Seated on a mauve velvet chair, she was a vision in layered powder blue and silver, every drape of the shimmering cloth an artistic creation. Uncountable tiny diamonds swirled along the borders of her garments. The effect was one of exquisite wealth and taste.

I could show off more, her appearance whispered. *But I'm too confident.*

Yasmin suddenly felt gauche in her ruby and orange silk outfit.

Never mind that, though. Aysa knew what suited Yasmin's figure and coloring. She looked as well as it was possible for her to. Safiye glanced up from her scroll version of *Town and Country* and widened her eyes at her.

"Good morning," she said. "You look nice."

She didn't sound entirely pleased—which made Yasmin think her travel clothes were fine after all.

"Thank you," she said, taking the chair opposite. "I had to go home to pack. The family maids pulled a cut-and-stitch refurbish on some of my old wardrobe. I didn't want to let you down by looking second rate."

The confession unbent Safiye at least a bit. "I rang for tea, but I expect the porters are swamped right now."

"No doubt. I'll try to find one later, once the rush settles down."

Safiye nodded and said no more as the train cars began to roll. Concluding her companion wasn't feeling chatty, Yasmin pulled her own scroll out of her shoulder bag. The city papers were loaded on it, plus a triple password-protected file of her research on Dimitriou. She'd add notes once she had anything to observe. Better yet, since her and her brother's scrolls shared a spy-proof link, she could message him if she needed information she couldn't access on site.

That sparked a thought that should have occurred to her earlier.

"I forgot to ask," she said. "How are the scroll signals out in Edgeward?"

"Scroll signals?"

"Are they chancy? Milion is awfully close to the In-Betweens. Sometimes that screws up magical messaging."

"I don't know. This will be my first trip. Up till now I've only socialized with Stefan in the city." A small crease appeared on Safiye's otherwise flawless brow. "The proximity of the mists is that disruptive? Having no outside communication wouldn't be convenient."

"I'm sure we'll manage," Yasmin soothed, though she disliked the idea too. "Someone in town is sure to have a signal stabilizer. Maybe even Stefan will."

"Maybe," Safiye said. Allowing her scroll to roll up, she set it on the small table between them. "You've been near the borders of the world before?"

"When I was younger. Because of my father's work. They're different sorts of places. Beautiful, depending on your taste. You have to get used to them."

Safiye raised her eyebrows. "Hopefully, I'll be able to. Stefan spends a good portion of his year out there."

Yasmin hesitated, unsure she ought to say what her personal attitude urged her to. After a moment, she gave in. "You know you don't *have* to marry him. Even if there's nothing categorically wrong with Dimitriou, a woman like you has her pick of men."

"Do I?" Safiye asked wryly. "Being cast off by the sultan rather brands me as damaged goods."

"Nonsense. No djinni worth his smoke could think of you that way. You're intelligent and cultured. And extremely beautiful. That the sultan chose you in the first place marks you as the ideal of what elite males desire."

"And yet Iksander didn't make me his kadin. Twice other djinniya won that prize."

"That doesn't mean there's anything wrong with you."

Unconvinced, Safiye shook her head.

"I'm not flattering you," Yasmin said, leaning forward across her knees. "I think Iksander simply wanted a . . . different type."

Safiye snorted sardonically. "You mean a type whose heart he didn't have to chisel down to with an icepick."

"There's nothing wrong with being cautious! No female who values herself bestows her esteem lightly."

"You might," Safiye said. "You're softer than I am."

"I *look* softer," Yasmin denied firmly. "The male who mistakes me for truly pliant risks having his ears pinned back." To demonstrate, she formed the index-and-pinkie gesture for a defensive curse.

Safiye laughed, her body relaxing into her chair. "You're better company than I thought."

Yasmin was glad she felt that way. They'd pass as friends more easily. Curious to see how far they'd progressed, she glanced out the compartment window. The rosy fringed shade was up, the landscape outside edging toward suburbs instead of town. Red-roofed villas, still close together but not as cheek-to-jowl, gleamed bright and cheerful within private walled gardens.

Her smile slipped as she spied one house with a crack jagging up its front. The palm by its gate had toppled, dead brown and moldering. No living resident would tolerate such eyesores, which meant the villa's owners probably were no more. Everything *wasn't* bright and cheerful. Despite Iksander and his friends' best efforts, some djinn hadn't survived Empress Luna's curse.

Unwilling to let dark thoughts overtake her, she blew out a breath and stood. "Why don't I nab us a tea platter? We'll be sitting a while. I may as well stretch my legs."

She hardly needed to justify taking the subordinate role. Accustomed to being served, Safiye nodded absently.

Because she couldn't go wrong appearing modest, Yasmin covered her hair before exiting. The side corridor was narrow. Coupled with the swaying motion, sidling down it demanded care. The conductors knew the trick of flattening against the windows to let wobbly passengers by. Not so adept herself, Yasmin sighed in relief as she spotted the lit-up sign for the dining car.

She'd let down her guard too soon. A gentleman stepped out of a compartment directly in front of her.

She gasped as a sudden lurch unbalanced her into him.

"Oh," he said, turning to steady her by the arms. "Pardon me. I didn't—"

Yasmin jerked and so did he. Joseph was the man who'd caught her, tall and strong and very much in the broad-shouldered flesh. He was dressed more flamboyantly than she knew to be his habit, his tunic a vivid yellow nipped by a lime green sash. He resembled a prosperous businessman more than a buttoned-up royal sorcerer. For one brief moment his striking face lit with pleasure at seeing her. A second later, disapproval wiped out the reaction.

"Yasmin, what are you doing here?"

A partial truth seemed easiest. "I'm traveling to Milion with a friend."

"A friend," he repeated.

"I do have them."

Her offended tone spurred a tiny flinch. "Of course you do. I didn't—" He paused to regroup his thoughts. "Yasmin, perhaps Edgeward isn't the best place to journey to. Not just now anyway."

Well, wasn't that a highhanded male utterance? Yasmin put up her chin. "Whether it is or not, 'just now' I need to reach the restaurant car."

Ignoring her racing pulse, she began to brush by him. Joseph caught her wrist. His hold was gentle but arresting. He lowered his voice to speak to her ears alone.

"Forgive me. I have no right to tell you where you can go. I'm simply concerned for your safety."

Did he realize his thumb stroked the sensitive tendon inside her arm? To say this was distracting understated the case by miles. Hot chills chased along her nerves, heating and softening her core.

Don't pay attention to that, she thought.

"What do you mean?" she demanded, matching his muted tone. "Why wouldn't I be safe? Are you going to Milion too?"

"I'm sorry, I can't—" He stopped as he caught sight of someone behind her. "Damn it. Say nothing about my warning . . . and don't ask more questions."

This last he said in a hiss. She might have argued if the situation had given her a chance.

"There you are, Joe, old boy," the newcomer said.

Yasmin turned to see what sort of djinni referred to Joseph the Magician in this familiar way. To her surprise, for the second time in as many minutes, she caused a man to stop short.

"Good heavens," he exclaimed. "It's Yasmin Baykal, isn't it?"

Yasmin could only blink. Did everyone on this train know her?

The man laughed. "You don't remember me, do you? Eamon Pappus. From the boys' school down the lane from your girls' institute." He winked at Joseph. "I chased this female to the abyss and back. Wouldn't give me the time of day."

Memory stirred belatedly in her mind. Two years older than she, Eamon's pursuit—if that was the correct term—had both put her off and embarrassed her. A twig on the branch of a loftier family than her own, Eamon had alternated between awkward arrogance and harassment. He'd finally left her alone when her older brother Ramis, of all people, thrashed him badly enough that he'd had to shift form to heal his injuries. Despite Eamon's superior lineage, Yasmin's mother once made her promise never to marry a male like him.

Eamon saw her recall return. A smile stretched across his face—a smug one, it seemed to her. When his gaze swept leeringly up and down her person, she lost all doubt of it.

"I feel compelled you to tell you, Yazzy, being shuffled off by Iksander hasn't spoiled your appearance. —Joking," he added insincerely, lifting his palms in response to her stony expression. "I'm sure he meant your departure as no insult. You do, however, look utterly yummy."

Yasmin concluded his personality was as bad as ever. His looks too, as it happened. He'd been unattractive as a boy, and age hadn't improved him. She'd heard humans thought no djinni ugly, but perhaps it took human eyes to find loveliness in him. Eamon's receding hairline did no favors to his oddly bulgy forehead. Plus, the way his limbs attached to his torso was subtly off—as if his creator hadn't understood body mechanics. She recalled he hadn't excelled at a single school sport he'd gone out for.

Because saying so would have been petty, she held her tongue.

"She hates me," Eamon laughed to Joseph as if it were a joke. "She'd burn me to the ground right now if you weren't here to watch."

"Eamon," Joseph said quietly. "You are a gentleman. Please treat Miss Baykal with respect."

"Oh, sure," Eamon responded. "I'm just funning. Listen Yazzy . . . You don't mind if I call you that, do you? Why don't you join us in our compartment, and we'll make it up to you?"

"I'm traveling with a friend."

"Your friend is welcome. Especially if she's as pretty as you are."

His smile was less of a leer, but she didn't trust it any more than before.

"Come on," he coaxed. "Loosen up. Aren't we all on holiday?"

He laughed as he said it. It must have been an inside joke, because who went on holiday to Edgeward? The area's proximity to the mists made all but the hardiest tourists uneasy.

"That's very kind," she said, "but my friend and I prefer to ride quietly."

Eamon snorted, unconvinced by her excuse. To her relief, he merely waved his hand. "Suit yourself. Come on, Joe. Maybe we'll find someone interesting in the bar car."

Joseph went without objection—a mystery in itself. What was he doing with that man, riding to Milion?

Maybe Safiye knew. Eamon was highborn like her. The sultanate only had so many aristocrats. Chances were they'd both crossed paths with Dimitriou. This, of course, didn't explain why Joseph was tangled up with Pappus. The magician's origins were humble. He'd risen due to talent.

Half her attention stuck to this conundrum as she continued into the dining car. Luckily, they had tea to take away. Thanks to the carry tray's complimentary anti-spill charm, she ferried it to their compartment without mishap. All was calm inside. Safiye gazed out the window, pretty chin in her elegant hand.

"Got it," Yasmin announced. "Biscuits too, if you're hungry."

"Wonderful. You sit and I'll pour for us."

Yasmin let Safiye slide a full cup across the table before broaching her question. "Do you know a man named Eamon Pappus?"

"Regrettably. Stefan collects eccentric acquaintances sometimes. Why do you ask?"

"I bumped into him on the way to the dining car."

Safiye wrinkled her nose. "I suppose he's attending this weekend's party. He's been promising to bring a special guest to meet Stefan. Made a big mystery of it."

Yasmin's mind clicked through what might be safe to say. "I saw him with Joseph the Magician. Maybe that's who he meant."

"Really? The eunuch is on the train?" Struck by this information, Safiye sat back and sipped her tea. "That *is* interesting."

Yasmin thought so too . . . but probably not for the same reason.

CHAPTER FOUR

Honored Guests

Due to soaking up decades of magic charges, older flying carpets made more reliable vehicles. Perhaps to signal how highly he valued his prospective fiancée, Dimitriou sent a gorgeous twelfth century antique to collect her and her companion. A second rug, nearly as notable as the first, carried Safiye's body men.

To Yasmin's relief, they didn't have to share the ride. Joseph and Eamon flew separately.

The man who piloted her and Safiye was a tall mustached djinni in livery. Wielding his guide pole with stolid efficiency, he lifted off swiftly. Yasmin would have preferred he be poky. For professional reasons, she'd hoped to survey their surroundings.

"Might we circle town before we head to Lord Dimitriou's estate?" she asked. "Lady Toraman and I are new to the area."

"Certainly," he said. "Mind you, it won't take long. Milion is a small hamlet."

He veered off from his previous dead-on course. Conveniently, he slowed down as well.

"How pretty!" Safiye cried, leaning over the folded-up side to see. "It must be market day. Look at the people down in the square."

There was a crowd, or what passed for one out here. The largest group milled in front of a stall with a red-and-white striped awning. As Yasmin watched, two djinn in bright blue guard uniforms rushed over. They seemed to be shooing shoppers from the vendor.

Hm, she thought. *Something happened there that shouldn't.*

Neither Safiye nor the driver seemed to notice the disturbance.

"There's the Temple of Demeter," Safiye said, pointing out a white, columned edifice. "Stefan said it was handsome."

"Very nice," Yasmin agreed. Was Dimitriou a follower of that goddess? The sect was small but respectable. They liked offerings, she believed. Sacrifices of doves and bread left on a stone altar.

Appropriately enough, fields of burgeoning green wheat spread out behind the temple. As they flew over, stalks rippled in the wake from their vehicle.

Their driver waved leftward with his free arm. "That way's the mists. Today's clear, so you can see them. They're about three miles off."

Curious, Yasmin looked. The distant drop off was hazy, as if soft white fog lay over a stretch of ground. Naturally, no actual ground supported the blurred vapor. The end of Iksander's world was precisely that. Step past it, and you'd fall into nothingness. She recalled her first visit to an edge. She'd been five, and she'd been afraid and captivated at the same time. Peeking at the mists was like contemplating the afterlife. What existed beyond the world they knew even her clever father could only speculate.

She'd clung to his hand so tightly he'd bent down and picked her up. What she hadn't done was ask to be taken away from it.

Her attraction wasn't universal. Many djinn found In-Betweens repellent. Safiye seemed to be one of those. She shivered delicately. "This is close enough for today, I think."

"As you like," replied the driver. Though his voice conveyed no judgment, Yasmin sensed Safiye had failed a local test. Perhaps Safiye sensed it too.

"Some other time," she said.

Banking gently, they flew past town again. The women held onto their scarves as an agreeably warm wind whipped the silk across their faces. The landscape stayed rural until, like a mirage, a splendid property appeared. Three large domes crowned a long palace—one gold, one silver, and one copper. Around this vision, many acres of groomed gardens stretched. Yasmin's eyes widened at paths lined with palms and flowers, at fountains and reflecting pools and antique follies crumbling artistically. The effect they created was one of civilized enchantment.

"That is the master's home," their driver informed them.

His words were unnecessary. Who else's could it be? A glance at Safiye's face told Yasmin her companion was impressed. Her brows were up, her lips parted in surprise.

"My," she said, her hand flattened to her bosom. "It's beautiful, isn't it?"

"Quite," Yasmin said. In truth, it was the equal of the sultan's residence.

The driver landed near a rise of creamy white marble steps. These led up to a columned front portico and—beneath its shadow—a huge pair of gilded doors. Had both halves been agape, a pair of elephants could have walked through without touching. Only one side was swung open at the moment. A djinni she recognized as Dimitriou stood smiling in front of it. His hair hung longer than in the pictures she'd seen of him, the gleaming caramel locks waving past his shoulders. His eyes were a crystalline aqua the photographs hadn't caught.

Though Yasmin meant to concentrate on gathering first impressions, the two trees growing up on either side of the steps stole her attention.

"Ruby trees," she breathed, stunned by the presence of such a rarity. She'd heard of them, of course, but had never seen any in person.

As if the nearer tree sensed her admiration, it let fall one of its bright red fruits. Yasmin picked it up in a daze. The cherry-sized uncut gem still bore its green leaves and stem. The stone 'fruit' was clear and perfect, like blood gleaming in the sunshine that hit her palm.

She shook herself. Ahead of her, Dimitriou and Safiye were greeting each other.

"Darling," Dimitriou said, kissing her cheeks in turn. His voice was deep and caressing. "The sight of you is a balm to my love-struck heart."

"Pull the other one," his inamorata retorted. Despite the words, her smile conveyed real pleasure. Their embrace was loose but familiar. Her hands rested on his arms as her lovely face turned up to him.

Dimitriou grinned at her skepticism, his green-blue eyes gleaming naughtily. "It's certainly a balm to something," he murmured.

Safiye blushed and swatted him. The girlish reaction wasn't one Yasmin expected to see from cool Lady Toraman.

Wow, she thought. *She really does like him.*

Dimitriou touched Safiye's hair, gently stroking an escaped lock beneath her veil again. If he were faking liking Safiye back, he did a good job of it.

Perhaps he felt Yasmin's attention. He kissed Safiye's cheek once more before releasing her. The smile he turned to Yasmin was amiable. "You must be Miss Baykal."

"Yasmin," she said, offering him a curtsey. "I'm very pleased to meet you, Lord Dimitriou."

His smile broadened. "If you are Yasmin, then I am Stefan. We're not so formal out here in the provinces."

Yasmin wasn't sure she believed that, but it was a nice thing to say. She held out the gem in her palm to him. "Your ruby tree dropped a fruit."

"You must keep it. Think of it as a souvenir of a hopefully enjoyable stay. Please," he insisted, curling her fingers gently back over it. "Those trees aren't even really mine. They sprang up not long ago. I assume the seeds blew into my garden across the mists. They seem to do well in Milion's climate. All the wild magic in the air, I guess."

Until he said this, she hadn't noticed the extra hum that enlivened the atmosphere. Then again, maybe the hum was the effect of his hand lingering on hers. His personal magic wasn't as strong as hers, but neither was it negligible.

He let go and smiled, taking Safiye's arm to escort her up the steps.

"Come along," he called jovially across his shoulder. "I wouldn't want you to melt out here in the sun."

No djinni would melt in this pleasant heat. Up the steps she went anyway. Passing through the doors, she found herself in a cavernous space beneath the palace's central dome. As promised, the interior was cooler. Darker too, scattered with the showy sort of furniture highborns liked to put in their foyers. Huge potted ferns framed two arched exits to either side of the large atrium. More elephants would have fit through those. Struck by the sense of space, Yasmin craned her head back instinctively. She'd seen a picture once of a famous human basilica. This cupola reminded her of that, though its paintings were different. They depicted scenes from djinn history—battles mostly, but also some romances.

The amount of gold accenting the architectural detail wouldn't have shamed an emperor.

"Wow," she said, unable to restrain herself.

"Feel free to look around," Stefan said. "The servants can take you to your rooms whenever you're ready."

"Sir," someone interrupted in a low but urgent voice. "Forgive me for intruding. There's been an incident in the marketplace."

That interested Yasmin. She glanced back toward the entryway. A guard in blue uniform—perhaps one of the pair she'd spied earlier—stood in the square of sunshine that blazed in from outside. The light was so bright he appeared as if he were outlined in fire.

"An incident?" Stefan repeated casually.

"Yes, sir. A stall simply . . . materialized without warning, and no one was manning it.

It was stocked with rather nice bed linens. Understandably, a few townsfolk were tempted to appropriate the unattended merchandise."

"You guards stopped them, I presume."

"We did, but now we're wondering what to do with the goods. As magistrate, it's your decision."

"I suppose it is." Seeming amused by this, Stefan tapped his lips. "Wait two days. If no one comes forward to claim the stall, draw a name from the pool of vendors awaiting licenses. They can start their career with a nice windfall."

"Very good, sir," the guard responded with a crisp bow. "I'll relay your judgment immediately."

As he left, Safiye drifted to Stefan's side. They both watched the man trot away. "Does this sort of thing happen often? Laden market booths simply appearing?"

"Now and then." Stefan squeezed her slim shoulders. "The In-Betweens are like the sea sometimes. We can't predict what will wash up on our shores."

Yasmin had never heard of mists behaving in this fashion. If transporting objects across them were that easy, her father's invention wouldn't have made him a fortune. With an effort, she shut her mouth against saying so. No one knew everything about the In-Betweens, on top of which contradicting Stefan seemed unlikely to win her an advantage.

"Darling," Safiye said, touching his chest lightly. "Would you mind if Yasmin and I went to our rooms right now? I'm sure we'd welcome a chance to freshen up after our journey."

"Of course," Stefan said. "Forgive me for not thinking."

He neither snapped his fingers nor lifted his beringed hand. A veiled female servant simply leaped forward from a shadow. She appeared so suddenly Yasmin wondered if she'd been waiting in vapor form. Apparently, she needed no instructions.

"Won't you follow me?" she asked politely.

She led them down a long corridor to a pair of adjoining suites. The chambers were luxuriously appointed and spacious. Yasmin struggled not to gawk.

"These are lovely," Safiye said. "Please thank your master on my behalf."

The djinniya curtseyed and withdrew.

"My," Safiye said, looking around wide-eyed.

"Shall I take this room?" Yasmin asked. "The other has a view of the back garden, but I believe they're similar in size."

"They are much the same, aren't they? Stefan is generous."

"No doubt he wishes to honor you by honoring your friend." Yasmin sat on the mattress and tested it. The giant silk-swathed bed was magnificent. The chamber's only drawback was that it had no locks. Were Dimitriou's servants in the habit of hovering invisibly? She'd have to install an anti-intrusion spell . . . perhaps an anti-surveillance one as well. She tugged her earlobe in thought. Hopefully, doing so wouldn't seem overly paranoid.

Her preoccupation annoyed Safiye.

"Yasmin," she scolded. "You can't mean to suggest Stefan is simply playing angles by treating you so well."

"Would you disapprove if he were?"

Safiye laughed. "You outdo me in cynicism. He is generous! Look at his decision concerning the market stall. Many in his position would have claimed the goods for themselves, whether they needed them or not. And he gave you that ruby. Your father can't be so rich you consider a magic gem a trifle."

"I don't." Yasmin refrained from saying it might be a trifle to Stefan. The memory of him pressing her fingers around the stone returned. The gesture had stopped just short of improper—a practiced calculation, she suspected. Safiye wasn't wrong in thinking her would-be husband was likely to cheat on her.

Safiye shook her head at Yasmin's less than ringing denial. "Never mind. I suppose I didn't bring you here to convince me of—"

"Forgive me." Yasmin popped up from the bed to cut her sentence short. "I've forgotten something I meant to do."

Safiye gaped at her until she pressed a cautioning finger against her lips.

"Security," Yasmin said. "After all those years in the harem, you know I'm fond of my privacy. You don't mind if I put up a spell or two."

Understanding then, Safiye's face cleared of annoyance.

"Fine," she said with convincing brusqueness. "But just do your room, if you please. I don't want Stefan thinking I distrust him."

Stefan might or might not have been offended by that idea.

"As you like," Yasmin said.

Safiye turned to go into her own suite but paused a moment more. "When you're finished, you may as well try to nap. Stefan is a night owl. We'll be up all hours tonight."

Yasmin's chest tightened without warning. Safiye meant they'd be up with Dimitriou's other guests. This wasn't just a visit. This was a house party.

But she'd deal with that when she had to. Joseph might be peeved she'd ignored his warning, but he'd get over it. He wouldn't monkeywrench her business here. Not deliberately anyway.

She strove to ignore that *business* wasn't her chief vulnerability with regard to him.

Slightly uncomfortable with her souvenir, Yasmin stashed the magic ruby at the back of a bureau drawer. Putting up security spells was a simple matter. She'd spun many such charms before. Convinced they'd be hard to breach, she dug out her personal scroll. Deciding to keep the message simple, she notified Balu that she'd arrived safely.

"P.S.," she added. "Please ask Father if it's possible for a market stall to float across the In-Betweens by itself."

She put more power than she thought she needed into sending the message off. The link felt weirdly spongy, but she believed it worked. Not the least bit tired, she jotted a few observations then paced the room until her brother responded.

Gld 2 fXsoGlrr M6nev NEV so!AR was his less than informative reply.

She supposed this answered the question of whether she could count on a clear connection in Edgeward. Sighing, she set the scroll aside. Maybe her luck would improve later, or maybe this was as good as the signal was getting.

You're on your own for now, she thought.

That is, she was on her own unless she wanted to rely on a certain too-handsome sorcerer . . .

CHAPTER FIVE

Dancing Fools

Her attempt to reach her brother fruitless, Yasmin decided to slip out and sleuth. The way owners ran their residences could reveal character. Her take on Dimitriou was only just forming. Sadly, she mis-timed her exit. Before she got five paces down the hall, a clutch of female staff appeared to help her and Safiye get ready for the evening.

This sort of fussing had always bored her. Yasmin could polish herself with spells in a tenth of the time being pampered by servants took. Then again, it might be best not to trumpet her magic skill. She'd learned in the harem that being underestimated earned more freedom.

Safiye enjoyed the primping as much as ever . . . and turned out breathtaking. Dimitriou sent a fabulous gown: a 'modest token' he hoped she'd honor him by wearing. The cloth was silver on glittering silver and skimmed her elegant figure alluringly. A matching diamond tiara gleamed like stars snatched down from the sky. The effect was a bit too much, actually. The blinding sparkle obscured the former concubine's own beauty.

Sensing this perhaps, she turned from the gilt-framed mirror to face Yasmin. "What do you think?"

"I think everyone will gasp when you walk in the room."

Her client seemed to hear the subtext under the compliment. She pursed her lips unsurely. "I don't own a veil nice enough to pair with this."

"No one's veiling tonight," one of the maids piped up. "It's a private dinner. Close friends and their close friends. Lord Dimitriou wants everyone relaxed."

"I look as if I'm trying to impersonate a queen."

"You're as beautiful as a queen," another maid averred.

"That truth cannot be disputed," Yasmin said honestly.

Safiye sighed at her reflection. "I suppose Stefan wouldn't send a dress that would embarrass me."

"Never!" the first maid declared. "My lady will shine appropriately."

"Don't worry," Yasmin said. "No matter what Lord Dimitriou intends, if anyone can carry off that rig, it's you."

The first maid shot her a scalding look for doubting her master's motives. Catching it, Safiye shook her head humorously. "Really, Yasmin, you are too droll sometimes!"

~

Droll or not, the prospect of joining the other guests gave rise to anxiety. Because it was the only outfit close to Safiye's in splendor, Yasmin chose the gold-embroidered deep pink tunic and narrow pants her mother had slipped into her trunk. Though the color was less juvenile than she'd feared, the tourmaline-studded garb fit her curves closely. When she'd been confined to the harem, dressing seductively wasn't simply permitted but required. Tonight, half her bosom was on display for males she didn't know. Leaving her hair down would have provided coverage, but that felt immodest too. A veil, regrettably, was impossible. She'd stand out like a sore thumb instead of blending in.

Despite the modern attitudes she took pride in, her longing to hike her neckline higher was almost irresistible.

Safiye had long since departed by the time the maids finished dressing her. Forced to proceed on her own fashionably late, Yasmin followed the clink of crystal to the salon. The soiree was already underway. The bursts of laughter that rang out coiled her nerves tight enough to snap.

What did she know of parties? She hadn't been to one with strangers—much less strange males—since she was a teenager.

Be a detective, she ordered, hanging back at the entry to collect herself. *Look around. Who are these 'close friends and their friends' the maid spoke of?*

Privileged djinn was her initial impression, well dressed and casually confident of their preeminence. The dozen or so couples split into two factions in the richly appointed room. The first she judged to be long-time friends of Dimitriou. They were his age and flamboyant in clothes and manner. They tossed back multi-colored cocktails and stood conversing in animated knots. Though it was difficult to be sure, she thought the females were wives. The second group was older and quieter. Dressed more conservatively, they'd established their social base in one of room's corners. Mostly seated, the men sipped strong spirits from heavy cut-glass tumblers. The djinniya who accompanied them either stood behind their chairs or perched on the arms. These females struck Yasmin as more like mistresses. They didn't look less expensive than the wives, simply less certain of their place at the gathering. Whatever the relationship, the men who'd brought them paid more attention to each other.

They were the type who thought of women as interchangeable.

At the moment, Stefan was with the younger group, leaning attentively toward a raven-curled djinniya in a bright yellow gown. Her breasts were practically popping out of her décolleté. When Stefan laughed at something she'd said, she playfully poked his bicep with two fingers. Far from minding the personal touch, his eyes glowed admiringly.

It wouldn't be a stretch to call the interchange flirtatious.

Safiye certainly thought it was. She'd glanced over from another chattering cluster and caught the tail end of it. Her face tightened briefly in annoyance before she turned away.

If Stefan hadn't looked at her just then, he'd have missed the expression.

He responded by patting the woman's arm and going to Safiye. Hugging her waist familiarly from behind, he nuzzled her neck and murmured in her ear. The communication must have been bawdy. Safiye rolled her eyes even as her cheeks pinkened. Dimitriou seemed so smugly pleased with himself Yasmin had to think he'd meant to cause jealousy.

Maybe he wanted his prospective fiancée off balance. If Safiye weren't sure of him—or herself—she might be more malleable. Undermining a woman's confidence was more difficult to establish than magical interference, and could work as effectively. That was plain-old psychology.

Yasmin gnawed her lip. Was this what Dimitriou was doing?

Her thoughts were interrupted before she reached a conclusion. Like a stink someone had spelled to stick, Eamon Pappus showed up in front of her.

"There you are, you gorgeous creature," he said convivially. Taken by surprise, Yasmin accepted the watermelon-colored cocktail he was holding out to her. "I'd begun to fear I'd be partnerless tonight."

"Partnerless?" she repeated, her stomach sinking at the thought of being paired with him.

"Well, except for Joe," Eamon laughed. "And he's not my type."

Why was Eamon's brow so shiny? Yasmin didn't think the man was sweating. But maybe the highness of his forehead overstretched its skin?

"Hel*lo*," Eamon teased, giving her brow a tap. "Anyone home in there?"

"Sorry," she responded, shrinking back automatically. "I wasn't aware partnering up was required."

One of the females she'd pegged as a mistress came up behind Eamon. Unaffected by repulsion, she hung one hand on his sloping shoulder. Her pout was probably intended as beguiling. "We're playing Pick the Dance. You know, where you draw a card from a covered dish and have to perform the style it says."

"I thought party games were for kids."

"It's fun," the woman insisted. "Stefan put up the prize. The winner gets a stupendous emerald ring."

Yasmin had a crazy urge to claim she had an emerald allergy.

"You have to play," Eamon said. "Only spoilsports sit out."

Their debate was drawing attention, other guests beginning to drift over. When she spotted Joseph among them, her heart did a little flip. Where had he been hiding? She hadn't noticed him before. He looked perfect in a scarlet and gold tunic, trim and straight and absolutely everything she thought a man should be. Almost everything anyway. His lips were grimly pressed together, his manner reluctant. That he didn't intend to save her from her dilemma was obvious. This being so, what she blurted next was doubly ridiculous.

"I can't dance with you. Joseph and I have an understanding."

"You do not," Eamon said as Joseph's jaw fell open.

"We do," she insisted, perversely digging herself deeper. "It's a private understanding. Nobody's heard of it because we kept it to ourselves."

"You're lying." Infuriated, Eamon spun to Joseph for support. "Tell this chit she's delusional."

Joseph managed to shut his mouth. "Miss Baykal . . . is correct. Yasmin and I hid our mutual regard so as not to enrage Iksander. The sultan has been known to act possessively."

"Iksander threw her off!"

Joseph brushed an invisible speck from his tunic front. "Aren't children sometimes reluctant to let others play with their discarded toys?"

Well, that insulted her *and* Iksander.

"You're both lying!" Eamon declared.

"We're not," Yasmin said since she had backup now. "We didn't want the sultan to assume we'd been . . . associating while I belonged to him."

Eamon's face darkened dangerously. "You're telling me you'd rather pair up with a man who can't even pleasure you."

His comment was a step too far, even for this worldly crowd. Most definitely, it was a step too far for her. She didn't care if Eamon thought Joseph was a eunuch. He deserved to be respected.

"Haven't you heard?" she said, smiling straight at him. "Some djinn do more with less."

It took a moment for their audience to grasp her insinuation. Once they did, they laughed—at Eamon's expense this time. Naturally, his pride couldn't tolerate the sting.

"Oh, I bet you two *associated* while you were in the harem. Ball-less men can sneak in there no problem."

No doubt he'd have spat more insults if their host hadn't come over.

"That's enough," Stefan cautioned, his hand supplanting the djinniya's on Eamon's shoulder. The emerald flashing on his pinkie was likely tonight's favor. "I realize Miss Baykal is a prize worth competing over, but you're insulting your own guest now. Or have you forgotten Joseph honors us with his presence because of you?"

Embarrassment washed into Eamon's face, diluting though not erasing his anger. "Forgive me. I shouldn't have said those things. Thank you for recalling me to myself." Stiffly, he bowed to Joseph and her in turn. "I hope neither of you allows my poor manners to spoil your evening."

He managed the apology with more grace than she expected. Also surprising, Joseph stepped to her side and slid an arm around her waist. Despite knowing the gesture was pretend, her nerves began fluttering.

"You've done me a favor," he said to Eamon. "If you hadn't tried to claim Yasmin as your partner, she wouldn't have confessed our relationship. Now, in this gathering, we may at last show our affections."

"Wonderful." Stefan clapped him and Eamon on the shoulder. "All is well. And of course, you can count on us not to share your secret outside these walls."

Yasmin spotted some of his guests exchanging glances. They weren't promising anything. It occurred to her, belatedly, that her self-serving stroke of genius might get Joseph into trouble.

Iksander wouldn't really be enraged at the thought of them pairing up, would he? He'd matured since banishing his original wife for seeming to cheat on him.

She bit her lip, but had little time for regret.

"Make them dance first!" suggested the mistress who'd spoken in support of the parlor game. "They look so cute in their pink and red outfits."

Were they cute? Joseph couldn't hide a grimace when she stole a glance at him. The gold embroidery on their tunics was rather similar.

Stefan smiled at the excited djinniya. "Tara, why don't you get the bowl with the dances? I think the servants left it on the table beside the door."

Tara scampered off and returned with a silver dish. Grinning, she tipped one side of the cover up. "Close your eyes and stick your hand in. No peeking, now—and no magical manipulation. The dance you pick is the dance you do."

With another grimace, Joseph allowed Yasmin the honors. She set down her drink and pulled out a folded card.

TIGER TANGO, it said inside.

Uh, she thought. *What the hell is a Tiger Tango?*

She looked at Joseph but, as Fate would have it, he was no help. Actually, for him, he looked somewhat terrified. His posture was ramrod stiff, and his normally sun-browned skin had paled. He leaned his head to her.

"Do you know what we're supposed to do?" he asked in an undertone.

His voice was raspy. He truly was nervous. She realized he probably hadn't gone to a lot of parties. Yes, he was in the sultan's inner circle, but he worked all the time. Seriousness was his defining trait. Making a fool of himself wouldn't be his idea of fun.

Come to think of it, would he have danced before?

"I, uh, believe I've seen Balu practice it. My brother and his friends like to play at all sorts of things."

If anything, Joseph went whiter. "You saw him *practice* it."

"I have a good memory. Follow my example, and we'll be fine."

Her first claim was true, her second wishful thinking. Possibly Joseph sensed this. He breathed a curse word she didn't recognize. Perhaps it was human. He'd been to their dimension.

"Enough consultation," Tara declared, nudging them toward the open center of the salon. "The musicians are ready now."

To her relief, the tune they struck up was similar to tangos she'd heard before.

"Wait," Joseph said as Yasmin stepped onto the parquet. "I think you need different shoes for this." He closed his eyes, spread his fingers, and sent his power rippling briefly from his palms. Without warning, her heels lifted off the ground. Yasmin looked down. Her slippers were gone. He'd spelled strappy black footwear onto her feet.

"I've viewed the human film *Take the Lead*," he said.

"Good," she laughed. "I won't have to explain which body part goes where."

For some reason, this made him blush. Slightly awkward but determined, he flattened one hand behind her shoulder blade. Identifying this as part of the opening pose, Yasmin slid her left leg back on the toe of her brand-new heels. After she'd done that, her and Joseph's hips almost touched. The color on her partner's cheekbones flared brighter. He acted as if their closeness was unheard of for him.

Oh, she thought. He must not have taken his now-healed body for all its possible flights. The thrill that swept through her was bubblier than champagne.

"You might need to pull me closer," she couldn't resist teasing. "This dance is supposed to be risqué."

"Yes," he said and cleared his throat. He tugged her the one inch more that brought them into light contact.

Heat sprang up along the line of his chest and groin. Was he growing aroused? He wasn't quite close enough to tell. The music swelled, the string players seeming to echo her excitement. The effect increased as Joseph unexpectedly took command. He didn't have to use his magic. The lightest pressure of his palm on hers guided her backward into a gliding walk.

Some kind spirit must have been watching out for her. She remembered how her feet were supposed to pause together and slide apart. *Don't rise up,* she reminded. *Direct your weight to the floor.* Done right, this dance was earthy and grounded.

Joseph lifted her hand to twirl her. Their eyes met as she completed the rotation. The gold in his gaze was molten. He was going to dip her. The subtle tension in his arm and leg muscles told her so. Smooth as silk, he arched her back and lifted her again. She wasn't dizzy but light as air. Though she'd wanted him forever, she hadn't guessed they'd connect this effortlessly. No one else existed. They were intimate and alone. She did a leg flick that curled her calf behind his. She brushed it caressingly.

He smiled as if he knew she dreamed of seducing him.

The contrast between his inexperience and his power titillated her. What would it be like to initiate the famous sorcerer, to free the carnal potential she sensed in him? Would she overwhelm him? Could she? Maybe it would be the other way around.

Joseph caused her blood to fire like no other.

"Oh, come on," someone called. "Get to the tiger part."

The interruption startled them out of their fantasy. Joseph looked at her with his eyebrows up. He had no idea what their heckler meant. She didn't either, but one of them had to come up with something.

"Rrowwr," she said, throwing caution and no doubt dignity to the wind. She circled Joseph while making clawing motions with her arms.

"Rrowwr?" he said less surely, mimicking her gestures.

"No, no, *no*," their critic scolded. Yasmin turned to see it was Tara. The djinniya seemed extremely put out by their performance. "Don't you two know how to play this game? You're supposed to change into your smoke forms, shape them like tigers, and prowl around each other."

"Um," Joseph said. "We could try that, if you prefer."

"Oh, forget it," Tara huffed. "You're clueless. You'll just make a hash of it." She sliced one hand across her throat to silence the musicians. "Would a *serious* couple like to compete next?"

Yasmin didn't know if the pair who raised their hands qualified. They were laughing, though they seemed unafraid of provoking Tara's wrath.

"They've given us the hook," Joseph murmured. "Time to exit, stage left."

It was more than time. The crowd was moving on without them. The next contestants were already drawing their selection from the dish.

"Levitation Waltz!" the female crowed, waving the card she'd picked.

"Lucky dogs," groaned another guest. "If we get the Particolored Polka, I'll die. That dance is the kiss of death. No one looks good doing it."

Presumably, the Levitation Waltz gave some advantage toward winning.

Still in synch despite their disrupted dance, Yasmin and Joseph slipped through the garden doors and into the fresh night air. Yasmin more than half hoped Joseph would take her arm, but had to be satisfied with him not drawing too far away. Because her tango shoes weren't easy to walk in, she removed them.

The quiet between her and the magician was almost comfortable.

"I can change those back for you," he offered, gesturing toward the heels she was carrying.

"That's all right. This grass is perfect for bare feet."

Satisfied with her explanation, he turned their steps toward a starlit reflecting pool.

"I'm sorry I embarrassed you," Yasmin said.

Joseph waved his hand vaguely. "Maybe it's wrong of me to admit, but I'm relieved we were disqualified. I'm not much of a party animal."

"Ha-ha," Yasmin said, thinking he'd made a pun on the Tiger Tango. Apparently not. He looked at her quizzically.

"Anyway," she went on. "Thanks for being a good sport. Especially about you and me 'having an understanding.' I shouldn't have pitched you into that just because I didn't want to get partnered with Eamon."

They'd reached the marble edge of the lengthy reflecting pool. The fountain in its middle created wavelets on which rafts of lilies bobbed. The oversized flowers were pink and white, their petals twinkling with a liberal coating of magic dust. Yasmin wondered if Dimitriou's staff had to fly over the pool on carpets to get them all sprinkled.

When Joseph looked at her, she forgot the prosaic question. If he were affected by the romance of their surroundings, it didn't show. His beautifully sharp features were solemn.

"Eamon is an acquired taste," he said.

"What *are* you doing with him?"

"We have interests in common."

She scoffed in disbelief.

"You don't know everything about me," he contended.

If she didn't know more about him than Eamon, she'd eat these shoes. Actually, she was pretty sure she knew more than Joseph realized. Keeping that from him was starting to weigh on her. It felt dishonest, for one thing.

"About the dance . . ." she said, wondering if she could ease into telling him. "Maybe it's just as well we had to stop when we did."

"Yes?" he said with his eyebrows up.

"Having to stop might have, you know, spared you a different sort of exposure, one you're maybe not ready for."

"What are you talking about?"

Oh, this was awkward. What if she'd misread his reactions? Their bodies hadn't been close enough for her to be absolutely sure. What if he'd gone hot for another reason than having an erection? Plain old embarrassment made people flush similarly to arousal.

"Um, maybe I'm assuming you responded more than you did?"

His forehead creased. "I don't understand what you're getting at."

Yasmin sighed. She didn't want to have to explain this. Yes, she'd lived in a harem and, yes, she'd probably talked about sex more times than him. That didn't make her the talk-about-sex expert.

Joseph registered her frustration. He reached out to rub her sleeve. "Could we discuss this some other time? I'm not certain we're—"

He stopped speaking to look back at the palace. When she turned, Yasmin saw what had alerted him. Their host was striding toward them across the springy lawn.

"Ah," Stefan said, "a thousand pardons for interrupting your tête-à-tête. After that scene inside, I wanted to make sure you two weren't upset."

"We're fine," Joseph said. "I was apologizing to Yasmin for not being more fun-loving."

Stefan's laugh came easily. "Everyone has their own ideas about what constitutes entertainment. I'll leave the pair of you alone if that's what you prefer."

"That is kind of you but unnecessary. We're here for a party. Even I can appreciate congenial company."

"Good," Stefan said. "Good. And perhaps I can coax you to enjoy it more with a human-style cigar." He laid his index finger beside his nose. "I have a shall we say shady connection who sometimes slips across dimensions."

By 'shady' he meant ifrit. The admission didn't surprise her. Most rich men knew a few dark djinn. Their lack of moral limits came in handy for skirting around light rules. What did surprise her was the readiness with which Joseph accepted.

"I wouldn't say no," he responded, falling into step with their host. "Humans excel at some things."

"Cigars being one," Stefan agreed with a male chuckle.

Yasmin was left to trail behind them . . . or thought she was.

"No, no," Stefan said, glancing over his shoulder. "Walk beside us. I'm infringing on your man's time with you. The least I can do is try to entertain you too."

His consideration weighed in his favor. When Joseph extended his hand to her, clearly meaning for her to take it, Yasmin felt grateful to the other man twice over.

CHAPTER SIX

Sweet Dreamer

Yasmin left the party late but not as late as some of Stefan's guests. Joseph still sat among the older males, puffing slowly on his cigar while they discussed who-knew-what very important matters around him.

Because Eamon was part of that circle too, she hadn't joined Joseph. Observing the traditionalists from a distance was easier anyway. Their women, for the most part, left them to their man-talk. Earlier, she'd watched Stefan drop in on them. Though he showed them deference and hadn't claimed center stage like he did with his personal friends, the men listened respectfully when he spoke.

Now, as Yasmin departed, Stefan and Safiye slow danced alone near the far windows. Safiye was good at playing docile. Her head rested sweetly on his shoulder. Then again, maybe she wasn't playing. Clearly, Stefan knew how to charm people.

Though guilt pricked her at abandoning her client, she was too tired for more sleuthing.

Her suite felt like an oasis when she reached it.

She checked her scroll, but no further messages—garbled or coherent—had arrived from her brother. She washed up, pulled on a plain silk gown, and crawled beneath the luxurious bedcovers.

The cool, smooth sheets reminded her of the nearby town's mysteriously appearing market stall. She couldn't tell if the puzzle was important or just random. Maybe her instincts were trying to nudge her, and that was why she hadn't forgotten it. Her instincts nudged her on Stefan too. He was off somehow, in more than the obvious playboy ways. Unfortunately, she had no facts to back up her suspicion. Without facts, Safiye seemed unlikely to listen to warnings.

Sighing, she wriggled around to her other side.

Was it her job to convince Safiye to refuse her suitor? Safiye's preference seemed to lean toward wanting reassurance that accepting him was okay.

Closing her eyes, she fluffed the already fluffy pillow. She'd think more clearly tomorrow.

Goddess, she prayed before she forgot. *You who oversee useful dreams, if it be Thy will, please seed my mind with the wisdom I need to fulfill my purpose well.*

The prayer sufficed to send her under.

Yasmin had left a tiny hole in her soundproof spell, to prevent being taken unawares by an intruder. She woke she didn't know how much later to the sound of voices in the corridor. Stefan seemed to be trying to convince Safiye to let him in. Yasmin thought it possible they hadn't had intercourse. Safiye—who was nothing if not tactical—might consider that as giving away too much gratis.

"This is the women's wing," she protested laughingly. "What if someone catches you leaving tomorrow?"

"When you inform them we're engaged, that won't matter."

"You're assuming I've decided."

"Haven't you?" he purred, followed by the thump of Safiye's back being pressed into a wall. After that came a long silence.

Almost silence anyway. Yasmin heard the pair kissing. Quiet groans soon joined the kissing noises, mostly but not entirely from Stefan. She debated covering her ears, but then she wouldn't hear if he left or stayed. If Yasmin wanted to sneak out later, knowing his location would affect her strategy.

One thing was certain. She wasn't recording *this* in her client notes.

Finally, Safiye pushed her suitor away from her.

"Darling," she said breathlessly. "I regret doing this, believe me, but I'm serious about asking you to go."

Stefan huffed out a breath. "You make me feel like a teenager."

"Is that so bad?"

He laughed, low and male. "Promise you'll burn for me in your dreams."

"That's an easy vow to make."

He kissed her once more and went. "*All* night," he emphasized as a parting shot.

Safiye's door shut a moment later. Yasmin waited but the other woman didn't tap on their connecting door. Maybe she assumed Yasmin was asleep, or maybe she'd rather dream about Stefan than recap the day's business. Either way, Yasmin was now wide-awake.

She hadn't said goodnight to the man she was interested in—much less said goodnight like that.

Her sigh was a bit too wistful for comfort.

She was debating whether to get up and do something useful when a pale blue glow flared along the pattern she'd drawn for her anti-intrusion spell. She scrambled out of bed with barely a pause to think.

"Lamp base," she murmured, thrusting out her arm to call the sturdiest one to her.

She knew how to swing it. She'd taken physical self-defense as part of her PI training.

Don't go crazy, she warned herself. *You probably don't want to kill anyone.*

The knob to her door didn't turn, but she didn't really expect it to. Someone was trying to enter magically—someone skilled, unfortunately. The keyhole wavered as if heated vapor were pushing through. She had a second to wonder if she should change form to defend herself.

One second after that, Joseph blinked into solid being inside her room.

"Don't attack," he whispered. "It's only me."

"Joseph," she said, relief fighting with annoyance. She lowered the lamp and spelled on its light in the same motion.

He wiped the glitter of sweat from his brow and grinned. "Whew. That was a serious anti-intrusion charm. You have to show me how you built that."

She didn't know why she'd bother since he'd gotten through it quickly enough. "You could have knocked."

"This is the women's corridor. I didn't want to wake anyone. As it was, Dimitriou almost spotted my vapor form. You can put that back where it belongs now."

He meant the lamp base. She still gripped it menacingly.

"Fine," she said, wafting it to its table and setting its shade in place. Because it seemed a wise precaution, she stoppered the final hole in her soundproof spell.

"May I sit?" he asked politely.

He didn't mean on the bed. The area around the lamp held cozy armchairs and plush footstools.

"Suit yourself," Yasmin said.

He glanced at her when she tossed her head, his gaze taking in the sheerness of her simple bias-cut white nightgown. This was standard harem sleepwear. Despite Iksander rarely visiting, the principle that his women always ought to be ready to entertain him had persisted. The gossamer silk displayed Yasmin's body and, if she said so herself, her body was very nice. In addition to being a healthy young djinniya, her curves were feminine and her limbs well shaped. Her pleasingly rounded breasts had up-tilted nipples, their hue roses set in cream. Her body hair was banished from the places fashion decreed. When she moved, she jiggled the right amount for her physical type. She met, in short, the basic standard for royal concubines.

Knowing this gave her more confidence than she otherwise might have felt. She stalked to the chair facing his and sat. As she did, her sleep-mussed hair fell forward. She didn't mind the locks hanging to her waist. Let him see she was a woman. Let him feel her female power.

Aware she had his attention, she crossed her legs slowly.

Joseph jerked his eyes away, the rush of blood to his cheekbones now visible. "Wouldn't you like to put on a robe?"

"Not really. I'm not cold."

When Joseph's lips thinned, she smiled. His expression looked disapproving, but she didn't think it was.

You have the advantage. Perhaps you should steer this encounter.

Yasmin smoothed her gown over her upper knee. "Did you see anything interesting while you were flitting around invisibly?"

"I wasn't flitting. I was coming here. And I didn't risk discovery just to repeat gossip."

"So you *did* see something." Interested, she leaned forward. Joseph frowned, possibly because her breasts swayed against the silk.

"You invaded my bedroom without permission," she reminded. "The least you can do is humor me."

His honey-gold eyes narrowed as realization hit. "You're not here as Safiye's friend. She's your client. She hired you to vet Stefan."

Privately irritated by his perceptiveness, Yasmin shrugged. "You still owe me an answer."

"What I saw has nothing to do with him."

"It's a rule of detecting not to take other people's word on which facts are important."

Joseph rolled his eyes but gave in. "I saw the djinniya Tara weeping pitifully on her maid's shoulder."

"Pitifully," Yasmin said, struck by his choice of words. "Could you tell why? I mean, I know Tara was upset when she and her partner drew the Particolored Polka, but was she distressed over more than losing the contest?"

"The particolor effect returned. She couldn't get the pattern to leave her skin. Her face was completely covered with squirming blobs."

"That's strange. I distinctly recall her dispelling the charm after their dance was done. Her technique seemed fine to me."

"I thought so too, but you know what they say about magic working unpredictably this close to the In-Betweens."

Yasmin sat back and thought. "You know, when Tara reached into the bowl of dances, I thought I sensed Dimitriou giving that card a magical nudge toward her. At the time, I assumed he wanted to punish her for embarrassing you."

"And you," Joseph reminded.

"I suppose he might care about that. Hopefully, he doesn't suspect Safiye hired me to vet him. If I were her actual friend, he'd expect her to ask my opinion on marrying him."

"He seems to have other reasons for wanting to get on your good side."

Yasmin grimaced and waved her hand. "Men like him flirt as easily as they breathe. I'm not saying he'd turn me down if he thought he could get away with it, just that his interest in me isn't serious. In any case, Safiye doesn't seem to consider his cheating nature a deal breaker."

"You would," Joseph said, watching her closely.

Would she? Her shoulders hiked unsurely. "I suppose I'd prefer not to share a husband if I had one."

"I'm not surprised Stefan asked Safiye to marry him. Between her family name and having been a sultan's chosen, she'd make a prestige partner."

His musing tone brought her attention back to him. "Why are you here, Joseph? I don't mean in my room. I mean in Edgeward with Eamon."

"I told you. We have interests in common."

"Well, that's a lie. He's even less your friend than Safiye's mine."

Joseph crossed his arms stubbornly. "If you choose not to believe me, I can't help that."

"You know what *I'm* doing here."

"Because I guessed."

"I can guess too," she warned, then double-checked her eavesdropping shield. "For instance, I happen to know Stefan Dimitriou is popular with djinn who dislike the liberal direction Iksander is taking our city. What's more, I wouldn't be surprised if that cabal you were smoking cigars with for half the night are precisely that sort of folk. They tolerate that idiot Eamon because he delivered you. The question is, what sort of service are *you* meant to supply them?"

"You're being ridiculous."

Yasmin crossed her arms like he had—but with different results. That the gesture hiked her breasts wasn't accidental. She'd use whatever weapons she had to fluster him.

"*Yasmin*," he said placatingly.

"You shouldn't call me ridiculous when you know I'm right."

He shook his head. "It's safer if I don't explain."

"Safer for whom?"

"For both of us."

"I disagree. If we know each other's business, we're less likely to step on each other's toes." Again, Joseph shook his head. "After everything we went through, I can't believe you don't trust me. I helped you defeat my own brother. Just like you, I risked my life for our city. I'm as loyal to Iksander as I believe you are."

She wasn't playing the emotional female card. She meant every word staunchly. Her plea didn't have the effect she hoped. Joseph rose from his chair. She pushed up too—automatically, it felt to her—as if they were attached by strings. She wanted to step closer but resisted.

"Perhaps I should go," he said. "I didn't come here to anger you."

"Why *did* you come?"

"I wanted to make sure you're okay with our acting like a couple."

"Of course I'm okay with that. It was my idea!" Her breath burst from her in exasperation. "Why do you think I apologized earlier? Lord, I never expected you to be such a *man*."

He still wore his evening clothes. At her exclamation, he tugged his scarlet waist sash straighter. "I know the pretense was your idea. When you came up with it, however, you couldn't have known—"

He stopped midsentence, and Yasmin threw up her hands. "Couldn't have known what?"

"When you spoke about me exposing myself while we were dancing, I realized you must have been surprised. The truth is, some men with my . . . deficiency are able to respond to female beauty."

"Goddess sake," she exploded, losing all patience. She stepped to him and poked his chest. "I know you're not a eunuch anymore."

"You know?" he repeated in amazement.

"I've known since the night I slipped into your room at the palace in my cat form. You were aroused. I noticed you . . . weren't missing any parts." Joseph had gone bright red, but Yasmin pressed onward. One of them being mortified to speechlessness was enough. "I don't suppose you want to explain how that came about."

"You want to know why I was aroused?"

His question caused her to laugh. "I assume that happened for the usual reasons. I meant how you came to be whole again. Something to do with the doubling process, I assume."

"Yes, I— When I copied myself to escape Empress Luna's curse, I accidentally made a healed version."

"*Accidentally?*" Yasmin blinked at this idea.

"The two versions of me were supposed to be identical. So I'd have no trouble recombining with my original after we returned to rescue our citizens. Then that villain Mario smashed my statue, and the only body I had was this." He indicated it with both hands, looking—to her astonishment—ashamed. She took a moment to find her voice.

"Weren't you glad?"

"Of course I was. Too glad. This body isn't as powerful as the one our Creator made for me. I may never recover my full abilities. Through my selfishness, I robbed our city of my best service when she needed it most of all."

"You didn't do that on purpose."

"I can't be sure of that. How many times did I pray to God to lift my burden? How many times did I fight the urge to curse Him for forsaking me? I wanted to be a normal man: to not spend my life alone. You and I both know longings that intense can distort spellwork." His muscles were shaking slightly, his eyes bright with the strength of his emotions.

"Iksander doesn't know," he added. "Only you and Elyse have guessed."

Elyse was a human he'd met in New York. The Glorious City's guardians Cade and Arcadius were now engaged to her. Iksander's acceptance of their unusual romantic arrangement was an early sign he didn't intend to continue doing business as usual.

"Why not tell people?" she asked softly. "Why keep this a secret?"

"I'm still damaged, Yasmin. Just in a different way."

The cracking of his voice broke her heart. "You were *never* damaged, and you aren't now." He started to wag his head, and she clasped it between her hands. "Your worth never came from your magic power—or from your body's abilities. When that evil sorcerer enslaved you, did you give in to his extortion or did you resist? Joseph, your strength saved your whole town and family."

"People who tell that story exaggerate."

"They don't exaggerate that you became a eunuch because you defied a murderer. Even as a boy, you had the courage to sacrifice yourself to protect others. Your worth is in your spirit, and you've always had the spirit of an amazing man."

"Less amazing," he rasped sadly. "I shall never be as I was before."

A growl of anger rolled in her throat. Djinn would kill to have a tenth of his skill and intelligence, to have seen the wonders he'd encountered, and to enjoy his devoted friends. He was still the best magician she'd ever met. Why would he waste his gifts by bemoaning they weren't more?

"You're being stupid," she said flatly.

His head jerked back from her hold, his spine stiffening as he took offense. "If that's the way you feel—"

She didn't care what he planned to say. She didn't have to bow to his supposedly superior male view. Her opinions might not be perfect, but they mattered as much as his. She was her own woman now, with the right to give herself—or not—as she wished.

***I** can take the lead*, she thought.

"I'm kissing you," she warned.

He gaped at her but didn't back away.

Good, she thought, and pressed her lips to his.

Her heart jumped at the contact. His lips were soft, his hands like iron on her upper arms.

"Yasmin," he said and then his arms wrapped her.

They wound around her to lift her off the ground, his mouth abruptly pushing hard at hers. She went hot all over as his tongue slid in and sucked hers. He'd done this before, enough to know what he was about, enough that nerves thrilled along the length of her vertebrae. Aching inside almost more than she could stand, she clutched his broad shoulders from behind. Clearly affected by this, Joseph's arms tightened on her waist and hauled her higher.

She felt unexpectedly and rather deliciously manhandled.

His hold changed again. He cupped her head, going deeper into the now savage kiss. His other hand gripped her bottom, his fingers digging into lush flesh to squeeze. Groaning then, he hiked her pelvis up to cover his completely.

This time, Yasmin couldn't doubt his condition. She shivered at the rigid swelling that rubbed her through his trousers. He was long, for certain, and thick, and as hard as if a sculptor had carved him from hot marble. Arousal crashed over her in waves, from her scalp to her core to the tingling soles of her naked feet.

The sensation was unprecedented. Her body had never responded to anyone like this. He was what she craved: her personal, perfect choice of bed partner.

"Joseph," she moaned, digging her fingers into his thick dark hair.

He groaned again, jaw working as his mouth plundered hers. Dragging up her nightgown, she wrapped her legs around him.

The clasp of her thighs sparked a reaction. He thumped her against the wall just as she'd heard their host do to Safiye earlier. With all his weight, he thrust his steely length against her, pushing and grinding and nearly fucking her through the scrap of silk that was left to cover her. Wetness flooded from her, permeating the flimsy undergarment and making it cling closer.

Joseph's tip scraped her clitoris.

Its swollen state seemed to excite him more. One hand shoved under her hiked-up gown, cruising around her bottom before coming out again to slide up her side. Had he touched a woman like this before? Did it feel as revelatory to him as it did to her? He pushed her breast upward from beneath and dragged his mouth off hers. When he closed his lips on her nipple, he didn't restrain his strength. He sucked the peak so hard through the silk she gasped.

The longing that inspired was more persuasion than she required.

"Take me," she said, pulling his head closer. "Please, Joseph, take me now."

He made a noise like he was in pain. His fingers tightened on her like pincers, his hot breath panting against her breast.

Then he pushed back from her.

When her legs slid down him, they shook so much her knees threatened to give out. Joseph's expression was regretful.

"Why are you stopping?" she asked, her voice shaking like her legs. "I thought you wanted me."

"I do," he said, gently stroking her sweaty hair from her cheek. "I— Now isn't the right time for this."

She couldn't believe him. Her spell assured their privacy. They were free, unattached adults. And, unless she'd utterly lost her reason, they wanted each other—one more than the other, apparently.

Her pride stung horribly at the memory of begging him.

She found her voice *and* her sarcasm. "And when might the 'right' time be? It wasn't after we faced danger side-by-side. After that, you smoked off and forgot me."

"I didn't forget you. How could I? Yasmin, you're one in a million djinniya."

One in a million but not the one for him.

He read the doubt in her twisting mouth. "Didn't I come to visit you at your office?

Didn't I bring a gift?"

"You called me 'Miss Baykal.'"

"Your brother was there. Shouldn't I protect your reputation in front of him?"

He was humoring her or, worse, treating her with pity. Unwilling to confront that directly and maybe hear an unpleasant truth, she lowered her brows at him. "You don't trust me."

"I do. More than you realize. My purpose here is important and delicate. What you don't know you can't give away, which anyone might do without meaning to. Honestly, I'm counting on you to act as if my presence here *doesn't* strike you as suspicious."

"You're counting on me to act as if I'm stupid."

He smiled. "A little bit, perhaps."

"If you explained . . ."

"No," he said and rubbed her shoulders. He was calm, his pulse barely drumming in his neck. That didn't seem fair. Yasmin's blood continued to feel like it was on fire. She drew her spine straighter.

"I officially disapprove of your decision," she said coolly.

Joseph's smile deepened to the point of crinkling his gorgeous golden eyes. "Duly noted. And now I really must depart."

She thought he'd release her shoulders. He leaned to her instead, pressing his lips to her scowling brow. Despite the gentleness of the gesture, she didn't betray herself by softening. With all her strength, she continued to glare at him.

"*You're* not my father," she said darkly. "You shouldn't kiss me like he does."

She startled the smile from him.

"No," he said soberly, his hands falling from her then. "I won't make the mistake of pretending I am again."

Perhaps his nerves were rattled, after all. Rather than smoke out like he'd come in, he strode off without changing.

CHAPTER SEVEN

Day Tripper

"Good heavens," Safiye exclaimed the next morning. "Someone didn't get her beauty rest."

She'd walked in on Yasmin attempting to charm redness from her eyes. Yasmin *hadn't* been crying over Joseph's rejection. That would have been pitiful. Nonetheless, her eyes were as bloodshot as if she sobbed all night.

"Try these drops," Safiye offered, digging a stoppered vial from her tiny purse. "Sometimes personal magic needs a mundane assist."

Yasmin tried them, blinked, and immediately felt better.

Nodding in approval, Safiye slid to sit on the bathroom sink's polished counter. Yasmin concluded she'd slept well. Her looks had no blot on them.

"So," Safiye said. "You've had a day to observe. What's your impression of Stefan?"

Yasmin had prepared for this question. "Lord Dimitriou is well respected, both by djinn under his command and social peers. He runs his house efficiently. His staff is loyal. He has a lofty opinion of himself but knows when to play diplomat."

"He's not the only one," Safiye said humorously, perceiving the care Yasmin had taken in her response.

"When he turns his charm on a person, he's difficult to dislike."

"Part of you wants to dislike him," Safiye guessed.

Yasmin let her breath sigh out. "I confess that's true. Though I can't pin down the cause for my reaction, I'm reluctant to dismiss it. I do think you're correct in your assumption that he won't be faithful."

Safiye's gaze sharpened. "Did he proposition you?"

"He did not. It was merely an impression."

Safiye's lips pursed with displeasure.

"I believe he wants you to see him flirting with other females," Yasmin added. "He may see this as a way to . . . heighten his value in your eyes."

"All djinn play games in relationships. To a certain extent anyway."

"I cannot disagree with that. I understand you'd prefer concrete facts to assist your decision. I shall continue to look for them."

Safiye's faint smile slanted higher on one side. "I see I picked the right woman for the job. You'll be honest with me, no matter what."

"As far as I'm able," Yasmin said, "I won't abuse your trust."

"Well." Safiye hopped down from the counter to regard her. "The maids inform me breakfast will be served shortly. They say it is buffet style and casual. Once you've done dressing, you should join us."

"I shall hasten to finish," Yasmin assured her.

Putting herself in order took a quarter hour longer. The corridor was silent as she stepped into it. Was she last to leave her rooms? That was embarrassing. Everyone shouldn't have been better than she at going short on sleep.

She'd just clucked her tongue in dismay when a female servant exited a room with a cleaning cart full of potions and fresh towels. She seemed startled to see a guest. Yasmin recalled her suspicion that, when possible, Dimitriou's staff must be instructed to remain invisible.

"Pardon, miss," the woman said, her edges blurring even as she apologized. "I didn't know you were there."

"Don't smoke off on my account. I have a question I'd like to ask."

"Yes, miss?" the djinniya said.

"This is embarrassing, but I don't know where to eat breakfast."

"Do you wish open service or just women?"

Yasmin hadn't realized she had a choice. Open service meant men and women. Chances were this was the group Safiye was eating with. The mistresses were likelier to observe gender segregation. Safiye was expecting her, but the traditionalists' women—being away from the gaze of men—might be freer in their gossip.

"The women-only service," she decided. "I haven't been awake long enough to face mixed company."

Smiling slightly, the servant pointed her down the hall. "Past the main entry. Second set of doors on the right. There's a bronze statue of Demeter before you get to it."

Not only were the directions simple, but the double doors the maid had mentioned were propped open. A dark blue curtain protected breakfasters' privacy. Rather than walk straight into an unknown situation, Yasmin paused outside to eavesdrop.

"I'm telling you he went to her," one woman was insisting. "I saw him leave her room afterward. They'd been doing something absolutely. His face was flushed like a beet."

"What time was this?"

"I don't know. Half past two or thereabouts."

"If it was half past two, he couldn't have stayed long. The party didn't break up much earlier."

"What reason was there for him to stay? He doesn't have the right equipment to accomplish anything worthwhile."

"Oh, I don't know," a third woman laughed. "He looks as if he has clever hands, not to mention a pretty mouth."

"Don't remind me. It's a crime for a man like that to be so good looking. Can you imagine the frustration?"

"Maybe she'll take a second lover to fill the gaps, like our new kadin with her two partners. Apparently, that's standard now for the royal set."

This was said scornfully. Others hummed in agreement. Iksander hadn't done his reputation any favors by sharing his human wife—not according to this crowd, at least.

"If the second man is Eamon," the first female who'd spoken added, "she'll have plenty of gaps left!"

Laughter met the joke, which gave Yasmin the chance to enter while pretending not to have heard what went before. That she and Joseph had been the topic of discussion was obvious.

With an extra forceful push of magic, she commanded her cheeks to cool.

"Good morning, ladies," she said, lifting the dark curtain and ducking through. "I hope you don't mind if I join you."

A few of the six djinniya looked abashed.

"Please do," said the elegant brunette at the table's head. "We're always happy for new faces. We were introduced last night, but I'm Antonina, in case you don't recall."

"Thank you," Yasmin said in an equally polite tone. "I grew used to female company in the harem. It's a pleasure to enjoy it again." Her presence thus explained, she filled a plate and sat.

"I don't see Tara," she observed after a casual interval. "I hope she isn't under the weather."

"She went home," Antonina informed her.

"Home!" Yasmin had assumed the blotchy, multi-colored woman was hiding in her room.

Antonina nodded, amenable to sharing this information. "Stefan's housekeeper broke the news this morning. Tara's trunks were already gone. Her personal maid must have packed like the wind. She only had the one servant. LaBass keeps her on tight purse strings. She'd probably have sold that emerald ring if she won."

"She should have spent more time practicing," another djinniya said. "If she had, her magic might not have gone awry."

"Well," Yasmin said, unaccountably uneasy. "That's too bad. Did LaBass remain?"

"I doubt a hurricane would blow any of our men from this house, not as long as there's business to discuss."

"Mm," Yasmin hummed around a nibble of buttered toast. Asking what business the men were here for seemed like pushing her luck—assuming the women even knew.

"Don't get ideas because Tara's gone," one mistress warned. "We don't approve of poaching here."

Yasmin put down her toast in shock. "I promise you, I have no such intentions. Believe it or not, Joseph the Magician is man enough for me."

She held the djinniya's gaze, refusing to blink or blush. After a moment, her accuser looked away.

"Forgive me," the woman mumbled, aware she'd been outflanked. "I shouldn't have implied that."

"No, you shouldn't," Yasmin agreed and picked up her toast again.

She told herself her satisfaction at defending Joseph wasn't because she a crush on him. She'd defended herself as well. That was equally important.

Antonina, evidently, had earned her seat at the head of the table. When she spoke, it was as the group's leader. "I'm sure we're all fortunate in our circumstances. And in that spirit, why don't I go over today's schedule . . ."

~

The centerpiece of the schedule was a group excursion to Milion, whose quaint charm—so Dimitriou claimed—merited more than a flyover. He appeared later in the morning, having slept in and skipped breakfast. His host's prerogative left him sparkly-eyed and brimming with energy.

Practically bouncing from high spirits, he joined his guests beneath the golden dome of the grand entryway.

"We'll land in the square," he said, "tour the shops, and finish up at the Temple of Demeter. The murals there are lovely, as good as any in the capital—not that I've always cared. For reasons I'm not at liberty to discuss, my interest in the structure has intensified recently."

He grinned at Safiye, who he held cozily in the curve of his arm.

Though she didn't comment, she smiled tolerantly, seeming not to mind his hint that the temple would be a good place to tie the knot. Yasmin couldn't help worrying the time to turn Safiye back from accepting her suitor was running out.

Unaffected by such concerns, Dimitriou's disembodied servants eased opened the huge front doors. In vapor form, they were nearly invisible, the only sign of their presence a slight shimmer in the air. This made an impressive visual by itself, but as the guests stepped into the sunshine, they gasped in amazement.

The whole estate twinkled, from pavers to flowers to towering palm fronds. The diamanté effect *couldn't* be magic dust. Even Stefan wouldn't be that extravagant.

"It's from the dew," he explained, laughing at their awe. "Every so often the mists deposit wild magic on everything."

"It's marvelous," Safiye said, craning around to see. "I shouldn't have doubted Yasmin when she said the In-Betweens could be beautiful."

At the mention of Yasmin's name, Stefan turned to her. His expression was pleasant and interested. "You've visited this area before?"

"Not this area precisely. When I was younger, I traveled to other towns near an edge. I confess I've never seen anything like this."

"Ah, yes," Stefan said. "Because of your father's work. How could I have forgotten? Still, I'm glad Milion takes pride of place for our special dews."

"It has pride of place in many things," Safiye complimented, lightly stroking the sapphire buttons above his heart.

He smiled into her eyes. "More things soon, I dare to hope."

Yasmin pushed aside her annoyance at their romantic tone. Did it bother her that Stefan knew what her father did? Her relation to him wasn't secret, and she and her father were—if not famous—at least in the public consciousness. Dimitriou might not even have had to research her. Then again, maybe it was his claiming to have forgotten who her father was that struck an off note with her.

*I just don't **trust** him,* she thought.

Someone she did trust stepped quietly beside her.

Her pulse skittered in her veins. When she turned, she had to remind herself to breathe. She knew what Joseph's tempting mouth felt like now.

"Good morning," he said. His tone was cautious, his gaze searching hers for consequences of their awkward parting the previous night. Doubly glad for Safiye's eye drops, she smiled at him. She didn't mean to smile, exactly. Her lips simply curved that way.

"Good morning," she said—also quietly but perhaps a bit warmer.

Joseph's golden eyes sparked with heat. He leaned an inch closer. "It is a good morning if you've forgiven me."

She wanted to say something tart, but her mouth had dried. She'd have kissed him in a second, no matter if he pushed her away again. What was wrong with her that he could resurrect her longing so easily? She couldn't even look away. Her soul seemed to want to drink him in.

He must have guessed what she was feeling. Suddenly, he breathed faster too. "Yasmin," he whispered.

He remembered himself too soon for her. He straightened and backed up a step. "People are choosing carpets. We should try to get seats on the same one. You know, because we're a couple."

Because they were pretending.

She took too long to respond. His eyes turned quizzical. Worried perhaps, he took her arm in a gentle hold. He slid his fingers down her sleeve until they twined with hers.

"Come on," he said, giving her hand a squeeze.

She followed his tug like a golem that had been charmed. No fool, Joseph chose a rug Eamon wasn't on. They sat together in a corner, legs crossed, sides bumping, warm air coursing around them as they flew. Milion sparkled just like Dimitriou's estate, coated with the same magic. From above, the town resembled a pretty toy for djinniya princesses.

She felt like a princess when they landed and Joseph helped her swing out. Shaking off the effect, she realized how opulent Dimitriou's carpets were compared to their surroundings. Milion was a well-kept town, but its people weren't made of money. They worked for their living. Stefan's guests alighted on the grass of the central square like a flock of exotic birds: wealthy elite descending on peons.

Even the mistresses—who might have known better—didn't try to act like they belonged to the same species.

Stefan flipped a golden coin to one of the djinn who'd come out to watch. "Keep an eye on our rugs," he said, his manner still pleasant but not as personal.

Taking no offense that she could see, the man bowed agreeably. "Yes, Lord Dimitriou. Your vehicles will be safe here when you return."

The drivers and guards would accompany them, she guessed.

Reminding herself she wasn't here to start a revolt among the lower classes, she looked around curiously. She saw a silk seller and a bakeshop and a store for refreshing worn slippers. She wondered idly if the apothecary carried the brand of teeth cleaning disk she liked. The one she'd brought was due for a replacement.

Then she spotted the post office.

If anywhere in town had a signal booster, this was a good candidate. Plus, if she could somehow separate herself from the others, she might be able to glean useful intelligence.

She wasn't aware her body language betrayed her interest until Joseph leaned closer. "Whatever you're thinking: stop. Stay with the group and don't attract attention. Let your snooping compulsion rest for once."

It wasn't a snooping compulsion, it was her job! She lowered her brows at him then decided he wasn't worth arguing with.

"Stefan," she said, raising her voice enough to be heard over the distance between them. "Do you know if the post office has a stabilizer? I've been having trouble getting a message to my brother."

Dimitriou walked back to her with more keenness than she liked. "An urgent message?"

"No, no. Balu lives at home with our parents. He gets bored there sometimes. If I don't keep in touch, he'll feel neglected."

"Ah, it's nice you're close. Families aren't always. My parents died when I was a teenager. Looking back, I wish I hadn't been so eager to cut my leading strings. I'd give anything to have them with me now." His tone was rueful, his confession seemingly genuine. All the same, it slid into her mind that if his parents had been alive, he wouldn't have been lord of a great estate.

"We don't know what we have until we lose it," she said gravely.

"You're very wise," he praised, though her statement had been banal.

She ordered herself not to look away from his warmly approving eyes.

"The stabilizer?" Joseph said, interrupting their moment.

"Ah, yes." Stefan scratched his cheek. "The post office has one certainly. Just tell the clerk to charge your boost to my account." Her question answered, he turned to her self-appointed protector. "Joseph, since you're the sultan's advisor on all things magical, I wonder if I might ask your opinion on a security system I'm thinking of installing . . ."

He led Joseph off by the arm, sparing Yasmin the bother of figuring out how to shake loose of his company. Before anyone else could think of joining her, she walked briskly to the small storefront.

Happily, her luck held. The establishment was empty but for a bored twentyish male clerk. A pile of magic dust, no doubt scraped up from outside, sat on the counter in front of him. He was sprinkling scintillating pinches onto postcards, thereby animating the scenes on them.

"I don't suppose you'd like to buy one of these," he said gloomily. "I've got, like, a zillion shots of the In-Betweens. Plus, for a little extra, I can project your image into them."

"Perhaps once I've sent my message. I'm told you have a signal stabilizer. I'm hoping to reach the capital."

"That's no problem. You can use the curtained booth over there. You're one of Lord D's guests, aren't you? He'll want you on his tab. Just go in, and I'll process everything."

Though she didn't like being in Stefan's debt, it seemed awkward to refuse. Yasmin went into the presumably private booth. A small desk and chair supplied her a place to write. In case Stefan had more arrangements with the clerk than who paid for what, she composed an innocuous message to her brother.

HELLO, "BRO"! GOT YOUR RESPONSE TO MY PREVIOUS LETTER,
BUT IT ARRIVED GARBLED. AM USING BOOSTER AT MILION
PUBLIC POST OFFICE FOR THIS ONE. IF YOU ABSOLUTELY NEED
TO REACH ME, SEND INFO TO THIS ADDRESS. KISSES AND
HUGS. DON'T DRIVE THE "'RENTS" CRAZY.
MUCH LOVE, YASMIN.

Satisfied Balu would understand they couldn't communicate openly, she pushed the folded note into the slot marked 'SEND.' A burst of enchanted flame dematerialized the paper. If the operation went as intended, her words would show up on Balu's scroll in seconds.

"Goddess willing," she murmured, in case divine aid would help.

Deciding a little primping also couldn't hurt, she smoothed her head scarf, pinched her cheeks, and went out again.

"All good?" asked the clerk, glancing up at her.

She flashed her most brilliant smile. "Thank you, yes, and I will take one of those of postcards now. They looked adorable."

The process of inserting her image into a shot entailed more friendliness. The young clerk was nearly cheerful by the time she paid for the souvenir. As she'd guessed, the animated postcards were his personal side business. He made her coin disappear into his sash pocket.

"You don't need to come back to mail that," he said. "It's pre-charged. Just write the address and say a prayer."

Yasmin nodded that she understood. "You must see all the goings on in the square from here. Do you know what happened to the market stall that showed up the other day? We were with Lord Dimitriou when the news arrived. I confess the story made me terribly curious."

"My theory is dragons are behind it," the young man said.

This seemed unlikely but not impossible. "Dragons?"

"Absolutely." The young man rested his elbows on the counter. "Mist dragons might swallow something down thinking it's good to eat, then spit it out on our shore. Or maybe the myth that we have a Nessie is true. If we could prove it, that'd bring the tourists out here for sure."

"A Nessie would be exciting," she agreed. "What about the booth itself? Is anyone investigating it for clues to its origins?"

"I wish. It's locked up underneath the assembly hall until Lord D sorts out ownership. As if a *person* will come forward to claim it."

He shook his head at that ridiculous idea.

"That's too bad," Yasmin said. She restrained herself from asking where the hall was. If this town was like most, it would be on the square. In truth, she'd already seen a building she thought was a contender.

"No imagination," the clerk was grousing. "That's the problem with most djinn."

She left the young man as she'd found him, resuming his gloominess. She, by contrast, was energized. She had a lead to follow! Before Stefan or his group could spot her, she hurried down a side street into the shadow of a few rubbish bins.

Changing into her cat form was child's play. She closed her eyes to focus, mentally recited her usual prayer, then visualized the scraggly black-and-white feline she'd turned into countless times. A heartbeat later, she padded forward on silent paws. Her crooked tail and whiskers felt as much a part of her as her djinn nose or feet—more a part, in some ways. She was free as a cat. No need to follow rules. No need to cover up . . . or wish she were able to. All those silly internal conflicts dissolved. She was her truest self, her own spirit animal.

She trotted toward the square with jubilation in her soul.

A loosened grate provided entry into the assembly hall's cellar. The vent's other end was a six-foot drop onto a cement floor. Since she was used to maneuvering as a cat, after a moment's fright she landed almost as lightly as a real one. A shake and a couple sneezes cleared her of dust and dirt. Sensing no one else on the basement level, she slinked forward to explore.

Conveniently, the first storage room she tried held a promising shape under a large dropcloth.

Unwilling to take too long and risk being missed, she changed back to two-legged form. Hands were better than paws for things like this. Pulling back the canvas revealed she had indeed found the mystery stall. With her heart beating faster, she spelled on a light and entered the small structure.

The unclaimed merchandise still sat on the wooden shelves. Skillfully embroidered sheets drew her fingers up to stroke. The stitching she found there caused her to start. The wavy cloud pattern on the trim matched the linens in Stefan's house. What were the odds that a booth coughed randomly from the mists stocked the same bedclothes? The pattern was distinctive. Yasmin, at least, had never seen it outside Milion.

"Huh," she said, unable to decide what this meant.

She bent down to rummage further. Before her father's invention made their family's fortune, Yasmin's mother had run a market stall. She'd sold pre-charged crib mobiles that played lullabies. As a girl, Yasmin often went to work with her. She recalled her mother having a secret hiding place for possessions she didn't want on her all the time: her purse or a story scroll to keep Yasmin occupied.

"Ah-hah," she said, spotting a concealment spell under the counter.

Yasmin had a knack for untangling other people's magic. A minute cracked the protection, revealing a small flat drawer. Inside, she found not belongings but the missing owner's license to run the stall. She pulled it out and smoothed it on the counter.

The parchment sheet included the vendor's picture. The djinniya didn't look more than thirty. She had a narrow serious face, dark straight hair that fell past her shoulders, and soft green eyes. A moment later, Yasmin gasped in surprise. As part of preparing for this job, she'd loaded a Milion walking map on her scroll. The vendor license listed a residential address two blocks from where she stood. If this paperwork was accurate, the In-Betweens couldn't have spit out the booth as alleged. The booth belonged here. Ivy Ozil—a local—had set it up on the square once a week for the last two years.

"How can this be?" she murmured. "The people here are your neighbors. They wouldn't forget you."

She shivered as another question occurred to her. If Ivy Ozil were alive, why hadn't she come forward to claim her stuff?

Yasmin needed to check out the address. Yes, the booth's connection to Dimitriou was slim. It was, however, there. She didn't believe in coincidences. This discovery mattered.

"*Hey*," said a harsh male voice. "You're not supposed to be in here."

She spun around to see who'd crept up on her. One of the Milion guards blocked the exit. She'd know that bright blue uniform anywhere.

Damn it, she thought. *You should have prepared a story.* As to that, she should have been paying more attention.

"I'm so sorry," she said as sincerely as she could. "I'm one of Lord D's guests. I couldn't resist trying to solve the mystery." She waved toward the bedding booth. "It's the market stall, the one that mysteriously showed up the other day. I was looking for clues to its origin."

Every word of this was true, a circumstance she hoped sounded in her voice. Disappointingly, the guard glowered harder. Despite her pounding heart, Yasmin attempted to keep her wits. The vendor's license lay on the counter in plain view, but the guard seemed not to have noticed it. Whatever happened, she wanted to preserve that evidence. Inspired by the postal clerk's handling of her coin, she spelled the parchment, folded, into the secret pocket in her waist sash. However suspicious the guard might be, he was unlikely to frisk a female of her status.

"Truly," she said to her challenger. "I meant no harm."

The guard wasn't buying her meek manner. "You day trippers are all the same. You think you can smile and spin some story, and we simple villagers will bend over to please you." He snorted and shook his head. "You can tell your tale to Lord Dimitriou after I report you for trespassing."

Damn, she thought and promptly scrapped the idea of offering the guard a bribe. That, she decided, would just make him angrier.

~

Perhaps it was a failure of courage, but Yasmin didn't rejoin Stefan's village tour. Instead, she returned to his house alone, paced her suite in agitation, and read the vendor's license a couple thousand additional times. No matter how finely she parsed the words, they didn't prove anything solid.

A maid arrived at her door an hour before dinner. The 'master' had returned. He wanted to speak to her.

Hold yourself together, Yasmin ordered. *Take your medicine, but don't give the game away.* Like any highborn male, Stefan would expect deference. She knew how to offer that—or at least its semblance. She had a lifetime of practice.

The maid led her to Dimitriou's private office, which was located beneath the smallest of the estate's three domes. Polished copper sheathed its high ribbed ceiling, the color a complement to the tufted aqua velvet that clad the curving walls. Stefan sat behind a large antique desk, his caramel brown hair tied back, his head bent over paperwork. A device she *believed* was a replica of a human phone, rotary style, gleamed black beside his elbow. Wires connected it to a port in the wall. She shook off her distraction over this oddity. Stefan was giving out the impression of a busy, important man—almost too busy and important to spend his time scolding her.

The posturing amused her. Calmed by that, she waited for him to look up. The instant he did, she realized relaxing even a smidgen was premature.

The easy charm she'd grown used to was nowhere in evidence. His face was colder than any person's she'd ever seen. Djinn were fiery creatures, naturally passionate. Stefan's features resembled carved alabaster more than warm flesh. His eyes were alive but icy and glittering. Their hue matched the pale blue-green walls. Though this implied vanity, and theoretically could have amused her too, his chill regard made it hard to swallow.

Her anxiety didn't lessen as he leaned back in his tall chair.

"You've been poking into matters that don't concern you," he said coolly.

"I'm afraid I have," she admitted, having no trouble whatsoever hanging her head. "I have no excuse except an overabundance of curiosity. I've never been able to resist a good puzzle."

"You're a grown woman. You can resist anything you choose."

"You're correct, of course. I can only throw myself on your mercy." She peeked at him from beneath her lashes, as any female might.

His expression didn't change. He placed his hands on the desk, spread his fingers, and sat straighter. He looked like a judge about to pronounce a sentence. She prepared herself to hear a verdict.

"You must face a consequence," he said. "Or you won't learn your lesson. I want you to sit out tonight's entertainment. I'll have dinner sent to your room. You can think about what you've done."

She could *think about* what she'd done? As if she were six years old? Stefan wasn't her father or her husband or anything but her host. By gender arrogance alone, he claimed authority over her. Too astonished to hold the reaction back, her jaw dropped as if weights were attached to it. If this was how he treated women, Yasmin's client definitely shouldn't marry him!

A glimmer of . . . something flared in the depths of Dimitriou's aloof eyes. Maybe it was amusement. Or satisfaction. She couldn't tell. Whatever the pleasurable feeling, it seemed intended for him alone to enjoy.

"Do you have a problem with my decision?" he asked calmly.

"No," she said, shaking herself back to respectfulness. "I'm certain it's precisely what I deserve."

CHAPTER EIGHT

Pleasure Seekers

The evening was the longest in Yasmin's memory. As agreed, she returned to her rooms and stayed. A meal of bread and water was brought to her by a maid. Admittedly, it was good bread, accompanied by a cruet of olive oil and herbs to drizzle onto it. Still, Stefan had to be 'trolling' her—as Balu claimed humans said.

Bread and water were prison fare.

Once the maid left, no one interrupted her punishment. Opening a window teased her with distant shouts of laughter. Stefan's guests were playing a game out on the grounds tonight. Carpet polo, possibly. She thought she heard mallets thwacking balls.

Annoyed that she was stuck here while people were having fun or—worse—dropping useful clues, she flounced back onto her bed.

Why am I obeying? she wondered silently. *No one keeps me here but me.*

She wasn't as adept at taking vapor form as Joseph. He was better than Stefan's servants, despite their extensive experience. She, however, could slip out in her cat form. The drawback was that if she were caught flouting Dimitriou's edict, he might banish her from his home. She'd never complete her assignment. Plus, her behavior would embarrass her client.

Obey for now, she decided. Goddess willing, Dimitriou would believe he'd succeeded in cowing her. He'd relax and she'd get another opening.

She stared at the flowery ceiling medallion, waiting for Safiye to return. That didn't happen, though the noises of partying quieted and ceased. Did Safiye know she'd been punished? Was she displeased and avoiding her? Another possibility was that Stefan had convinced her to spend the night with him. She could be in his bed chamber that minute.

"Shit," Yasmin murmured. Was she too late? Had Safiye already accepted his proposal?

She was heaving a sigh when a scratch sounded on her door. That bolted her upright. The steam drifting through the keyhole confirmed that Joseph was entering.

"It's me," he whispered as he reformed. "I came to see if you were okay."

She smoothed her hair before she could stop herself.

"I am," she whispered back.

He sat on the end of the bed, dangerously elegant in his evening clothes—or at least dangerous to her. She should have minded his presumption but didn't.

"You didn't listen to me," he observed, one nimble-fingered hand petting the coverlet. "About not drawing attention to yourself."

"Don't you scold. I already took my licks from Dimitriou."

"Was it worth it?"

"Maybe," she answered sullenly.

His smile was faint but visible. She liked his amusement less than the simple fact of his company.

"I'm not telling you what I found," she warned. "You haven't earned that from me."

Suddenly he was scooting closer, moving all the way up the mattress to sit by her. His hand rose to touch her hair, and her pulse leaped wildly. His golden eyes were gentle, his thumb like velvet caressing her cheekbone.

"I'm sure I haven't earned this either," he said softly.

His lips molded softly, warmly over her parted ones. He didn't push inside her mouth but brushed across it from side to side. Every spot he glided over tingled. Her breath went shallow, and he sat back.

They remained connected. She'd laid her palm on his chest while he was kissing her. Now she couldn't bring herself to withdraw it. His body heat was amazing, his heart drumming strongly behind his ribs. Hers drummed too. In her skin. Between her legs. Everywhere, it felt like. She realized her mouth hung open. He'd barely touched her, but she'd unraveled utterly.

She really was in trouble if he affected her this strongly.

Seeing her reaction, Joseph laughed breathlessly. His cheeks were flushed, his eyes dancing. He cupped her face like before. "I *worried* about you when you didn't rejoin the group."

Was that why he kissed her, because he'd been worried?

"I was fine," she said proudly.

"You weren't fine. You were getting into trouble where you weren't supposed to be!"

"Well, I'm fine now. See. Not a scratch on me."

"You are the most infuriating—" He stopped and shook his head. "God help me, I couldn't get you out of my mind all day. Wondering if you were all right. Trying not to remember kissing your gorgeous lips. My mind's a shambles. I don't know how anyone resists you."

She knew she wasn't thinking clearly. His words didn't allow it.

"You don't have to," she blurted.

"Don't tease," he said.

He was the tease, not her.

"I'm not," she said firmly. "If you want me, I'd rather you not resist."

Though his color deepened, he abruptly went solemn. Angry, she took him by the ears. "Make your move," she said. "Or never try this again."

She guessed he believed her. He blinked and then he wound his arms around her. The kiss he pulled her into was bruising but welcome. This time, he used his tongue. As it sparred with hers, his hungry hands roved her body. She wore a sheath nightgown like last night. Tonight, he seemed to relish how thin it was. He cupped her breast, squeezing it through the silk and thumbing circles around her taut nipple.

She swallowed an excited cry, sensation winging from his touch straight to her clitoris. Arousal spilled from her in a rush. Maybe he knew. He let out a sound, muscles tensing as he shifted in preparation for moving over her. One hand slid her nightgown higher. He stroked her bare thigh from knee to hip, caressing the muscle there.

She moaned as he pushed her into the plush mattress.

"Christ," he gasped and writhed full length against her.

He was so hard it amazed her. She caressed his back through his tunic, waist to shoulder, every plane and bunching muscle delighting her. Joseph drove his hands underneath her bottom, hauling her closer still.

An incredible ache of longing coiled in her core.

"Yasmin," he panted, his erection grinding the softness between her legs. "I want to make you come."

"Keep doing that and you will. Better yet—" Groaning with impatience, she tugged at his snug waist sash. "Magick off your clothes and make me come with you inside me."

His eyes flared hot gold, the trademark light of their kind almost blinding her. "I can't do that. People will know if we have intercourse."

"No, they won't. Not for sure. And who cares anyway?"

"They'll know," he insisted. "You and I aren't average, magic-wise. Having actual sex will change our auras. The difference will be noticeable."

Yasmin stopped trying to tear his sash away. "Why does having people think you're still a eunuch matter?"

"Don't ask what I can't answer."

"You mean what you won't."

He looked at her, not denying it and not seeming sorry either. She huffed and began to speak, but he was too quick for her. He covered her mouth and kissed her blisteringly.

Her hands made fists on his back as the kiss drew out. After a bit, as he realized she wasn't going anywhere, his incursion slowed. This turned out to be even more seductive. Every lick of his tongue seemed to stroke lower parts of her, while every undulation of his hips actually did. *Stop that,* she protested . . . but only inside her head. She couldn't push him away. She craved what he did too much. He had her other breast in his hand now, his thumb and finger lightly pinching the lengthened tip. He must have been reading her energy. He knew exactly what pressure to use on her; knew when to let go so her nipple would throb with loss.

He also knew when to start over.

Then again, the way she gasped and wriggled probably shortened his learning curve.

By the time his mouth shifted to her neck, she could barely think. Her body buzzed all over with excitement, and his breath came as short as hers. The broken gusts fanned her perspiring skin. If that hadn't been so arousing, she might have enjoyed a feeling of victory. As it was, her strongest reaction was surrender. With a moan that melted her even more, he nipped a tendon she hadn't known was sensitive.

Her thighs were taffy. They rose up either side of him as if he'd spelled them there. In truth, he didn't need a spell. Of her own free will, she wanted to open herself to him.

He sat up unexpectedly. Her legs sprawled around his hips while he gazed down at her. Djinn fire continued burning behind his eyes, but it was steadier. He knew what he'd done to her; knew she wouldn't refuse whatever he wished to do.

Regardless of what he knew, he gave her a chance to tell him to stop. Inch by inch, he pushed her nightgown higher, the silk tickling her skin as it went. With him, being bared felt liberating rather than immodest. Needing no coaxing, she lifted her hips for him. He slid the silk to her waist.

Only her undergarment covered her. Joseph stroked the opening to either side. "May I spell these away?"

He could have asked more than that. Rather than say so, she pushed up on her elbows. This gave her a better view of what she'd done to him. She touched the hump that lifted his tunic front, petting the thick arch along its length. His breath sucked in. He was very excited.

"I'll be careful with you," he said.

Another man would have meant because of his size, but he'd said he wasn't taking her that way.

"Why do you need to be careful?"

"Because—" He broke off and swallowed. "Because I haven't done many sexual things before."

He'd switched the place he caressed her undergarment. Now his nails strafed lightly up and down the cloth that covered her pussy lips. She couldn't control a shiver . . . or the breathiness of her voice. "So far you're doing fine."

The glimmer of a smile broke his seriousness.

"I think I should set a rule," she added.

"A *rule*."

"What you do to me, I should be allowed in return."

"Ah," he said unsurely. "I, uh, don't think you should feel obliged to do the things to me that I'd like to do to you."

"I said you ought to allow it, not that I'd feel obliged." She smiled when he squirmed uneasily. He really was entertaining to push this way. "You can't deny my request is fair."

"It is fair," he admitted grudgingly. "I agree that you may . . . if you wish . . . do to me what I do to you. However, you must wait until I'm done."

Her laugh for this was throaty. "For a djinni, you're not much of a bargainer."

"Other males are welcome to have other priorities." The dignity in his tone didn't cancel a hint of humor.

"Well," she prompted. "Aren't you going to spell away my clothes?"

He hesitated. "If I spell yours away . . ."

"Yes," she grinned. "You'd be giving me permission to make you naked too."

"I'd rather not be."

"I know you're beautiful."

He grimaced. "I fear I'll be too tempted to . . . go farther than I should if we are skin-to-skin. You could make an exception on that one thing."

He sounded so hopeful she wagged her head. "I want you naked from the waist up. That's my final offer. I won't relinquish any more privileges."

"Agreed," he said.

To her amusement, they shook on it. Because she had his hand in hers, she pulled his palm to her mouth to kiss. He shuddered when she slipped her tongue out to lick the spot.

"Yasmin . . ."

"Am I distracting you?" she asked innocently, sliding the wet tip downward to flick nerves beneath his wrist. His skin was salty, and his fingers curled in reaction. "Surely a big, fancy magician like yourself can work a little spell no matter what I do."

His eyes narrowed. She felt the energy around him thicken as he focused. He flicked the same fingers she'd caused to bend, and suddenly air puffed against her skin all over. He'd stripped her bare without uttering a charm. Not only that, her nightgown now hung neat as a pin on the back of an armchair.

"Showoff," she accused.

She let him have a heartbeat to enjoy that.

Then she magically whisked his waist sash and tunic onto the floor. Two garments were better than one, weren't they?

"You didn't fold them," he pointed out smugly.

She didn't admit she wasn't as slick as him. "I'm not your valet!"

When she started to stroke his naked back, he caught her wrists. With firm but not brutish pressure, he pulled them beside her head. "You're a minx."

"I'm a woman."

His pupils swelled at the statement, darkening the center of his glowing eyes. His respiration turned sexual as she wriggled between his thighs. The time for humor was over. Desire ruled their choices now. He fanned her wrists with his thumbs, stimulating her nerves as she'd so recently done to him.

The fact that he crouched over her in a classic posture of male control didn't escape either one of them.

"I'm at your mercy," she reminded, aroused just by saying it. "You have my permission to do what you like to me."

He bent lower, his tongue curling out to wet his parted lips. He kissed her neck so lightly shivers coursed down her spine. Her collarbones came next, kisses dropped like dew on her skin. He traveled left, then right, then nuzzled the dip between. His hands stroked up and down her forearms, somehow making her tingle all over. The inner slope of one breast received his tribute next, his breath coming faster as he neared her nipple. He claimed that like an erotic dream, soft lips surrounding the peak to tug.

Had he ever touched a woman as he was touching her? She didn't think so. His manner was too enrapt. She let him explore her body as he desired. To her, this was exciting, no matter how careful his technique. He sucked her second nipple as tenderly as the first, his hands sliding lower to chafe her waist in a matched rhythm.

When he dragged his palms to her hips, she squirmed.

Theoretically, a man could use a hold like that to subdue his female.

Though Joseph wasn't gripping her hard at all, she'd just grown so wet arousal spilled from her.

His head lifted from her breast. "Do you like this?"

She nodded, unable to speak aloud.

"You're biting your lip," he observed. He seemed to take this as a good sign.

His hold slid to her knees, which he caressed lightly as a feather on either side. Her left leg jerked in response to the skimming touch.

"Does that tickle?"

"Only in a good way," she gasped.

He smiled and pushed his palms up her thighs, seeming to savor their shape and feel. "I believe I need leverage for this. Please let me know if you'd like more pressure."

What he meant by 'this' soon became obvious. He moved backward on the mattress between her legs. He was going to kiss her sex. Though one rather insistent part of her wanted exactly that, being pleasured in such a fashion seemed highly personal.

"Wait," she gasped as his head lowered.

He looked up at her with a furrow between his brows. Would telling him this act was also foreign to her make him more nervous?

"I kiss you here, yes?" he asked, his thumbs sliding inward to touch her clitoris from either side. "Or suck you, rather, and perhaps rub you with my tongue. I've read about it and seen animated pictures. It doesn't seem that difficult."

She had just enough breath to laugh. "I suppose it's not 'rocket science.'"

He knew the human term. "Then why do you wish to wait?"

"It's . . . intimate."

His eyes flared a few lumens brighter. "I want to be intimate with you." His voice was husky. He kissed her gently to right and left. "You haven't been shy with me up till now. Let me learn what pleases you."

She stroked his hair, the dark locks silky as she combed them behind his ears. Evidently, the rims of his ears were sensitive. He shivered as her thumbs skimmed them. "I've barely touched you . . ."

He smiled like a thief who spies an unlocked door. "You can touch me later. If we get around to it."

If they got around to it! She drew breath to object, but the air came right back out as a moan. He'd put his mouth on her. He was sucking her swollen bud. The tug on the epicenter of her sensation was deliciously direct. It felt better—to be honest—than anything she'd ever experienced. Encouraged by her reaction, he hooked his arms firmly around her thighs.

She hadn't realized his biceps were so formidable. They felt hot and steely next to her bottom cheeks.

"There," he said, panting a bit against her. "That should keep you where you need to be."

It kept her squirming, was what it did. Apparently, being controlled like this lit her sexual fires. His strength held her in place even when she began to thrash. His technique barely had to be good at all. She was too wound up to contain her excitement. Fortunately, he didn't try to get fancy. He stuck to steady and effective. And thorough. Thorough was very much his style. He sucked and flicked and used his thumbs to rub along her side channels, until she couldn't help crying out. He growled at that, a rumble against her pelvic floor. The small of her back arched uncontrollably off the bed.

Joseph lifted his mouth off her. "Did you—?"

"Don't stop," she gasped, too close to the edge to be self-conscious.

"No, no stopping," he agreed, returning to his self-appointed task.

She was glad for his seriousness then. He didn't flinch when her hands clamped behind his head. Goddess bless him, he went harder and faster. *Probably* he could breathe. He'd mention if he couldn't, wouldn't he?

An instant later, she lost her ability to concern herself with his physical comfort. She groaned as all the ecstatic feelings he'd inspired gathered together and leaped high. She came in a series of powerful pulses, the pleasure so intense, so protracted that it literally stole her breath. She gasped for air as it ended, then let out a pleasured sigh.

"Okay," Joseph said from a fuzzy distance. "That was you coming, wasn't it?"

She laughed softly. She was limp, her hands no longer imprisoning his head. "That was me, most certainly."

He moved up to lay beside her. After a minute for her lungs and strength to recover, she rolled toward him. His face was close, their heads resting on the same pillow. His expression was calm but watchful, his body understandably not as relaxed as hers. His lashes were amazing up close like this. The back of her hand fell naturally onto his naked chest.

Too naturally maybe, though she didn't pull it away. Since they were so convenient, she turned her hand to pet his pectorals.

"Did I suffocate you?" she asked.

One side of his mouth twitched. "No more than I could stand." He hesitated and spoke again. "That was all right?"

"Far better than all right. I believe you're a natural."

"Maybe I should get more practice."

"Nuh-uh," she contradicted and slid her palm slowly down his centerline.

"Yasmin," he cautioned as her fingertips skated across his navel's dip. Muscles jerked in his belly . . . and not just from nervousness. The heat that poured off his muscled body was tropical.

"A deal's a deal," she purred.

"I'd rather you didn't— I mean, obviously I wouldn't *dislike* if you did to me what I did to you, but—"

His breath caught sharply as she palmed the substantial ridge of his erection. A hard-on this stiff really had to be squeezed a bit. Yasmin felt gratified when his eyes crossed briefly.

"But?" she prompted agreeably.

"I'd rather you did that," he rasped.

"This?" He surprised her. Taking him by hand would be easier, of course, given that most of her experience was with inanimate training tools. Despite this, she had to ask. "Wouldn't you like me to do something you can't do for yourself?"

"Well, I have done it, naturally. When I was younger. Before."

"Before?"

"Before the sorcerer unmanned me."

"And not since?"

He heard her astonishment. "I thought giving myself a release would differentiate me too much from my double. I didn't want to hinder rejoining it. Our city needed me at full power."

According to him, the statue of his double had been destroyed months ago. Once it was, he'd had no reason not to act like a normal male and give himself whatever release he wished. Maybe he wasn't the orgy type, but some form of self-indulgence would have been understandable.

"Your restraint is extraordinary," she observed.

He colored at her tone. "I thought I ought to have . . . an occasion."

She smiled at that idea. "Am *I* an occasion?"

"Yes," he said, perfectly serious.

Her hand still cupped his erection. He laid his hand on top, his fingers sliding between hers. "Won't you pleasure me this way?"

There couldn't be any real doubt she would. "I'm loosening these," she said, undoing the front of his trousers.

He gasped as her actions gave his erection room to rise.

"Better?" she murmured. The answer being obvious, she reached into his garment.

He gasped again, a hint of a curse in it, as all four of her fingertips slid down his underside. This was delicious to her as well. His skin was velvet beneath her touch, the veins that fed his hardness raised and pulsing under the taut surface.

"You feel good in my hand," she said, stroking down and then up his thick length again. "Smooth and strong and fiery."

He'd clenched his jaw, his body coiling against a pleasure that likely threatened to overwhelm. She abandoned the idea of him giving her direction; expecting him to talk would have been too much. His speechlessness was all right. She liked the idea of taking charge of this.

She guessed she enjoyed being bossy as much as being bossed.

"Hitch your leg over mine," she said huskily. "I need room to reach all of you."

He obeyed after a small pause. The weight and tension of his leg on hers was unexpectedly arousing. Ordering herself not to get distracted, she pushed her hand deeper into his garment.

"God," he breathed as her fingers brushed over and clasped his testicles.

"Are you sensitive here?"

His hand had been between her shoulder blades, but as she asked her question, he slid it lower. "Yes. That part of me is new. It might as well have never been touched before."

Oh, she liked that idea. Before she could say so, his fingers traced a circle on one half of her lush bottom. The pattern he drew sent electricity through her nerves. Was he trying to arouse her, or could he just not resist exploring more parts of her?

"You're biting your lip again," he said.

Because this seemed like surrendering the upper hand, she released her lip and nipped his. That led to a probing kiss neither of them could bear to stop for a few minutes. Each taste made her long for more, each suck and pull a spur to their excitement.

When she pulled back at last, both their lungs worked like bellows.

"Rub my cock," he panted. "Before I lose my mind."

She was a bit embarrassed for having forgotten.

"Can't have that," she panted in return. "Your mind is a lovely thing."

Despite her words, she didn't rub his cock right away. She hadn't finished investigating his testicles. She ran her fingers around them gently, not wanting to inadvertently cause him pain. She was pretty sure she was inspiring the opposite. His neck arched back, his Adam's apple standing out. The texture of his skin intrigued her, the heft of the hidden structures inside the sac. Tendons jerked and shortened as she stroked him with her thumb's pad.

"*Yasmin*," Joseph rasped. "Don't make me wait so much."

"Sorry," she said. "The way you're made interests me."

He was looking into her eyes, his gaze so close, so intense that it made her feel things she couldn't put names to. Her irises must have been glowing too. Magic seemed to sparkle in the space between them. Was this what people meant by two souls becoming one? Should she be worried if it was?

"You're a miracle," he murmured. "The way you touch me . . . The way you feel underneath my hand . . ."

She wanted to give him everything he wanted, everything he dreamed of.

She didn't say that. She had *some* self-preservation left.

"You want me to get down to business."

"Yes."

"You want to come."

His gaze heated even more. "You'll be in no doubt if you slide your hold up me."

She took his cock by the base and pulled. His thickness leaped in her hand, and his neck sagged back with bliss like before, eyes closed, muscles all over his body tightening. She tried picking up the pace, then realized how awkward doing this with her arm shoved inside his trousers was. Without asking, she magicked the fabric to his hips. His startled eyes flew open.

"I know you're modest," she said. "I'm just being practical.

He looked at her. "All right," he said finally.

She didn't glance down, though she wanted to. She learned him by touch, pull by pull, stroke by stroke, until he felt like he was trembling inside and out. His shaft was as hard as iron, swollen to a size that both fascinated and alarmed her. Maybe, even without her gawking at his penis, he felt exposed. He dropped his brow to her shoulder, hiding his face from view. The leg he'd slung over hers coiled and shifted—as if he were too restless to keep it still. His body had instincts that didn't require experience. He was almost thrusting, almost mimicking taking her.

She was no expert, but he seemed as if he were fighting not to explode.

"Are you holding back your climax?" she whispered.

"Should I not?" he gasped.

"You should do what you want." Whether this was the proper answer, she didn't know. It simply seemed right to her. Something else seemed right as well. "Hold on," she said. "I'm pushing you onto your back."

She didn't give him time to resist. She shoved, he rolled, and she straddled him where he'd sprawled. Her eyes took a quick but thorough drink of him. A hundred illustrated pillow books couldn't have prepared her for his appeal. He looked good enough to eat: sweaty and tight and carnal with his diaphragm heaving in and out. His cock stretched hugely up his belly, lying flat against it from the change in his position. Because she could, she clasped it from either side. He groaned and twisted on the covers as she pushed her thumbs up the distended under-ridge.

"That's better," she said, giving him the two-handed rub again. "One hand really isn't enough for a man your size."

"*Yasmin.*" Caught off balance, at least metaphorically, he grabbed onto her hips. She'd temporarily forgotten she was naked, but as he blinked at his new view, she remembered. She guessed he liked what he saw. He rolled his lips together and then licked them.

"You look nice too," she teased.

He was flushed all over, like he'd been baking in the sun. His cheeks and nipples and glans were the darkest places, drawing her eyes irresistibly. His crown was spilling pre-come, the flow like oil shining on his skin. Yasmin decided maybe she ought to give him a warning.

"I want to rub this into you," she said, touching the silky wetness with two fingers. "It will make my hands slide better. When I slick it around your tip, that will probably cause you to ejaculate."

He looked down at himself, seeing what she did. "I . . . have noticed I am more sensitive there."

The way he admitted this made her smile. "You don't object?"

"I would—" He stopped and sucked in more air. "I would like you to make a fist. A tight one. And drag it up and down me quickly."

She had no doubt she'd like this too.

"As you wish," she said.

Like any concubine worth her smoke, she'd practiced this on stone dildos. Confident she'd do well enough, she set her knees for balance. She began as he had with her: simple and steady. He liked when the fist she'd made crossed the flange of his crown. His fingers dug into her hipbones, and his breathing deepened—deliberately, she thought.

He was trying to last, to savor every moment of the journey.

Though he trembled, his restraint amazed her. Her arm was going to give out before he did. Come to think of it, maybe he could stand a trick or two.

That idea sent a palpable thrill through her. Why not make this as memorable as her training enabled?

"How about fist over fist?" she suggested throatily.

Before he could do more than suck in a breath, she put her words into action. One tight hand replaced the other as each fist flipped off his tip. He moaned as she went faster, and that was a thrill as well. His head rolled from side to side on the pillow, his back beginning to arch off the bed for her squeezing pulls. He was in his head, his eyes screwed shut with pleasure, but she didn't mind at all. She liked watching him lose himself, liked being the one to push him over the precipice.

She saved massaging his glans until his choppy gasps informed her his control hung by its last thread. She caught his shaft between the heels of her palms, trapping it for her special treatment no matter how wild his thrashing got. With his penis steadied, she rubbed the slippery crown, quick and hot, with all her finger pads.

Probably, this was over-stimulation. Joseph's spine bowed, and he choked out a cry. Because she knew too much feeling was exactly right sometimes, she didn't lose her nerve. Instead, determined to send him over with all possible fireworks, she worked her thumbs into the nerves that concentrated where his foreskin attached beneath the head.

He swelled in her hands and gasped.

This was her only warning. He came like a fountain that had been shut off too long. One short burst shot out and then a long stream of seed. His body shuddered, head to toe, threatening to jostle her off her knees. His energy jumped and sparked all the while, making her feel as if her nerves shared the climax too. She certainly panted like they had. Her thighs were even a bit goosey.

A minute passed before the climax eased. Yasmin sat back shakily on her heels. Because she thought he'd prefer it, she spelled his ejaculate to smoke.

Joseph's eyes blinked slowly open, taking a moment to focus on her face. "Well," he said hoarsely, swallowing to clear his throat. "That didn't disappoint."

Yasmin smiled. "I'm glad to hear it. And remember, now that I've broken you in, you're allowed to do that for yourself."

"Of course, I— I wouldn't presume to—"

She laid two fingers across his stammering mouth. "You didn't presume. I loved doing that for you, the same as I believe you enjoyed pleasuring me."

His golden eyes fired at the memory. "I did find that gratifying."

"So I'm only saying, if you want a climax and don't happen to have a partner, this is a thing normal people do."

He cocked his head at her. "Do the women of the harem pleasure themselves?" His fingertips touched her knees, stroking them lightly. He seemed not to know if this was all right to ask but was too curious not to. Yasmin supposed he hadn't discussed such things with male friends.

"It wasn't forbidden—not by Iksander, anyway. And harem women are flesh and blood, the same as anyone."

"Ah," he said, slightly awkward. "Of course, you are."

The intimate mood they'd been sharing broke. Joseph shifted in a non-sexual way.

"Shall I let you up?" she asked.

She swung off him and he sat up. He raked one hand back through his damp, dark hair. She knew what his next words would be before his mouth opened.

"I should probably go," he said, confirming it.

Her pride held a private war over stopping him. Why should she look like the clingy one? She sighed internally. She *did* have a valid reason for asking him to stay.

"Actually, I'd like to discuss something with you first. About what I found today."

"I thought I hadn't earned your confidences."

"I guess, maybe, I worked off my annoyance."

He smiled, which she managed to be resentful of and pleased by at the same time. Lifting his hips, he hiked his trousers and fastened them. "My ears are at your disposal," he said smoothly.

Deciding she'd don some covering too, she summoned her silk nightgown from the chair Joseph had spelled it to.

"I went looking for the mysterious market stall," she said once she'd pulled on the garment. "The one the townspeople claim showed up the day we arrived. It was locked in the basement of the Assembly Hall. Before the guard caught me, I discovered two facts of note. One: the stall sold the exact same bedsheets you're lying on—quite a coincidence if it blew here by chance across the In-Betweens."

"And two?"

"Two is that I found this." Feeling a need to move, she hopped up to retrieve the jeweled waist sash she'd worn earlier. She removed the license from the hidden pocket and handed it to him.

"The vendor is local," she said as he smoothed the folded parchment across his thigh. "I recognize her address. Everyone in Milion ought to know the stall belongs to her."

Joseph finished reading and looked up. The furrow he had so much practice making incised his brow. "This is suggestive, I admit."

"I *have* to visit that address," she said.

She'd been encouraged by his first reaction, but now he frowned. "How do you figure that? Who knows if this has anything to do with Dimitriou? Even if it does, you must realize by now what your client wants your report to say. Maybe marrying Stefan is a mistake, but I doubt Safiye is paying you enough to risk your safety chasing leads whose relevance is, at best, dubious."

"Am I only supposed to care about things I'm paid to investigate? What if Ivy Ozil is dead?"

"Her being dead wouldn't explain why people here forgot her."

"Exactly. Forgetting spells require sophisticated magic, possibly the sort a man like Dimitriou could afford. I'd say 'do,' but I don't think he's that powerful."

"That's a stretch," Joseph said.

"I notice you're not claiming he's too much of saint to be involved."

Joseph scoffed through his nose. "Like most of the djinn at this party, he's verifiably dangerous. I simply question the benefit to him."

Like *most* of the djinn? The admission, however nebulous, startled her.

"Don't ask," he said, both hands raised to fend off inquiry. "And for God's sake, don't poke this bear. What do you think Dimitriou will do if he catches your nose where it doesn't belong a second time?"

Abruptly, she wasn't sure being sent home was all she'd face. She crossed her arms regardless. "I don't need your approval to check this out."

"Of course, you don't. You're an 'independent female.'"

"If you're going to be sarcastic, I'll follow your example and keep my worries to myself."

"You're my main worry at the moment," he muttered.

That was vaguely flattering. What he said next was just a shock.

"I'll come with you."

She was speechless for two seconds. "Who says I'll let you?"

"I'd provide cover. You can pretend we're doing something romantic. If I'm seen leaving your room again, no one will doubt it."

Her arms stayed crossed. She wasn't ready to admit he had a point.

Joseph rose from the bed and spoke. "We'll visit the address first thing tomorrow. Maybe claim it's a sunrise stroll. If we're lucky, we won't be missed. Stefan's guests do seem to be late risers."

Yasmin wasn't exactly an early bird—not by his standards anyway.

"I'll be ready," she said, rather than bring that up.

Joseph nodded curtly. His previous romantic mood was behind him. He didn't kiss or even touch her before turning toward the door.

"You're forgetting the rest of your clothes," she called.

He stopped and blushed the teensiest bit. "Ah, yes. I, ah—" He scratched his barely heating cheek. "Perhaps I shouldn't put them on but just carry them."

He collected them from the floor in a loose bundle.

"You'll look more convincing if you sling your tunic over one shoulder."

"More convincing."

"You've been fooling around with a former royal concubine. If you don't swagger, who'll believe you got lucky?"

He smiled, belatedly registering her humorous tone. When he'd arranged garments as she suggested, he lifted his left eyebrow. "Do I look lucky now?"

"Lucky enough. You can save any extra strutting for if you get luckier later."

That brought a full flush into his face. He still didn't kiss her, but he did bow respectfully.

CHAPTER NINE

Team

Unsurprisingly, Yasmin's forlorn hope of catching up on missed sleep was dashed. What rest she got was fitful, and Joseph collected her before dawn. They snuck out in smoke form together, resuming their natural shapes as the sun's first rays hit the clock tower on the square. No special dew spangled the grass this morning. The town was picturesque but basically normal.

A two-block walk brought them to the address on Ivy Ozil's license. Her house was a nice thatched cottage with a gorgeous tangle of red roses in its garden. It looked lived in but not run down.

"Lights are on in the kitchen," Joseph said. "Someone's here—three someones if my nose for energy isn't mistaken."

Yasmin's nervousness rose. "Should we knock? Ask if they know what happened to Ivy?"

Joseph considered. "One stranger at the door might seem less threatening. I'll hang back in vapor form. You can signal me if there's trouble."

She'd have preferred not to commit this social awkwardness alone. He was right, though, on top of which it was her wild hare they were following.

"Am I straight?" she asked, indicating her headscarf.

"Perfectly," he confirmed, one hand lifting to smooth it.

The gesture caused other feelings to stir in her. His gaze held hers, its steadiness settling her. They'd faced graver dangers than knocking on a door. Why wouldn't he assume she could handle this? To think otherwise would have been insulting.

This was a step forward in the faith he afforded her.

"Go on," he said. "I'll keep an eye out."

She straightened her shoulders and went up the front walk.

A girl about three years old answered her triple knock. Garbed in what appeared to be Nessie-themed pajamas, she had straight black hair cut in bangs and an adorably somber face. She couldn't have looked more like Ivy if she'd been popped out of a mold.

On seeing Yasmin, her soft green eyes went wide.

"Hello," she said, swinging slightly from the—to her—high door knob. "Are you here to see Daddy?"

Yasmin crouched down to child level. "Actually, I'm here about your mother."

"Don't have one," the girl informed her. "Daddy 'dopted me and 'canthus from the temple."

Yasmin didn't know what to say to that. Stumped, she straightened to full height.

"*Acanthus!* Get back here," a stern male voice called from another room. The scold failed. An even younger child scampered barefoot into the alcove before the door. Dressed only in a diaper, he, too, was black-haired and green-eyed. Shrieking joyfully, he flapped his hands excitedly at Yasmin.

Maybe he was waving hello to her?

The man from the other room tried again. "Columbine, stop letting the cool air out."

"Daddy, I'm not," Columbine protested. "A lady knocked."

This answer got action. A fair-haired man with a long blade nose came out to stare at her. He seemed harried, as if unused to wrangling children by himself. Yasmin couldn't help noticing he resembled his offspring considerably less than the woman she'd come seeking.

"Please pardon the intrusion," she began. "I'm hoping to track a djinniya named Ivy Ozil."

"I'm Cedric Ozil," he said. "No one named Ivy lives in this house."

"Are you certain? This was the address I was given."

"No adult female lives here at all."

He seemed certain, but Yasmin wasn't ready to give up. "I have a picture of her. Perhaps you could look at it."

Cedric Ozil was polite enough to study the image she'd copied onto her scroll. "No," he said, shaking his head firmly. "This isn't anyone I know. Not a relative or an acquaintance. I'm afraid whoever told you she lived here was mistaken."

"Forgive my asking, but could she possibly be the mother of your children? Your daughter mentioned they're adopted."

The man's head jerked back angrily. "Demeter is their mother," he snapped, referring to the goddess. By tradition, followers called her the mother of orphans. "You'd better leave before I call the Watch."

Not wanting this, she curtseyed and stepped back. Cedric didn't try to be polite as he slammed the door. Confused, Yasmin pinched her lower lip. Though she didn't have definite proof, logic said Ivy was those children's mother . . . and that as recently as two days ago she'd been Cedric's wife. She shook her head. It took serious magic to erase someone that completely from the minds of people close to them.

She wasn't sure what made her look up. Hope for divine inspiration, possibly. When she did, something shiny caught her eye. Tucked among the eaves was a disk the size of her open hand. Ever so faintly, it buzzed with spent magic. Though she knew she had no right to do so, she stretched on tiptoe to grab it. As soon as the object was in her grasp, and before she could be seen and stopped, she strode around the side of the house out of view of the front window.

Joseph materialized while she was examining her find.

"Did you hear?" she asked.

"Some. I flew a circuit around the house in case anyone approached. What have you got?"

"I believe it's a cake made from wild magic—you know, the sparkly stuff the mists deposit. I found it hidden above the door." She tried to snap or bend the disk by holding either side. The pressure had no effect. The thing wasn't simply hard, it was damage resistant.

"It could be a spell anchor." Joseph leaned closer so he could see. "Or a delivery system for a charm. Obviously, it used to have more charge."

She showed him the other side.

The surface held a carved wave pattern reminiscent of the one embroidered on Dimitriou's sheets. What looked like a boat oar lay crosswise over it.

"Huh," he said. "I recognize this sign. It's an old pictogram for Lethe, the mythical river that separates this world from the afterlife."

"The River of Forgetting."

"Yes. The dead drink from it as a means of relinquishing earthly attachments. The oar symbolizes the ferryman." He traced the symbols cautiously. "This is very clever. A whole town's memories have been erased, thanks to specks of magic that should have dissipated within hours of depositing. I wouldn't know how to turn what the mists leave behind into a stable form like this."

"Neither would I. Then again, the locals have had generations to learn the trick. The other day, I watched a postal clerk sprinkle magic he'd collected to animate postcards. That's a simple charm compared to this, but he must make it last long enough for the card to reach its recipient."

Joseph tapped pursed lips. "I suppose the forgetting spell didn't affect us because it had already shot its load."

"Should I put this back, do you think? I don't believe it can cause more harm, and we don't want whoever set it to discover it's missing. I could waft it back magically. Cedric won't notice I haven't left the property."

"Yes," Joseph said. "That seems a safe precaution."

Once she'd returned the disk, he put his hand on her shoulder. "Before we leave, I want to show you something. When I flew around the cottage, I discovered an . . . oddity in the back yard."

She followed him there, ducking below the windows the same as him. The rear garden provided cover for them to stand. The plantings were as pretty as those in front, with shady fruit trees and vibrant flower beds. She had no trouble imagining Ivy out here, showing her kids how to weed and water among the butterflies. How sad that the people she loved forgot her! Yasmin's eyes pricked, but she blinked the sting away. She couldn't let emotion blind her—not when there might be clues to uncover.

"Here," Joseph said, hunkering down beside a stone bench to point.

"It's a hole."

"It's a pair of holes. The second one's over there. I'm no gardener, but it appears as if two young trees have been removed, roots and all." He grinned at her confusion. "I know. I thought it was nothing too until I spotted this."

Yasmin bent closer.

Gingerly, Joseph pulled a half-buried pebble from the dirt. Except it wasn't a pebble, or not an ordinary one. It was a gem from a ruby tree. A stem and two browning leaves were still attached to it.

"That's from the same kind of tree Dimitriou says landed spontaneously next to his front entrance!"

"Yes, it is," Joseph agreed quietly. "And if you were a magic seed blown across the In-Betweens, where would you choose to sprout? My money is on the garden of a loving mother with a green thumb and a beautiful family."

"So the ruby trees were Ivy's. Probably, at least. Dimitriou isn't hurting for money, but maybe his ego demanded the special seeds choose him. Or he could have stolen them to impress Safiye. Either way, if Ivy knew he took the trees and tried to get them back, he'd have a motive for killing her."

"We don't know for sure she's dead. Or that Dimitriou placed the forgetting charm. Come to think of it, if he killed her, why hasn't he turned ifrit? A soul's shift from light to dark is difficult to hide."

"My brother Ramis managed it."

"For limited periods. And your family is very gifted. Dimitriou strikes me as average on the magic scale."

Yasmin rubbed a knuckle across her lips. He struck her that way too. "Can you contact the Ministry of Justice? They'll listen to you even if our evidence is slim. You could let them know we suspect Dimitriou might have harmed this woman."

"You're assuming I can get messages out any more reliably than you. Also, unfortunately, me appearing too friendly with the current administration is awkward at this moment."

Before Yasmin could press him to explain, he stiffened and looked up. Curious, she lifted her head too. An unidentifiable djinni smoked across the sky in a rush. The gray-tailed cloud moved swiftly, disappearing behind a line of palms within a few seconds.

"I think that was Dimitriou," Joseph said.

"You could tell with him zipping by like that?"

"Well, I'm not a hundred percent sure, but the smoke was headed toward his estate. It could be someone on his staff. What urgent errand would they be on, I wonder? Unless Dimitriou is an earlier riser than we thought."

He craned in the direction they'd initially spied the traveler.

"The mists are that way," Yasmin said. "I remember from our flyover."

"The actual end of the world drop-off?"

She nodded in confirmation.

A frown twisted Joseph's mouth. "I have no idea if that's significant."

"Me, either," Yasmin said.

The shiver that gripped her nape implied it meant nothing good.

CHAPTER TEN

Eyes and Ears

Smoking back to Dimitriou's estate seemed a logical next action. With luck, their absence wouldn't have been noticed. Though it wasn't on the way, they detoured across the scrubland the unknown djinni had come from. No houses marked the rough landscape. Even for locals, the atmosphere near the In-Betweens was uncomfortably uncanny. One lonely shell of a building stuck up from the wild grasses. What it had been Yasmin couldn't guess. Currently, it had no roof, only crumbling stone wall remnants.

Inevitably, the mists pulled their attention from the ruin. The great billows of sunlit and shadowed cloud heaved sluggishly in the immeasurable abyss. The shapes the clouds formed were hypnotizing: almost faces of almost creatures that almost seemed alive.

"That's close enough," she warned when Joseph's smoke form began to drift toward the cliff-like edge. He jerked and flew back to her.

"Forgot where I was," he said.

"It's not forgetting. In-Betweens possess a slight siren call. My father claims the mists *want* to lure people in. You learn to steel yourself against it."

Joseph turned glowing eyes to her. "Apart from that, it's hard to imagine what would draw Dimitriou to this place." He considered the mists once more before shrugging hazy shoulders. "I suppose we won't discover the reason this minute. We'd better get going while we can."

Since Yasmin had no argument against this, they continued to the estate.

They arrived early enough that only servants moved in the corridors. Relieved to have slipped in undetected, Yasmin crawled back into bed for a catch-up nap. Though she recited the standard prayer for illumination, her dreams left her no wiser.

On the bright side, she rejoined Dimitriou's party with her energy restored.

She found a pleasant buffet-style meal set up on the lawn under fluttering white awnings. Apparently finished eating, Stefan's personal friends played a raucous game of croquet in the bright sunshine. The males she privately thought of as the cabal relaxed on cushioned lounge chairs loosely grouped around Stefan and Safiye. Joseph wasn't among them, though she noticed Eamon Pappus sullenly forking up cantaloupe.

She continued to glance around as she filled a plate. She didn't see the mistresses. Perhaps they were brunching in seclusion.

"Over here," Safiye called, spying her. "I saved you a place to sit."

This was nice of her. Yasmin wouldn't have blamed her client for being angry over her unsanctioned snooping fiasco. But it seemed all was forgiven. By Stefan too. As she passed his chair, he shaded his eyes and smiled.

"Glad you could join us, sleepyhead."

His voice was an indolent purr, his posture relaxed in the extreme. The ice she'd seen in him during their confrontation might never have existed. She recalled Safiye's failure to return to her rooms last night. Cutting her gaze to the djinniya revealed she appeared as putty-limbed as Stefan.

It also revealed other things. Safiye's cheeks were flushed from more than the warmth outside, her lips rosier than cosmetics could account for. Her morning tunic was multilayered gold-on-gold diaphanous silk. The glittering stuff draped her figure in an ideal mix of seduction and elegance. Empresses didn't always strike that balance so perfectly. In lieu of embroidery, a fortune in canary diamonds ornamented her bodice. Yasmin was willing to bet this outfit was another present from Stefan.

She'd also bet the couple had consummated their relationship.

"You look . . . in the pink," she said as she sat beside Safiye.

The djinniya smiled like a well-fed cat. "A good night's rest will do that."

Her tone suggested an inclination toward female confidences—even toward a female she was paying to act friend-like. That suited Yasmin. She had one confidence in particular she wanted to pin down.

"I didn't hear you come in," she said, her voice as muted as Safiye's. "Were you and Stefan together the entire night?"

Safiye caressed the extravagant fabric that draped her thighs. "Perhaps," she said coyly.

"Are you sure? He couldn't have slipped out while you slept?"

Safiye's expression changed from self-satisfaction to annoyance. This time when she answered, she hushed her voice magically. "Are you suggesting Stefan left our bed to visit another woman? Trust me, Yasmin—whatever his usual habits—pleasuring me didn't leave stamina for that."

That was an interesting way to put it. Didn't being a concubine mean placing more emphasis on pleasing your partner? But maybe Safiye's strategy was better. Joseph hadn't had any trouble tearing himself away from her.

Joseph stepping onto the lawn distracted her from posing more questions.

"Well, well," Stefan drawled from Safiye's other side. "You two must be on the same schedule."

LaBass—the allegedly tight-fisted business mogul whose mistress Tara had left early—was first to greet the newcomer. The only of the males with a beard, LaBass was a sleek but solid djinni Yasmin found hard to read. He decided the best seat for Joseph involved chucking Eamon out of his.

"Don't pout," LaBass chided the younger man. "You're done eating. Joseph needs somewhere to set his plate."

"He hasn't got a plate," Eamon said.

"So he doesn't. Why don't you fill one for him? Or find a servant who will, if you're too proud for that."

Eamon could be obtuse, but even he knew performing the task wasn't optional. He strode off, huffing slightly, toward the buffet tables.

Looking a little awkward, Joseph lowered himself into Eamon's chair. "I could have done that myself."

"It's good for Eamon to learn his place."

That, evidently, wasn't meant to be argued with either.

Eamon returned shortly with a generously laden plate. To his credit, he handed it over gracefully.

"Thank you," Joseph said with grave politeness. "These are precisely the foods I like."

Too stubborn to leave or perhaps encouraged by Joseph's thanks, Eamon floated a drum table into the privileged circle and perched on it.

LaBass seemed to find this ploy amusing. His laugh shook his broad wrestler's chest. "If we're rearranging furniture, we should float Joseph's lovely partner and her chair over too."

Joseph looked startled by the idea. "That's not necessary. I'm sure Yasmin is comfortable sitting with her friend."

"Nonsense." LaBass waved a beringed hand. "You mentioned you two haven't had the chance to keep company openly. Young romantics belong together. I'm not so old I don't know that."

"Oh, go on," Stefan encouraged. He took Safiye's hand and squeezed. "Safiye and I will entertain each other."

Yasmin wasn't asked her preference. Clearly, it was irrelevant. Resigned, she gripped the chair arms and clenched her teeth as LaBass and Joseph joined their magic to levitate her across to them.

"There," LaBass said, neatly shifting his lounger so that she landed between the men. "Now we're cozy. And, look, we didn't spill anything from her plate."

"Which I appreciate," she said, breathless from her spur-of-the-moment ride.

LaBass smiled approvingly. Up close, she saw he was older than she'd initially believed. Deep lines of amusement appeared around his eyes. He patted her knee like an uncle. "Tell me about yourself. Who is the pretty lady who caught our favorite promising young man's eye?"

He asked as if Joseph's associations—and therefore *she*—were somehow his business. Rather than try to fathom why, she answered.

"I'm Yasmin Baykal, sir."

"That much we all know," he laughed. "And your father is Aydin Baykal of Baykal Shipping?"

"Yes, sir."

"Call me LaBass. Everybody does. Even my mistress!"

"LaBass," she complied. "And please call me Yasmin."

"Excellent." He patted her knee again. "Your name is a flower that perfumes the tongue. I imagine your life has changed since leaving court? Not so long ago, wasn't it?"

Unlike Eamon, he didn't claim Iksander 'tossed her out.' Nonetheless, his expression was sympathetic. That was natural, she supposed. He and his group would view her previous status as the highest a female could aspire to.

"Outside life has been an adjustment," she admitted cautiously. "But it hasn't been all bad."

"Yasmin's parents were understanding," Joseph volunteered.

"Of course they were," LaBass said. "I can tell you're a good daughter. What happened with the sultan wasn't at all your fault."

It was a *little* her fault. She hadn't forced the issue, but in her own small way, she'd maneuvered circumstances so that the breakup of the harem would come about. She'd longed for personal freedom more than she'd feared disgrace.

In case her face betrayed this, she bowed her head. "That's kind of you to say."

"You'll find a new husband," LaBass assured in a wink-wink tone. "Maybe even someone we know."

Oh, she wanted to snap at him. She didn't need a husband, not even one as appealing as Joseph. Maybe she wasn't the queen of being independent, but she was learning. Her hands curled tighter around her plate.

"May it please the goddess," she said respectfully.

"You hear that?" LaBass chortled to Joseph. "That's womanly modesty."

Eamon coughed into his fist. Yasmin guessed he had his own opinion about her modesty.

"Yes?" LaBass peered at him narrowly.

"Nothing, sir. Just it's a shame her harem training will go to waste."

"Eamon," LaBass pronounced. "Sometimes you're a bigger idiot than Iksander."

This was too much for the djinni not to defend against. "*I* wouldn't disband a perfectly good collection of concubines. I think a leader should have a harem, for the prestige of his territory, if nothing else. Certainly, he shouldn't commit himself to some human whore *and* her male lover. What's more, I know you agree with me." He spread his arms to indicate their sunlit surroundings. "This is how life is meant to be for djinn like us. Men being men. Women being women. The ranks sticking to their place. All that jabber about improving conditions for the lower classes is absurd. If the poor can't raise themselves, they belong where God put them."

Murmurs broke out as he crossed his arms. To Yasmin, they didn't sound like murmurs of disagreement—disapproval, maybe, for Eamon speaking so openly.

LaBass didn't react to Eamon's speech, not that she could see, anyway. He surprised her by turning to her instead.

"What's your opinion on that?" he asked.

"Me?" She blinked, her pulse speeding up at the direct inquiry. Joseph tensed on her other side. Obviously, LaBass's question was a test, but maybe Joseph didn't know she understood this. Meanwhile, the older djinni was watching her. Would he guess if she lied? Some djinni were good at that. She tried to speak carefully. "I hadn't really thought about it. I don't suppose anyone likes too much change all at once."

LaBass stared a few heartbeats longer. "No," he said, seeming to nod mostly to himself. "No one likes too much change all at once. Better to go step by little step when bringing about the world one wants."

She doubted the world he wanted was the same one she did. Too aware of this, she fought to breathe evenly and look amiable.

Without warning, his smile broke out.

"You're a clever girl," he announced. He reached across her to slap Joseph's arm jovially. "Don't let this prize slip away from you."

"I . . . shall attempt to avoid that," Joseph said haltingly.

His lack of enthusiasm tempted Yasmin to roll her eyes. Hopefully, LaBass would chalk his reaction up to shyness. The scroll network's pitiful local access suddenly struck her as fortunate. LaBass couldn't easily deep-search her. He had to discover what he could by means of old-fashioned questioning. As long as Safiye watched what she said, he wouldn't unearth her real reason for being here.

That information getting out might be awkward for her and Joseph both.

This thought triggered fresh annoyance over him keeping her in the dark. Really, if she were going to be drawn into these sorts of interrogations, he ought to share what he was up to.

Her private fuming was interrupted.

"Listen," one of the male croquet players called. "I think I hear Nessie."

Yasmin's eyebrows rose, but everyone fell silent . . . most everyone, anyway.

"I thought Nessie was a myth," Safiye objected.

Stefan patted her knee. "We locals like to give her the benefit of the doubt."

"Hush," the croquet player scolded. "You need to be quiet. The call came from far away."

Yasmin held her breath. A moment later, she heard a distant rising and falling moan. The noise came again, faint but discernible. The hair on her arms stood up.

That was the kind of sound that haunted djinn nightmares.

"Good Lord," Safiye said, vaguely horrified.

Stefan laughed. "It's lucky to hear Nessie. Locals claim it augurs good fortune. I've certainly found it to be the case."

"You're kidding," Safiye said. "That horrible wailing is lucky?"

He kissed the tip of her nose, amused in the manner of someone enjoying a private joke. "If you're frightened, darling, you must allow me to hold you tight."

She laughed when Stefan embraced her, her repulsion dissolving in the face of his playfulness.

"Young love," LaBass commented, watching them. He employed the same indulgent tone as when describing her and Joseph.

"They are an attractive pair," Joseph said.

"They'll go far together," Eamon added while studying his fingernails. "All the way, one might say."

His tone was fraught with suggestion. LaBass sent him a sharp look, which reminded Yasmin to guard what her face revealed. What did Eamon mean by them going 'all the way?' More than to the altar, it seemed to her.

"What did we miss?" Antonina asked, leading her fellow mistresses into the bright garden.

Yasmin's heart jumped at their arrival.

I'm relieved, she thought, startled by the realization. When she hadn't seen Antonina's group with the other guests, part of her had wondered if they were safe and sound. Ivy's disappearance was making her imagine all sorts of awfulness. Come to think of it, had LaBass's mistress Tara truly fled? People said she left in embarrassment, but did any of them know?

Despite the warmth of the day, she shivered. As fate would have it, Stefan turned his head in her direction.

Their eyes collided, crystalline aqua to luminous gray. The effect was a parody of lovers locking glances across a room. The world and the people in it metaphorically fell away.

It simply wasn't romantic.

Yasmin blanked her expression as completely as she could. A second shiver threatened to seize her shoulders, but she suppressed that too.

She didn't suppress it well enough. Stefan's lips curved, a fresh sparkle of humor lighting his blue-green eyes. He winked at her, and somehow, she knew no one else witnessed it.

I see you seeing me, the tiny act seemed to say.

A moment later, Safiye touched his arm. As he turned back to her, he was perfectly casual—perfectly affectionate, for all anyone could see. Safiye was his ideal partner, his hoped-for future bride.

Goddess help us all, Yasmin prayed.

~

For the next little while, she couldn't have said what topics Dimitriou's guests discussed. Her thoughts—which she hadn't yet made sense of—whirled through her mind too quickly. She nearly failed to notice the alfresco meal ending.

"I'll walk you into the house," Joseph said.

He was already on his feet, offering his hand to her. She let him take charge of her, though normally she'd have minded being led along like a child. When he increased the impression by patting her forearm, it had the salutary but probably unintentional effect of clearing her mental fog.

Joseph had stopped walking.

They stood beneath the golden dome of the entryway, halfway between the men and women's arched corridors. Yasmin sensed no one else around, not even invisibly. The potted ferns rustled slightly in the breeze from the back garden.

"Well," she said. "Are you going to explain what that was about?"

Joseph's expression twisted unhappily.

"Honestly," she exclaimed in disgust.

"Yasmin, I . . ."

"There you are," Stefan said. "Just the djinni I need to speak to."

Per usual, Joseph had drawn too much of her focus. Without her noticing, Stefan and Safiye had entered arm-in-arm. Yasmin certainly *should* have noticed. Despite the atrium's shifting shadows, the diamonds on Safiye's tunic glittered like trapped stars. She stroked her suitor's bicep as if reluctant to part from him.

Stefan smiled at her before turning to Yasmin. "I hope you'll forgive me if I drag your friend to my office. We've a bit of business to discuss. LaBass has promised it won't take long."

Yasmin stood close enough to Joseph to feel him come to alert.

"I am at your disposal," he said with a polite bow.

Of course, he was. Leaving gave him an excuse to avoid the tongue-lashing he knew awaited him. "How could I stop you even if I wished?" Yasmin said. "You men will do what you men will do."

Perhaps to provide a contrast to Yasmin's tartness, Safiye kissed Stefan's cheek. "I'll do my best to console her, darling. You need not worry about us."

He kissed her back in the same light fashion then waved for Joseph to come with him.

Safiye's face lost its sweetness the moment the males were gone. Yasmin recognized the look from their days in the harem. There, Safiye had been the queen of icy disapproval. The trait had helped her maintain supremacy over the concubines.

At least, over the ones who shared her ambitions regarding Iksander.

Knowing this aspiration hadn't applied to her, Yasmin fought an unhelpful urge to smile. It occurred to her that Stefan hadn't outdone Safiye's glacial stare. Then again, she never claimed the couple had nothing in common.

Lost in the small amusement, she jerked as Safiye strode past her.

"Come," Safiye said, barely turning her head to issue the low order.

Safiye didn't wait for her to catch up. She was a strict mother duck who assumed her chick would follow. She wasn't wrong. Aware she was in for it, Yasmin hurried after her.

She's your employer, she told herself. *If you've got a scolding coming, you'll take it like a professional.*

Safiye wasn't so angry she forgot Yasmin's room had shields against eavesdropping. In silence, she thrust its door open.

"Yes?" Yasmin said after she'd shut it behind them.

Safiye seemed not to like her relative composure. Her cheeks flushed dark as she wagged one elegant, stern finger. "I saw that look you shot Stefan in the garden. You're not spoiling this for me!"

"What look?" Yasmin asked, genuinely confused.

"Like he horrified you!"

"Ah," Yasmin said. Her after-the-wink dismay.

"Yes, 'ah,'" the former concubine bit out.

"You hired me to dig into him," Yasmin reminded. "I've been doing so, and I have concerns."

"What concerns? I've seen no evidence you found anything wrong with him."

"I believe he's been less than honest in some of his dealings."

"What if he has? Name one highborn male who does everything on the straight and narrow."

Yasmin considered how specific she ought to get. It could be argued her client had a right to know everything. On the other hand, anything she said might get back to Dimitriou. "He may have stolen the ruby trees in his garden from the women they belonged to."

"*May* have," Safiye huffed. "Did this woman give you proof?"

"She can't give me proof. She's disappeared."

This silenced Safiye for a space. Her mouth worked as she struggled to deny the information might be important. "That's unfortunate," she conceded. "I pray she's well wherever she's gone off too. However, if—*if*—Stefan did misappropriate her trees, perhaps he did it to impress me."

Yasmin had thought the same herself. "The woman disappeared as if she'd never existed. Magic was used to accomplish it."

"That doesn't mean Stefan was involved."

"Okay," Yasmin said, committing to the devil's advocate position. "What about Tara then?"

"Everyone knows why LaBass's mistress left. She accidentally covered herself in spots from that stupid Particolored Polka."

"But is that really what happened? Did she actually leave? And was it she who botched the spell?"

Safiye crossed her arms. "What are you implying?"

"I'd swear Stefan nudged that choice toward her in the game. He was angry with her because she embarrassed Joseph and me."

"Oh, please." Safiye's arms slapped her sides as she dropped them again. She shook her head contemptuously. "I thought you'd be a good detective. In the harem, you always seemed coolheaded and observant. Now I realize you're prone to flights of fancy—and ludicrous ones at that."

Safiye had good instincts for pricking people where it would hurt. The knack didn't fail her now. Yasmin couldn't stop her cheeks from warming.

"I'm concerned for you," she said as levelly as she could. "I think Stefan may be dangerous."

This was too much for her client's patience. "That's it. I'm firing you."

Yasmin temporarily lost her breath. "You're firing me?"

"Yes. I'll pay you what you're owed, but you're officially out of here."

She hadn't seen this coming—though she should have. Her mind raced for a way to undo the disaster. Never mind her pride. If Safiye fired her, she'd marry Dimitriou for sure. Her relatives already considered him a catch. She'd be at his mercy with no one to protect her.

"I—" Yasmin rephrased a question inside her head. "Won't people think it's odd if I go? I'm supposed to be at this house party as your friend."

As she'd hoped, this caused Safiye to stop and think. "Fine. I'll pay you to stay for that but nothing else. No more poking your nose into Stefan's business."

Yasmin began to say she didn't care about being paid then thought better of it. Safiye was unlikely to believe that.

"I mean it," the other woman said. "You're not ruining this for me."

Her voice was stubborn and passionate—hardly the imperturbable courtesan Yasmin knew. Sentiments deeper than ambition were driving her. "You care about Dimitriou that much?"

"He's a good man. He—" Safiye smoothed her gown as if this would also smooth her agitation. When she'd done, she lifted her chin coolly. "I don't have as low an opinion of our sultan as some of Stefan's friends, but no one can call Iksander selfless in his lovemaking. Can you imagine him—or any man—telling a concubine to lie back and enjoy? I couldn't until I shared Stefan's bed. He wanted nothing but my pleasure; refused all my offers to use my arts on him. I was his everything, he said. I deserved to be worshiped on a high pedestal. I felt—" Her voice broke. "I felt as if I'd been waiting all my life to meet a man like him."

Yasmin might not find such a passive role appealing, but she couldn't doubt Safiye did. The emotion behind her words wasn't about recovering lost status. She honestly seemed dazzled. Her cheeks had flushed with remembered pleasure, and her eyes were as bright as stars. By accident or design, Stefan satisfied a predilection Safiye might not even now recognize she had.

"I'm glad you enjoyed the experience," Yasmin said carefully.

Safiye rolled her eyes. "I should have known you'd judge."

"Whether I do or not doesn't matter. I would point out, however, that his ability to please you doesn't negate my suspicions."

"It speaks to his character! As do a hundred other—" She broke off and shook her head. "I'm not debating this with you. Your opinion no longer holds sway with me."

Proud though it sounded, this didn't ring completely true. *I could still convince her,* Yasmin thought. *I mustn't give up without a fight.*

"I shall consider your words," she said diplomatically. "Perhaps you'd be kind enough to excuse me so that I may."

Forgetting they were in Yasmin's rooms, Safiye grimaced and waved her off.

CHAPTER ELEVEN

Teller of Tales

Yasmin left by the door she'd come in. She strove not to be rattled by what had happened, but her knees were a bit jellied. She hadn't imagined being fired would be so uncomfortable. Joining the working class required some toughness, apparently.

She was more than a little grateful for the emptiness of the corridor.

What now? she wondered, rubbing her chin with fingers that shook slightly. More than anything, she wanted to speak to Joseph. Partly, she found his company comforting, but they had a conversation to finish too. That was the important thing—at least if she were listening to her head.

She didn't think she could wait for him to slip into her suite again. If he even planned to, he wouldn't try until darkness fell. Could she locate him unnoticed now? Would he be finished talking to LaBass and Dimitriou?

Her cat could sneak to his room. No one in the house but Joseph knew she could turn into one.

She glanced around with all her perceptions. She was alone. She'd transformed so often she could do it in a twinkling. Galvanized by having a plan, she changed into her cat shape.

As she pattered from shadow to shadow on silent paws, she regretted not originally making her alternate self all black. Her three white socks stood out too much for stealth, but adjusting her coloring now would make the form less stable. Rather than try, she thought a concealment prayer. Perhaps it helped. She reached Joseph's quarters—which she tracked down thanks to his scent—without being spotted by anyone.

He wasn't there when she slipped inside. His rooms were smaller and more modest than she expected. Decorated in shades of bitter chocolate and paprika, they weren't half the size of hers. The single window was deep and narrow, the table beside it stacked with scholarly books he'd probably brought with him. Judging it safer, in case a servant came, she decided to wait for him as her cat. She jumped onto his bed, circled once, and curled up tail-to-nose. Being surrounded by his things was soothing. It was easy to close her eyes and nap.

She woke to his gentle hand stroking her.

"Yasmin," he whispered next to her twitching ear. "Cute as you are like this, our conversation will be one-sided if you don't shift."

Before she did, she took a moment to calm herself. Despite the precaution, when she reformed beside him on the edge of the mattress, she sat closer than intended. Was it flattering that he didn't scoot back from her? The question made her nose itch, so she rubbed it.

"I'm not cute," she denied. "I'm a scraggly alley cat."

"Very," Joseph agreed with insincere seriousness. His hand lifted to her ear to give the spot behind it a teasing scritch. His eyes were warm, his lips curving slightly in amusement.

"Safiye fired me," she blurted.

Joseph's dark eyebrows rose. "She fired you?"

"Yes. I tried to warn her Stefan might be dangerous, but she's convinced he's a prince. She's not sending me home, though. She doesn't have anyone else to pretend to be her friend."

"I see," Joseph said.

"I don't think I told her anything I shouldn't. I didn't mention you helped me snoop this morning."

"She's your client. Concealing what concerns her would be unethical."

"That's what I thought," she said, perhaps too pleased by his agreement. Less pleasing was the realization that she shouldn't share Safiye's account of Dimitriou's eccentric lovemaking style. Those details were personal.

I wonder why he left her afterward, she mused. He'd certainly appeared satiated at today's brunch. Then again, she and Joseph couldn't be sure they'd seen his smoke form streak over the Ozil house. Maybe—as Safiye claimed—he'd spent the whole night with her.

Joseph was having his own thoughts. He finished them with a resigned sigh.

"Yasmin," he said, gathering her hands and holding them on his knees. "I'm truly sorry for dragging you into this."

"Joseph—"

"Don't take my head off. I haven't kept my business from you because I don't trust you to keep a secret. Not anymore, anyway. The truth is I don't want to endanger you."

"You're endangering me more by keeping me in the dark."

She said this as simply as she could. She'd noticed he responded better to logic than emotion.

He rubbed her knuckles as his finely cut mouth turned down. "Perhaps I am. In any case, I no longer have a choice. LaBass has asked me to read you in."

Her pulse sped up with interest a breath before she registered the insult. Joseph couldn't decide on his own to confide in her? He had to be forced to it?

"Read me in on what?" she asked levelly.

He sighed again, more reluctantly than before. "I'm not sure where to start."

"The beginning usually works," she said.

* * *

Joseph's Tale

My purpose here came about by chance, as these matters do sometimes.

I don't suppose you know I have a fondness for antique animated maps. Not only are they beautiful, but they offer clues to how djinn did magic in the old days. Though I'm not wealthy, I am careful with my money, and Arcadius and Iksander pay generously. I've become known among city auction houses as someone who'll go the distance for a unique item.

Some months ago, such an item came up for bid: an authentic "Here be Dragons" atlas from the sixteenth century. Excited, I arrived at the auction house in good time to study the article. I'd just entered the drawing room, where the various lots were laid out on tables, when I noticed another djinni eyeing the map I was interested in.

You know this man as Eamon Pappus. Though I hadn't met him in person, I recognized him as a buyer who'd outbid me on occasion. I know you thought I lied when I said we had tastes in common, but in truth our preferences as collectors are similar. Further bonding us that afternoon was the fact that neither of us won the object of our desire. A carpet mogul outbid everyone and took the prize home with him. I still feel bitter when I recall it. I'd rather a public library or museum vanquished us.

Afterwards, Eamon invited me to his club for a consoling drink. Like many city dwellers, he knew who I was. Given my history and my role at court, I'm unable to travel anonymously—at least not without magical camouflage.

Suspicious by nature, I presumed Eamon's interest in cultivating my acquaintance hinged on me being Joseph the Magician. Curious as to what his true motive was, I accepted and went with him.

His conservative bent was obvious before we'd finished our first raki. Though my personal politics lean toward the liberal, I thought it wise to listen without comment. This choice proved providential. Eamon is less skeptical than I and, as you've observed, surer of his social skill than his charms warrant. He took my silence to mean I was—or could become—a fellow believer. He began probing my opinions on Iksander's recent reforms. Not wishing to appear too eager, I claimed I hadn't thought about them. I enjoyed my work and was grateful for the prestige of my position.

"What if you could retain that prestige," Eamon asked, "but in service of a group with values more like your own, djinn who truly are worthy of respect? What if our Glorious City could return to former perfections?"

I scoffed at his suggestion, telling him I was no wide-eyed child to believe in nursery tales. Utopias didn't exist, and all change came at a cost. The fantasy he spoke of would be no different.

He pretended he'd meant nothing specific. A 'pleasant speculation' was all it was, something to natter about over alcohol. We left the matter there and parted, though I expected he'd contact me again.

Before he did, I wanted to share what he'd said with Iksander's inner circle, among whom I'm proud to be counted. We knew the changes the sultan was enacting would spark opposition in some quarters. Inevitably, those who possess advantages resist adjusting the status quo. Other than murmurs of dissatisfaction, however, we'd heard nothing too worrying.

My master Arcadius, his double Cade, the vizier Murat, Iksander of course, and myself met in Iksander's private dining room. Interestingly, a modern animated map—a weather chart of our city's bay—ribbons its curving walls. In the glow of those sunny scenes, I summarized my encounter as lucidly as I could. The others endorsed my theory that Eamon hoped to enlist me in a traditionalist movement. Ever seeking to improve his status, delivering the sultan's sorcerer to their cause would be a coup for him.

After a bit more discussion, we decided I ought to let him recruit me. As you know, opposition parties aren't forbidden. With few historical exceptions, it's not the Glorious City's custom to tolerate tyranny. Different perspectives are allowed expression. The exception is the sort of group Eamon alluded to. Its nature struck us as conspiratorial—as if ethics or legalities necessitated concealment. Passing up a chance to investigate would have been irresponsible.

Thus resolved, I accepted Eamon's overtures of friendship.

In a shorter time than one might expect, he introduced me to LaBass and his associates. Understandably, they didn't unveil their whole plot at once. Though Eamon vouched for me, his sponsorship only went so far. I had to demonstrate to more exacting judges that I was trustworthy. Until today, when LaBass read me in, I'd only pieced together hints. I had nothing concrete to testify to—nothing, in short, that Iksander's lawyers could prosecute.

What did he read me in on, you want to know?

I'll answer by revisiting a civics lesson we learn in school but sometimes forget. Though our system is hereditary, two mechanisms exist for overthrowing a ruling line. The first is simple revolution. The people rise up in anger and heave out those in power. The second involves the fifty-nine district leaders declaring a Ruler's Quest. This declaration, which requires a two-thirds majority, has to be sincere. Speakers can't be magically persuaded, bribed, or threatened with violence. They must genuinely long in their hearts for a new dynasty.

In the past, factions have tried to rig the process, but it didn't turn out well. The power that undergirds our city—its guardian angel, if you will—ensures evildoers receive their just desserts.

This, at least, is what happened to past cheaters.

I see on your face you have guessed the truth. Past cheaters never had Joseph the Magician to help them wiggle around fallout. With me on their side, LaBass and his cronies hoped to bypass the process of laboriously convincing voters, one by one. Theoretically, my skills are so subtle I could spell the entire two-thirds without discovery. Then, once they'd ratified the quest, I could ensure the conspiracy's candidate won.

To use a human example, I'd guarantee their Arthur and no other drew the sword from the enchanted stone.

* * *

Yasmin blinked as Joseph fell silent. That was quite a story he'd just told her! A moment later, her mind leaped to an unwelcome conclusion. "Dimitriou is their candidate? He's the djinni they want to put on Iksander's throne?"

"You have to admit he wouldn't trigger a revolt. We know he's no Arthur, but he is personable: a seeming doer of good deeds with a sympathetic past. And he's an aristocrat. He'd appeal to the upper classes and moneyed folks alike. Those groups have many common priorities."

"You aren't wrong. When my mother heard I'd been invited here, she gushed. Lots of djinn in my parents' circle admire Dimitriou. They think he'd have found a way to prevent Luna cursing us."

"Good Lord," Joseph said, shocked by this.

"I know. The only way to escape her spell would have been to capitulate. I shudder to think what our lives would be like today under her." Yasmin shook her head. "Dimitriou knows what LaBass and the others want from him?"

"Oh, yes," Joseph said. "They'll have vetted other djinni before settling on him, but he's been privy to their plans for a while."

"I suppose that explains his sudden interest in marriage. You can't start a dynasty without a child bearer. —Safiye doesn't know," she added, in case there was any doubt.

"I agree Lady Toraman appears to be in the dark."

Yasmin's lips twitched in amusement. Joseph wasn't kidding when he said he was suspicious.

"Oh," she gasped, hands flying to her mouth as a new realization occurred to her. "This is why you want everyone believing you're still a eunuch. If they knew your original body was destroyed, they might think your power isn't up to giving them their shortcut."

"Yes," he confirmed soberly.

She didn't assure him he was still plenty powerful. She'd tried that already. Only he could make peace on that topic.

"LaBass may have misjudged Dimitriou," she said instead. "I don't think he'll be the compliant puppet they're counting on."

"You may be right. I researched him myself, but this business with Ivy Ozil took me by surprise. I knew he wasn't a boy scout, but—"

"A 'boy scout?'"

"A human term. It means a person who behaves honorably, who learns the rules early and follows them. The point is, Dimitriou has extremely well-concealed skeletons."

"I'm wondering something," Yasmin said. "LaBass and I barely had one conversation. He couldn't have decided to trust me so easily, yet he told you to share their plan."

Joseph shrugged. "He trusts that idiot Eamon . . . and Dimitriou. Clearly, his judgement has blind spots. Perhaps your beauty swayed him. Your version of that trait is potent. When you gaze into a person's eyes, your natural warmth makes them want to confide in you."

His comment surprised her. She knew he found her attractive but not that he'd thought about it to this extent.

"Some djinn managed to resist telling me their secrets," she observed sardonically.

"With difficulty," he said, understanding she meant him. "On top of which, the idea of recruiting *two* former royal concubines may have heightened your appeal. In a game like this, public perception matters. You and Safiye are celebrities of a sort. Winning you over would reflect badly on Iksander. Or perhaps LaBass is testing me, seeing if I'll obey instructions even when I'm reluctant."

Remembering what he said about protecting her, Yasmin slid her hands around his. Joseph looked at them intertwining. Though he didn't pull away, he didn't appear happy.

She probably couldn't change that. Maybe, though, she could change his focus.

"Joseph," she said. "I know you've got some evidence of wrongdoing by LaBass, but wouldn't it be better to have more? That's why you're not running back to Iksander, isn't it? You haven't gathered quite enough for his lawyers to use in court. If we unearth Stefan's secret, maybe we can improve the odds. If his skeletons are as awful as I suspect, they'll taint LaBass's whole movement."

Though he seemed wary, his gaze lit. "That might be useful," he admitted.

"We'll do it then." Grinning, she squeezed his fingers in excitement. "Fortunately, I know just the place to start . . ."

CHAPTER TWELVE

Truth Seekers

Safiye didn't question Yasmin's desire to retire to bed with a bad headache. From her perspective, being fired, or nearly, would naturally upset her. What excuse Joseph made for escaping she didn't know. Yasmin presumed the lie was convincing. Perhaps he claimed to be hand-patting her.

He'd agreed they shouldn't delay making their next move. Today was Sunday. Stefan's gathering would start breaking up tomorrow. While not impossible, poking around Milion after that would risk tipping off their targets. Joseph didn't want to put the conspirators on their guard or—worse—drive them underground.

On her part, Yasmin would rather not give Stefan the chance to disappear more people.

Working on the premise that there was no time to spare, they flew in smoke form to the ruin they believed they'd seen him coming from. Landing in the decaying building was eerier than circling over it. Though the sun was out, the wind had kicked up since morning. Like unmoored spiderwebs, the magic of the In-Betweens blew sporadically through the air. Solidifying a heartbeat after she did, Joseph shivered as some brushed him.

He glanced doubtfully at the crumbling walls. "I hope you're right about this. I don't sense anything other than the usual In-Between weirdness."

"The weirdness is camouflage," she asserted. "Or it could be. Plus, the nearness of the edge keeps other djinn away. If you were up to skullduggery and didn't want to be interrupted, this would be an ideal spot."

"Okay," he said, seeming to believe her. "Give me your hand. I want to borrow a little power and do a deeper scan."

She laid her palm in his without hesitation. Joseph was very gentle. She barely felt the draw on her energy as he closed his eyes and went quiet.

"Hm," he said after a few heartbeats.

"Hm, what?"

He opened his golden eyes. "There's a stairway. A break in the ground that leads downward. Over there in the left corner."

They waded through overgrown grasses to get to it. Yasmin *thought* she saw an opening. The tufts grew so thickly around the spot, shoving them aside was a two-djinni job.

"It *is* a stairway," she exclaimed.

The stone steps were cracked and spackled with pale lichen. Barely wide enough for a single djinni, gloom hid their lower reaches, making it difficult to gauge how far the treads descended. A greater concentration of wild magic—which felt oddly hot and cold at once—radiated upward from the bottom.

Yasmin took a breath to steady her resolve. "Down is the logical way to go."

"I'll go first," Joseph said and clasped her hand again.

Down and down they went—twenty steps, then fifty, and then she stopped counting. Joseph called up a palm light to illuminate their way. Though this was basic magic, the glow he'd summoned ebbed and flared fitfully. The magic of In-Betweens seemed to interfere with his.

When Joseph spoke, he sounded like he couldn't quite catch his breath. "Why do I feel as if we're approaching the cliff edge? I know we're moving in the opposite direction."

"That could be a spell. An illusion to discourage intruders."

Joseph started to respond but halted in his tracks.

They'd reached the end of the steps. A strange, ancient-looking door blocked their way forward. A bad paint job scabbed its peeling surface, an assortment of ugly colors exposed by the different layers. The knob was tarnished, its decoration spartan in the extreme. Yasmin identified a peephole but no bell—manual or magic-powered. On the landing, just ahead of their dusty feet, a brown, bristled mat bore the dubious word 'WELCOME.'

No proprietor she knew would own any of these items.

"That's an old human door," Joseph said. "Someone must have spelled it through a portal."

He tried the knob, but it didn't turn. A telltale hole pierced the plate under it.

"Do you suppose we need a physical key?" she asked.

He shook his head. "I'm sensing an open sesame. Usually, I can crack other people's codes, but this one is evading me. Something about it feels slippery."

"The wild magic could be helping to disguise it."

"Maybe." He bent toward the bristly mat and lifted one corner. "Ah, there's one of those magic cakes under here. Like the disk you found in the Ozil house's eaves."

She thought he'd remove it, to try to depower the protections. Instead, he dropped the mat and straightened.

"Our slipper soles are dirty. Before humans enter someone's home, they wipe their feet on mats like these. Perhaps that's the open sesame."

"Surely that's too simple."

Joseph smiled with half his mouth. "One way to find out."

"All right," she said, because he seemed to be waiting for her okay. "Go ahead."

He stepped onto the mat cautiously. He swiped his left foot, his right, and then his left once more for good measure. Yasmin held her breath but didn't sense anything altering. When he tried the knob again, it refused to budge.

Joseph sighed. "Well, it was a worth a try."

"Wait," Yasmin said, her heart abruptly beating faster. "I hear movement behind the door."

She heard footsteps approaching.

The door creaked open before they could retreat.

"Oh," the person behind it said. "You're not Stefan."

"Tara," Yasmin exclaimed, relief flooding her at the sight of the djinniya. Other than looking wan, Tara seemed unharmed. Yasmin told herself she *wasn't* disappointed this secret bunker was, evidently, just an unusual love nest. Tara must be two-timing LaBass with Dimitriou.

"Thank goodness!" she went on, ignoring the shameful reaction. "We were worried about you."

Tara cocked her head. "Why would you be worried? I've never been better."

"But . . . why are you here? We heard you'd gone home."

"I am home," she said simply.

Actually, she didn't say it *simply* but like a simpleton. The djinniya Yasmin remembered was livelier than this. Tara's clothes were out of character as well. She wore a sleeveless, powder-blue human dress whose bodice conformed to her lush figure. Shockingly, the full, swingy skirt ended at her knees. Her calves were as bare as her arms, her feet teetering in heels. Another foreign garment—white with pale orange checks—tied snugly around her waist. Yasmin believed humans called it an apron.

Perhaps Joseph recognized it from his stay in New York. Ignoring Tara's eccentric garb, he keyed in on something else. "Yasmin," he said in a low aside. "Look at those red marks on her neck."

The shapes were faint but reminded her of hands, as if someone had gripped Tara's throat too hard.

"Manual strangulation," he explained.

"Do come in," Tara said, before his words could add up in Yasmin's head. "I mustn't forget my manners, not when you've come all this way."

Yasmin and Joseph exchanged glances. *May as well,* his expression said.

They followed Tara into what appeared to be a home. It had chairs and couches and carpets on the floor. Windows were built into the walls but, this far underground, the scenes they looked out on were made of paint. In Yasmin's opinion, the depictions of Milion farmland were too slapdash to fool a child. No one had bothered to animate them. They sat still and did nothing.

"Martini?" Hostess-like, Tara gestured to a brass bar cart on wheels. "My master likes one when he arrives."

"You master?" Yasmin asked, suddenly unsure of her conclusions. "Do you mean LaBass?"

Tara waved as if swatting away a fly. "No, no. I've traded masters. I belong to Stefan. My existence is perfect now."

Her voice didn't sound like a real person's. Horror hit Yasmin in a cold, curdling wave. Tara *wasn't* a real person. Tara was a dead body with some leftover memories. Manual strangulation was a thing that killed people. Being stuffed full of magic was what allowed her to walk around.

She gasped too loudly. Joseph cleared his throat to cover the betraying sound.

Tara turned to both of them with her brows lifted in question.

"Could you show us around?" Joseph asked. "We'd love to see where you're living now."

She beamed at him. "I'd be delighted."

"One thing first." He stuck his hand in his trouser pocket and pulled it out, seemingly empty. "Do you see what I have in the center of my palm?"

Tara rose on the toes of her heels before leaning in. "There's nothing there but a tiny speck."

"Watch." Joseph's lips moved with a silent spell. The speck expanded until a shiny black rectangle filled his hand. It reminded Yasmin of human phones she'd seen pictures of. Hope flared a second before it died. Obviously, they couldn't use this device to communicate. Scroll networks ran on magic. Humans used different stuff—'radio' waves, or some such thing. Otherwise, Joseph would have contacted Iksander and Arcadius already.

"What's that?" Tara asked.

"It's a toy. It records sounds and video. A friend brought it back from a trip for me. Would you mind if I filmed this place and you?" He asked this very gently.

He's sorry for her, Yasmin thought.

"I wouldn't mind," Tara said, "but this place is a secret."

"That's all right. These pictures are for me. I won't share them with anyone who shouldn't see."

Yasmin sensed loopholes behind his words, but they satisfied Tara. Smiling, she turned and began walking. "We'll start with the kitchen. That's my favorite of the rooms."

Yasmin wouldn't have sworn it was a kitchen if Tara hadn't said. The spotless counters were colored plastic, the oven a metal box.

"Someone has a fetish for the Fifties," Joseph muttered beneath his breath.

Yasmin vaguely understood what this meant.

"We have canned SPAM and Campbell's Soup!" Tara crowed, stretching up to open a turquoise cabinet. "They're vacuum packed to last forever. My master is so clever."

The food seemed unfit for anything but looking at. Then again, did Tara eat anymore? Without making a fuss about it, Joseph recorded everything.

"Take a picture of my Coldspot," Tara encouraged, stroking a tall white box with turquoise side accents. "We chill orange juice in it."

"'We?'" Joseph asked. "Do other djinn live here too?"

"I didn't mean *them*," Tara said with less enthusiasm. "I meant me and Stefan. But, yes, there are others. If you want, I'll show you the dormitory."

The word gave Yasmin a sinking feeling.

"We'd like to see it," Joseph confirmed.

They followed her down a murky hall. The air smelled musty, as if it weren't regularly refreshed from the outside. Yasmin noticed Tara only breathed before she spoke. Otherwise, her lungs remained motionless.

"Here they are," the djinniya said, opening a door. "Don't expect much. They aren't interesting like me. You'll have to do the lights. My master says I shouldn't waste magic."

Joseph spelled on a line of dim ceiling pendants. Unlike the rest of the residence, which was painted in flat dull colors, the room she'd led them to was tiled. The tiles weren't fancy, just tan ceramic laid in a brick pattern. The courses ran up the walls and across the ceiling. The only departure from the monotony was a large brass drain in the floor.

Joseph had a question. "If this is a dormitory, where are the beds?"

Tara pushed up a lever they hadn't noticed on coming in. Immediately, light shone out through a number of large glass squares in the walls. Yasmin estimated twenty windows altogether. Each provided a view of a room with a narrow cot and a single body laid out on it.

None of the bodies stirred when the lights came on.

"See," Tara said. "Unless my master wakes them, they just lie there."

"We'll look at them all the same," Joseph said.

Yasmin accompanied him down the line. At the third room, she let out a cry. She recognized the inhabitant.

"That's Ivy," Tara said. "Stefan tried to make her the favorite, but she wasn't any good. I'm better, the master says. I'll last a long time, he thinks."

Familiar hand prints reddened Ivy's unmoving throat. They were darker than the ones around Tara's neck . . . more violent and bruised looking. Yasmin swallowed uncomfortably.

Ivy hadn't given up easily.

"Why are you better?" Joseph asked Tara.

"I have my personality." Tara's hair was loose and wavy and considerably shorter than was traditional. The unfamiliar style had required a dramatic cut. With one hand, she flipped some behind her shoulder. "If you fight too much, you lose it."

She meant if you fought being turned into a zombie.

"Tara," Yasmin said, pushing that aside. "Do you remember how you came to be here?"

"What do you mean?"

"You used to live somewhere else, didn't you?"

Tara's nose wrinkled. "I was in the master's upside house for a while. In the pretty room with my maid. It's hard to be sure, but I might have been crying." She touched her cheek where the multicolored spots from her haywire spell had danced. They were gone now, the same as the spark that had given her true life. "I don't recall why I was upset. Probably it's not important. The next thing I know I was here." Trying to remember distressed her. When she stopped, her expression cleared. "Stefan says not to think about it. Living here is everything any female could desire."

Joseph walked ahead of them, filming each window with his phone. As he went, he dragged the fingertips of his free hand along the tile, a seemingly idle gesture Yasmin wouldn't have attempted. She was too unnerved to want to touch anything.

"Oh," he said, stiffening in surprise as he turned the corner. "This room's occupant is male."

"I don't know his name," Tara said. "Stefan calls him the Handy Man."

"Well, he has big hands." Joseph pursed his lips thoughtfully. He glanced briefly sidewise at Tara, then lifted his arms and mimicked a strangling grip. "Yes, about the right size, I think."

Obviously, he thought Stefan used a proxy for his killing.

His gesture triggered no response in Tara. Whatever she remembered about her death, it wasn't specific. She pointed to a door whose presence was camouflaged by tile.

"My bedroom's through there," she said.

Of course, it was. Who *wouldn't* want to sleep in a morgue? Joseph nodded for Tara to show them.

This room was foreign in style as well. Mint green paint clad the walls, between which two flowery yellow beds shared a small lamp table. The windows were curtained in more yellow and looked out on an alien world. Though animated, the scenes of the human town convinced even less than the farmland ones. Here, doll men in doll suits strode up dollhouse walks where their doll wives greeted them with cheek pecks. Wearing aprons like Tara's, the women's arms hugged bowls whose mystery contents they never ceased stirring.

Tara sighed happily as the window loop recommenced. "Isn't it nice? The other night, when we first tried it out, Stefan made Ivy lie on the second bed. He said it's exciting to have an audience."

Yasmin's stomach clenched. Dimitriou had sex with what remained of Tara here, while what remained of Ivy watched. *This* was why he'd encouraged Safiye to lie back and enjoy. The human decade of the Fifties wasn't all he had a fetish for. He wanted—or needed—his partner to pretend to be deceased. When he'd left his prospective fiancée on their first night together, he risked everything to fly here. That was more than cheating. That was a compulsion. For him, this charnel house offered the only sort of union that sated him.

The realization horrified her. On the other hand, it would probably put an end to Dimitriou—and LaBass's—political ambitions.

"Dimitriou *likes* sleeping with dead people," she blurted.

She'd grown accustomed to Tara not understanding what she said.

"That's not nice," the female reproached, unexpectedly comprehending this.

She frowned strongly, her fists planted at her waist where the blue skirt poofed.

"Sorry," Yasmin said. "I, uh, didn't mean to suggest you weren't . . ."

She trailed off, not sure what she ought to explain. Did Tara know she was dead? If she found out, would it upset her?

"You acted like you thought my house was nice," the soulless corpse accused. "As if you were my friend. You're not, though, and I think you're not the master's friend, either. You'll be sorry when I tell him!"

She ran from the room—zipped, really—leaving Yasmin to stare in shock. She hadn't imagined a dead woman could move that fast.

"We'd better go after her," Joseph said.

"She can't be meaning to go outside. People will see her."

"She might have another way to contact Dimitriou."

Okay, that would be bad.

They ran through the dormitory, down the murky hall, and across the living room. They weren't catching up very well. Tara knew the territory . . . or had better gloom vision. She didn't trip on rugs or knock into tables the way they were.

"Shit," Joseph panted, skidding to a stop. "I can't hear her. How did we lose the trail?"

Could living-dead people smoke? Maybe Yasmin should try. To even the playing field.

"No," Joseph said, catching her wrist as she began to blur. "We're too close to the In-Betweens. I don't want them to lure you in."

She stopped dematerializing. She didn't think she was at risk of that, but who knew, really? The mists weren't predictable.

"There," she whispered, her arm jerking up to point. "I heard a door click shut."

The sound came from the double doors to an adjoining room. Joseph reached them first and flung both open. Inside, Tara stood by a waist-high desk, lifting an ominously familiar object toward her ear.

Dimitriou had an old-style human phone like that.

"No!" Yasmin cried, leaping for Tara before her pink-manicured index finger could turn the rotary dial.

Determined to tattle to her master, the female fought for control of the receiver. She was stronger than Yasmin was prepared for. They wrestled back and forth without either gaining ground.

"Help me," she urged Joseph, who seemed not to know how to intervene. "That phone doesn't use the scroll net. It's connected by actual wire to Dimitriou's home office."

Joseph joined her in the fight. The two of them together managed to press Tara back onto the desktop.

Disconcertingly, she hissed through bared teeth and thrashed.

"Let go," Joseph ordered, his hold clamped around her wrist. The strength required to subdue her brought out his ruthlessness. With all his might, he slammed the Tara's hand against the hard surface. Yasmin heard dead bone break, but the pain a living person would have felt didn't register for Tara. Though she seemed to lose steam with both of them fighting her, her fingers gripped her prize like steel.

"*Let go*," he repeated, magical influence behind the command this time.

"She won't obey you," Stefan interrupted from the door, jolting all three of them around. "Only I can compel my pets."

"Master!" Tara cried, wrenching free to run to him. Like a child whose parental savior had arrived, she hugged him tightly from the side. "How did you know I wanted you? Did you read my mind?"

"How could I, kitten? You have to have one for that to work. I found pillows stuffed under that one's covers, and followed her trail out here. Really, Yasmin," he clucked to her. "You might have put an effort into your subterfuge. A spell to imitate your sleeping self, at least. Your laziness insults me."

"You checked my *bed* to see if I was in it?"

"Who was going to stop me? I'm master of that house too. I simply said I wanted to patch things up between you and Safiye. Friends shouldn't be at odds when there's so much to celebrate." He smiled in anticipation of the news he was going to drop. "You'll be pleased to hear Lady Toraman agreed to marry me."

They were engaged? Yasmin tried to hide her dismay. She did a better job than Tara. The undead djinniya pouted like a teenager. "You're marrying that awful woman? Whatever for?"

Dimitriou stroked her hair like the kitten he'd just called her. "For appearances, darling. You're the female I care about. Here, I brought you a treat." He drew a silvery wild magic cake from his sash pocket. "This is all for you. You can use it to heal your wrist."

"You're the best!" Tara seized it from him, then ran to the corner and turned her back. They heard her whispering a spell but not the words she said. Yasmin sensed Joseph straining to magically augment his hearing.

Possibly Dimitriou sensed it too.

"I must say," he observed, drawing Joseph's attention back. "I had my doubts about the wisdom of clueing Miss Baykal in, but your participation in her nose-poking disappoints. I thought your political principles genuine."

"That's not worth debating," Joseph said. "I'm more interested in how you make those things."

Dimitriou's eyes half-hooded with amusement. "Of course you are." He thought a moment and then shrugged, seeming not to mind answering. "A childhood nurse taught me the formula. She learned it from her mother, who learned it from hers in turn. All

Milioners benefit from the wild magic hereabouts. It gives us more power to draw on. Alas, it evaporates. My nurse's method preserves the advantage for later use."

"Why would she share it with you?"

He smiled. "Why does any servant serve? In this instance, a mutual resentment toward my parents bonded us. As you might imagine, I won't be giving up visits here when my bride and I relocate to the capital. One does have to refill the well."

Yasmin couldn't hide her disgust. "That isn't the only reason you'll return—unless you intend to set up a bunker there. Living women just aren't the same, are they? Not even when they're willing to roll over and play dead."

Dimitriou laughed unashamedly. "You're quite right. They're not the same at all. My pets can be anything I desire whenever I desire it."

"So long as they don't run low on power."

"Yes, preserving them does pose challenges. In their not-quite-alive condition, they aren't always reliable. Memories linger, but intelligence dissipates. It's sad, really. Do you know, the first djinni I reanimated was a lucky experiment? A friend of mine, a long-time, valued associate who for years had handled my most sensitive challenges—"

"You mean your fixer," Joseph interjected.

"Yes, my fixer. But he thought he was my friend, and he was marvelously loyal. He died by accident, fulfilling a task for me. Since no one knew he was dead, I thought I'd tinker with his remains. See if I could bring him back and continue to get good out of him. Not being a prodigy like yourself, I exhausted my whole store of cakes reviving him. I did it though. And he was more attached to me than ever afterward."

"He's your Handy Man," Joseph guessed.

Dimitriou seemed to enjoy his quickness. "Tara mentioned him, did she? He's forgotten his name, and I've discovered it's best if I don't remind him. Upsets him quite a bit. Other than that, he's better than obedient. I don't have to tell him what to do. I simply hint at what I'd like. Wishing to please me, he decides on a course of action by himself. I suspect I'm splitting hairs with the universe, but as of yet, I've not turned ifrit. I am glad of that. That would take energy to hide."

"You're a gray practitioner," Joseph said.

"Is that what it's called? Good to know."

"Your charity school for orphans," Yasmin said, another conclusion springing into her mind. "You killed their parents!"

"Some of them," Dimitriou admitted pleasantly. "Knowing that gives me a pleasant buzz when I visit them. And thank you for reminding me I need to arrange for Cedric Ozil to encounter some mishap."

"You . . . you're—"

"A monster?" Dimitriou suggested mockingly. "The universe doesn't think so. In any case, you're a fine one to talk. Aside from Iksander's other irregularities, rumor has it your former master likes to make love in his smoke form. Your current partner can't get it up, despite which you don't hesitate to use him for *your* jollies. Maybe, Miss Baykal, you shouldn't be shaming others' kinks."

"I wouldn't equate a fetish for corpses with either of those things. Nor would your new best friends."

"What makes you think LaBass and Co. don't know? I believe they might. I know their sort. They'll have vetted me down to my last ass hair. They'd might prefer having a shameful secret they can hold over me. To their mind, our city's people would never stand for it."

"They wouldn't! You'd be tarred and feathered and tossed into a dungeon for good measure."

"Perhaps you're right. In any case, that theory need stand no test today. Not when I can so easily counter the threat you pose to me."

CHAPTER THIRTEEN

Daredevils

The universe might not have branded Dimitriou a demon, but the slow curving of his mouth made him resemble one. Probably Yasmin shouldn't have provoked him. She didn't want to find out how he meant to stop them. She wanted to escape with Joseph and his clever phone *and* all the proof on it.

Joseph had the same idea, it seemed.

"I'm sure there's some mutually beneficial agreement we could come to," he proposed.

Dimitriou laughed. "You two delight me. You really do. You especially." He wagged his head at Yasmin. "Beauty and brains—not to mention charisma! You make me sorry I have to incite your demise. If you'd been a bit more compliant, or willing to pretend, I'd have enjoyed marrying you. Safiye can be a tad socially standoffish. You, however, would have secured every citizen's devotion."

Yasmin gaped at him. What did a woman say to this sort of speech? Not 'thank you,' she was certain.

"Ah, well," Dimitriou sighed. "No point delaying the necessary. Tara, dear? If you're done with your treat, turn on the generator and wake the others. I'm feeling threatened by these two. My life may be in danger. I suspect I need defense."

Tara zipped off so quickly Yasmin and Joseph gasped in unison. The cake had done more than heal her. Now she was super-energized.

"Don't even try," Dimitriou said to Joseph, who was gathering his resources. "I've set wards in this office. You can't attack me magically."

Joseph was quicker in a corner than Yasmin. Seizing a carved mahogany guest chair, he ran at Dimitriou. The piece was heavy enough to bash in the other's head. Sadly, he didn't get the chance to try.

Tara and her living-dead friends arrived—the full twenty, by Yasmin's count. The glimpse she had time for told her these bodies contained no souls. Their eyes were flat, their skin an odd greenish white. Older than Tara, they resembled not-quite-as-fresh corpses.

"Protect!" The sole male in the group commanded: the handyman, she presumed. "Protect the master!"

The females swarmed Joseph in a mass. Helpless before their numbers, he went down under them.

Yasmin's effort to drag them off was futile.

"Stop!" she demanded anyway, putting her will behind it.

Dimitriou laughed delightedly. "Strong, aren't they? I do remind you they're immune to any spells but mine."

Enraged—and stubborn—she yanked the cold arms harder. The zombies were slapping and pinching Joseph . . . maybe from former girly habit? Despite their poor fighting skills, they were having an effect. They hummed excitedly when one of them drew blood.

"You could try assaulting me like he did," Dimitriou pointed out to her. "I think I'd enjoy that."

"*Don't*," Joseph warned as he struggled beneath the pile. "You'll just convince his pets they need to attack you. They respond to any threat to him."

"Damn it," she cursed in frustration. *This* was how Dimitriou squirmed out of responsibility for his kills.

Their laughing host had another offer. "Perhaps you'd like a chance to escape. As luck would have it, there's a secret door in the paneling. Yes, behind the desk. It opens when you press and turn the third brass flower."

This had to be another trick, but Yasmin didn't care. A chance was a chance, and at the moment she'd take it.

She vaulted the desk and wrenched the small flower around. A section of wall made a grinding noise as it swung open. Revealed behind it was a rough stone passage, lit by veins of something that glowed pale blue.

Her best guess was that the veins contained concentrations of wild magic.

"Come on," she urged, reaching down to grab Joseph's arm.

Dimitriou must have given his pets a signal. Her tug succeeded in pulling Joseph free. Though he cursed, he scrambled up into the tunnel along with her.

"He's not letting us go," he panted as they ran. "The minute he gives the word, that gang will come after us."

"A chance is a chance. Maybe he wants to make this a game."

"A *rigged* game," he retorted.

She refused to waste her breath arguing. The tunnel was sloping upward and bending left. Fresher air blew down it.

"Crap," Joseph said. "Now we really are headed toward the cliff."

She feared he was correct. The tingly spiderweb sensations they'd felt outside were strengthening.

"And here they come," Joseph said as the noise of their pursuers grew audible. Still running, he twisted around to see. "Dimitriou isn't with them. Tara is out in front."

"She's the strongest. Maybe the others will tire out."

Joseph grunted. This, she supposed, was better than flat out saying he doubted it. To make matters even more dire, they didn't have much runway left. Something that looked an awful lot like daylight brightened the too-near distance. Her muscles faltered from their swift pace.

Daylight didn't mean safety if it came from the In-Between.

"We have to make a stand," Joseph said. "We can't let them drive us into the mists. We might as well commit suicide."

He dug his heels in and caught her wrist.

"Damn it," she said, letting him yank her to a halt. To her dismay, she was trembling and sweating all over.

"We'll make them work for it," he said. "Maybe that will be enough to turn Dimitriou dark."

If he hadn't turned dark for killing his other victims, she didn't see why he would for them. Grinding her teeth together suppressed the words. An idea that was likely pointless occurred to her. Because pointless was all she had, she spoke firmly.

"We're farther from Dimitriou's influence now. I'm going to try to wake up their consciences. —They have memories," she added when Joseph pulled in a breath to speak. "At the least, we can appeal to the people they used to be."

"Very well," he said, though he looked as skeptical as she felt. "If you need extra power, I've got some stashed."

She didn't know what he meant. Her magic was still partly damped by Dimitriou's wards. Worse, the increasing nearness of In-Betweens confused it too much to rely on. Was Joseph so much more powerful he wasn't affected? She didn't have time to ask. Dimitriou's undead slaves had caught up. If she hadn't been about to die, she'd have laughed at them bunching up and stumbling when their leader Tara stopped.

"Hey," Tara pouted. "You're supposed to keep running."

"If we keep running, we'll fall into the In-Betweens."

"Good," Tara said. "You can't hurt our master then."

"But he's trying to hurt us. And he's using you to do it. Once upon a time, you'd have known that was wrong."

"Pah," Tara scoffed. "He's the master. Everything he does is right."

The gang she led rumbled in agreement.

"He killed you," Yasmin said, deciding she had nothing to lose by reminding her. "He had the Handy Man strangle you. His hands match the marks on your throat."

"They don't," Tara denied, though she touched the bruises reflexively. "You're a big fat liar."

The Handy Man shouldered up beside her.

"I *protected* him," he corrected, thick and slow.

"From Tara?" Joseph said scornfully, joining her campaign to win hearts and minds. "Look how tiny she is. Plus she adores him. How could she be a threat? Your master didn't need to kill her. She was simply an annoyance."

"Hey!" Tara said. "I'm the favorite."

"Safiye is his favorite. He's marrying her. And he'd have been glad to marry Yasmin. You heard him say so yourself."

Tara shook her head stubbornly. "Nuh-uh, your smoke is on fire!"

"Stop that," the Handy Man interrupted.

To Yasmin's surprise, he didn't mean Joseph. One of the other zombies had taken hold of his meaty hands and was lifting them to her throat.

"They *do* match," the female said in a tone of discovery. "I remember him strangling me!"

"Ivy," Yasmin breathed, recognizing her.

The pallid djinniya turned. Her widened eyes held a spark of—if not life—then intelligence. "People called me that when I was alive."

"You *are* alive," Tara scolded. "The master perfected you."

Ivy ignored her. She took a step toward Yasmin. "You know the truth, don't you? I was . . ." She furrowed her brow and frowned. "I wasn't like this. I didn't follow mindlessly. I was a good person."

"You were. Your name was Ivy Ozil. You were a good person and a mother."

"A mother."

"You had two children, a boy Acanthus and a girl Columbine. They have black hair and green eyes like you."

"Acanthus," Ivy said, testing out the name. "And Columbine is my daughter. She . . . I think she likes chasing butterflies. My husband says we should have—"

She stopped, her dim eyes welling up with tears.

"Your husband's name is Cedric," Yasmin said softly. "If you don't help us, Dimitriou plans to kill him and take your children into his orphanage."

"You're telling the truth," Ivy whispered. "I can hear it in your voice. I was always good at that. I was . . . I *knew* he lied about stealing those ruby trees!"

Apart from Tara and now Ivy, the other zombies seemed not to have much initiative. They'd barely moved while Ivy spoke, simply walling off the tunnel with a barricade of bodies that didn't blink or breathe. Yasmin didn't think they were out of power, more like conserving their energy. Still, Ivy switching sides might be sufficient to turn to the tide.

Yasmin focused her voice to reach only her.

"You'll stand with us," she said, praying this was true. "You'll help us fight for your family's sake."

"I want to," Ivy said. "But there are a lot of them. And Tara is very strong. Dimitriou gives her the cakes now."

"What if you had one?" Joseph asked softly. He reached into his pocket. To Yasmin's amazement, his hand came out with one of Dimitriou's silver disks. Where in the world had he gotten that?

"I magicked this from behind a tile in the dormitory. While Tara was distracted. Do you know how to draw energy from it?"

"Oh, yes," Ivy said, both hands reaching out longingly. A moment later, she pulled them back. "Even if I eat that, I can't destroy them all. Maybe not even Tara. The best I can try is to hold them back while you look for a safe way out."

They had no reason to think a safe way out existed.

"We'll take it," Yasmin said. "Goddess bless you."

Ivy pulled a face to say what she thought about the prospect of a deity helping her.

"You never know," Joseph said, and passed the cake over.

As soon as she had it, he grabbed Yasmin's hand and ran.

The zombies woke up then, uttering animal cries of protest and—from the sound of it—flinging themselves at their newly powered-up opponent. Ivy must have eaten her boost quickly. She was keeping the others from pursuit, enough that Joseph and Yasmin soon put the mob behind them.

The downside was that as they ran, the light of the In-Betweens grew brighter. Soon the tunnel mouth was more than a fuzzy glow. Yasmin saw heaving clouds in the opening.

"Can you smoke yet?" Joseph panted. "You could try phasing through the earth."

"I can't change any more than you! We're stuck in our solid bodies. Plus, I wouldn't dare pass through those wild magic veins. Goddess knows what it would do to me. — Don't slow down," she ordered when Joseph instinctively began to. "Maybe we can scale the cliff above the tunnel mouth."

He cursed but forced himself onward.

Grateful for that, she didn't scold when he dropped to his knees six feet from the passage end. She closed the final distance, shuddering all over as she gripped a rock and leaned out the opening. The mists swallowed up her head, blinding her. She couldn't see the nose on her face, much less a safe path upward. Determined not give up, she ran her hand up the outside wall.

Shit, shit, shit, she swore in her head at what she found. Though her shrinking nerves didn't want to, she moved to explore the other side.

"Damn it," she bit out, retreating into the tunnel.

Seated on his heels, Joseph looked up at her.

"The stone is smooth as glass," she admitted. "As if the mists polished it. There's not a single handhold to grab onto."

"Okay," he said, his golden eyes strangely calm. "We take the only choice we have and go down fighting."

She knew Stefan's pets would kill them. So did Joseph, it sounded like.

"That's not our only choice."

His calm face twisted. "Yasmin . . ."

"We can jump," she said stubbornly. "Maybe the In-Betweens will kill us, but maybe we'll last long enough to escape. *Things* survive in there, Joseph. Even living things, if you count ruby trees and that damned Nessie. I think we can do it. I think we're strong enough."

Joseph swallowed. "I'm not sure I can force myself to leap."

"You'll be with me," she pleaded. "We'll be leaping together."

His eyes went shiny. He seemed to understand what her words betrayed.

"I *can't* leave you behind," she said, willing to destroy any possible doubt. If she lived to regret it, she'd count herself lucky. "If the chance I make it is one in millions, I don't want that chance without you."

He shifted on his heels. "We—" He cleared his throat. "We . . . probably do have better odds of surviving together."

In spite of everything, she smiled and held out her hand to him.

He grinned back—a bit wryly—and then all hell broke loose.

A grisly object sailed in her direction, coming at her so fast she didn't have time to jerk away. The object missed her face by inches, close enough to reveal that it was Ivy's head. Her black hair trailed like a banner, her neck ripped bloodlessly from the rest of her. Her widened eyes and mouth gave her a look of horror.

Half a heartbeat later, the mists made her disappear.

"I ate her cake!" Tara exulted. "Ivy tried to save some for later, but I got the rest of it."

Tara truly was charged up now. Her eyes were fiery, her hair and her poufy skirt floating out with the power surplus. Though she'd arrived before the others, their growl and clatter were close behind.

"Jump!" Tara screamed. "Jump and be gone like that traitor!"

She chucked another body part toward the gulf: Ivy's severed arm this time. A hand followed and then a foot, both of which vanished instantly. Tara and her crew must have literally torn Ivy limb from limb.

Joseph was on his feet now, his fingers iron on Yasmin's wrist.

"Jesus," he breathed in shock.

"The fish man won't save you," Tara taunted. "You'll die like the master wants."

"We have to jump," Yasmin urged. "While we have the chance. If they tear us apart, we're done."

"KILL!" came the Handyman's bearlike voice. "PROTECT THE MASTER!"

The zombies behind him roared like a crowd whose team was winning a polo match. They surged together toward her and Joseph.

Yasmin wouldn't have thought she'd be thankful for such a thing, but their advance broke Joseph from his paralysis.

"Shit," he said, spinning with her to face the wall of mists.

They didn't need more than one running step to reach the final ledge.

With Joseph pulling her after him, they leaped into nothingness.

CHAPTER FOURTEEN

Riders on the Storm

Immediately, they couldn't see anything but cloud. Yasmin knew they were lucky to see that much. Vision deteriorated quickly in the In-Betweens, but the mists caused all kinds of sensory blindness. Concepts of up or down, of distance and time, soon failed. The ledge they'd jumped from could have been feet behind them or many miles. Neither was likely more accurate. The confusion ended—so her father warned—with the loss of one's sense of self. Then they'd be finished, their very souls swallowed by non-being.

Already, Yasmin had the sensation that she floated weightlessly.

"I can't feel your wrist," Joseph said.

She could tell he was trying to sound calm.

"My wrist is in your hand," she responded, "and I've twisted mine around yours. We're gripping each other firmly."

She didn't raise her voice. That would worsen Joseph's impression that his solid existence was dissolving. She couldn't let herself think about it either. She needed real things, strong things to hold onto.

When she was little, her father taught her emotional things would do. *If you ever fall in accidentally, remember how much your mother and I love you. Remember everything you care about. Remember your favorite toy and all the ways your brothers annoy you. Those responses rise from your heart. Anything you feel intensely will anchor you.*

"Do you remember the first time we kissed?" she asked.

"Of course," Joseph said. "I could never forget that."

He sounded mystified that she'd brought it up, but a moment later an understanding "ah" left him.

"I see," he said. "Thinking about that triggered an improvement. I can feel your arm now. I'll keep remembering kissing you."

"You can think of anything personal that moves you. Anything that matters will ground you."

"I don't mind thinking about kissing you."

He made her laugh. The sound was muffled . . . but not much, she told herself.

"Sorry if I shouldn't," he said, "but, um, I can't help wondering how long we can keep this up."

That was the trick, of course. The fact that she could *barely* feel her pulse speed up with anxiety troubled her. Had they been in here even a minute?

"We're together," she said. "And the Goddess is with us both. She's strongest in places where people fear they're weak."

"I'm not a follower of your goddess."

"That doesn't matter. She's here for everyone."

That wisdom came thanks to Yasmin's mother. When Yasmin was a girl, they'd attended temple every week, no skipping.

"Would you like to pray?" Joseph asked politely. "I usually do that silently in my head, but I wouldn't be offended if you want me to join you in reciting a favorite psalm."

She squeezed his wrist, appreciating his consideration for her comfort. He really was a lovely djinni. She promised herself that, if they got out of this, she'd never again be embarrassed that she carried a torch for him. Her feelings for him should be a source of pride: a proof of the soundest taste.

"It *is* nice to have escaped Dimitriou's zombies," he observed.

"Yes, it is. I—"

Before she could finish agreeing, a haunting wail cut through the nothingness. Her connection to Joseph was firm enough that his shudder shook her too.

"God," he groaned in a now-what tone. "That's Milion's Nessie."

The wail came again. Yasmin's blood leaped inside her numbing veins. Goddess be thanked, she perceived an actual ray of hope. "That's not Nessie. That's a train!"

"A train?"

"Yes. With an old-style steam whistle. We can take shelter in it. If it's survived the In-Betweens, it must have protections."

She didn't wait for him to agree. She pulled him after her. "We need to fly toward it. I *know* that's the right thing to do. My father used to coach me how to survive if I ever fell off an edge."

"Your father would know." He was struggling to sound sure.

"Yes," she agreed, more certain than he could be. "Of all the djinn in this world, he would know."

She convinced herself they were moving toward the whistle, though it felt more like swimming through jellied broth than flying. *Goddess guide us*, she thought, then spied a distinctive shape breaking through the cloud.

The passenger car floating ahead of them was attached to others, though they faded out of view. On the nearest, the silver lettering on the lacquered blue side was clear. 'GLORIOUS CITY – MILION – EXPRESS,' it said.

Since he was closer, Joseph stretched to grab the stair handle.

"Got it," he said and pulled them both inside.

As soon as they crossed the threshold, they took on weight. With matching gasps, they caught themselves on their feet.

"Gravity," he said. "You were right about the train being protected from the In-Betweens' influence."

Still breathless, Yasmin nodded and glanced around. After their trip through the mist, the non-clouded interior of the car seemed especially vivid. "I think this is Second Class. The seats are narrower, and the decoration is less fancy. I wonder how long Milioners have been hearing their Nessie. Everything in here looks brand new."

"And spotless." Joseph ran his finger along the dust-free back of an upholstered chair. No signs of previous passengers were anywhere. Curious, he considered the next connecting door. "Do we dare explore?"

"As long as we're careful. We don't want to end up in the mists again."

Sparing a grimace for the unvarying gray behind the windows, he began walking down the aisle. A sleeping car was coupled to Second Class, after which that end of the line finished.

"I don't see an engine," he said. "Not that its propulsion would necessarily help us here."

Yasmin had ducked into a small bathroom. "The taps work. I suppose we ought to run them sparingly. We don't know how much is left in the water tank."

"Some is better than none."

She couldn't argue, though they'd want food soon enough as well. "Should we walk the other way? See if there's a dining car?"

He waved for her to go ahead. When she tried the connecting door on the other end of Second Class, it stuck. Peering through the glass revealed a promising slice of tables and booth seats.

"Shall I try the lever?" Joseph offered. "It might need more muscle."

Unoffended, she let him squeeze past her. He pushed, grunted, and the mechanism gave way for him.

"Be careful," she cautioned as he swung the door open.

"It seems all ri—" He drew in a short, sharp breath. "Uh," he said. "Brace yourself. There are passengers, after all."

"Passengers!"

"They're not going to be much company, I'm afraid."

He moved farther in so she could see.

"Good Lord," she exclaimed, though he'd warned her.

A pair of well-dressed male and female mummies sat facing each other in the second booth on their left. Oddly upright and proper, they wore clothes that would have been in fashion a decade or so ago. Tea plates were arrayed before them, the little sandwiches and sweets as dried up and preserved as them.

"Well," Yasmin said, unable to get anything past her throat but that.

"I hope you don't mind," Joseph said. "I feel compelled to see if I can discover who they are."

Or were, she thought. Spooked by the macabre tableau, she hung a step behind as he poked through the male's garments. Halfway through his search, something crisp-sounding snapped, and the corpse fell sideways against the window glass. The impact caused the jawbone to drop. The mummy now looked aghast at the unsolicited frisking it was suffering.

"Eesh," Yasmin said.

Joseph grinned. Did all men delight like boys when women turned squeamish? Any moment he'd be teasing her with frogs. "Sorry. Found a billfold in his sash pocket." He opened it and rifled the contents. "Large denomination banknote. *Very* large denomination banknote. No-longer-secret code for a scroll. People really shouldn't write those down. Ah. Visiting card."

This last he removed. His brows shot up when he saw what was printed on it.

"Huh," he said and handed the card to her.

Yasmin read aloud. "'Georgios Aelfric Dimitriou, Lord Milion, Edgeward Province. Scroll address: To the stars from the Edge.' This is Stefan's father! The one who died in the train accident."

"And his mother, presumably, though perhaps the accident wasn't one. You might want to look away while I perform my next operation. Now that his mouth is open, I see something wedged in the throat."

Yasmin winced but—mostly—watched him extract it. She was the detective here. Someday, Goddess grant they survive this, she might need to do something similar.

Joseph's prize turned out to be a rolled-up scroll. He unfurled it carefully but it was neither damaged nor delicate.

"It's a legal document, disinheriting his son for 'egregious immoral habits.' A younger cousin, one Ubba Halfdan, is designated as heir instead."

She had no trouble guessing what Georgios might consider egregious immoral habits. His son's obsession with deceased bedpartners couldn't have sprung up yesterday.

"That's motive for murder," she observed. "Plus, that hedge witch nurse of his could have helped. You know, supplied him wild magic cakes to plant on the track so the train would derail. *And*—" she went on, her deductive powers warming up "—he might have sent the then-alive Handy Man to shove the scroll down his father's throat. It's a message. 'You want to punish me? Choke on it!' Then the Handy Man leaps off, triggers the cake bomb, and the train is catapulted into the In-Betweens, taking any evidence of un-accidental contributing factors along with it. A wild magic explosion might explain why the adjoining cars survived. Fragments from the cakes could have embedded in the structure."

"That scenario does seem possible." Joseph mused a moment more. "If Dimitriou's parents reserved the train for a romantic outing, they might not have wanted a lot of staff. Dimitriou's confederates could have been disguised as, say, the engineer and cook. That would account for these bodies getting stuck here alone." He pulled a face. "It certainly adds a gruesome twist to Dimitriou's claim that hearing Nessie brings good look. He must have liked the reminder of what he'd done."

Yasmin sighed. "Too bad we won't get a chance to prove it. Probably not, anyway."

"You never know. Look how many challenges we've hurdled already."

He spoke truly, though she couldn't, at present, see a way out of this.

"Come on," he said, giving her arm a squeeze. "Let's see what's left in the galley stores."

~

They found crackers, champagne, and a small supply of tinned caviar. Eschewing the company of the dining car's current occupants, they carried their meal to Second Class. Using the hinged pull-down trays for tables, Joseph poured champagne while Yasmin spread fish eggs on crackers. The atmosphere wasn't precisely festive, but it was better than starving.

"I think we should toast," Joseph said, clinking her bubbling flute with his.

Yasmin tried to put on a good-sport face.

"To having a chance," he said, "because a little hope is better than none at all."

"Do I look *that* glum?" she exclaimed.

A small smile flickered across his mouth. "Not *that* glum perhaps, but glummer than I expected, considering it was your gumption that got us here."

"I guess reality is settling in." She hunched her shoulders. "I keep seeing Ivy's head flying past me into the gulf. She was so brave, facing the rest of the zombies to help us. I feel like we got her killed."

"She was dead already."

"I know, but she had some sort of existence."

"Her death, if it was a death, could be a blessing in disguise. Her soul might prefer its former shell not wander. It might be resting easier."

"Tara's probably gloating over her victory."

Joseph's grin for this was broad. "She's dead too. We, on the other hand, are enjoying this fine—" he paused to survey the label "—fifteen-year-old champagne."

"I just wish we hadn't done what she and Stefan wanted. We jumped of our own free will. Yet again, Dimitriou will escape the consequences of murder."

"We're not dead," Joseph reminded her.

She had to look down, away from his eyes, before her own overflowed. Joseph seemed to guess he hadn't gotten through to her.

"You were right to convince me to jump," he insisted. "We are strong. And together. Even if we die here, that's better than being apart."

She watched her fingers twist around her glass's stem. "I suppose no djinni wants to pass over by himself."

"Yasmin." The way he huffed her name brought her head up. "You're not alone in caring. I'm . . . attached to you. In all the world, I doubt there are a dozen people I'd tolerate having beside me if I were dying."

She supposed it was good to be in the top dozen. Top three might be better.

"I'm not the only person you care about," he said. "You're more adept at making friends than me."

"Only because you don't let people get to know you."

One corner of his mouth twitched. "To know me is to love me?"

"People who don't know you love you too. Idolize you, at any rate."

His expression turned somber. "I hope that isn't the case with you. I hope you know me and love me nonetheless."

He laid his hands over both her wrists. His thumbs rubbed circles on their delicate underside. Was it fair of him to want her to love him when he made no equivalent claim? Fairness didn't seem to matter. Whatever he did, she loved him impossibly.

The tears she'd been trying to control spilled over.

Joseph let out an odd, helpless laugh, then took her wet face between his hands. "Why does my saying that make you weep? I swear, I don't understand women."

"I think . . . you . . . understand me well enough."

His serious eyes probed hers. "Creator grant that be so."

He kissed her. She was certain no one's lips had ever covered hers so gently. She jerked nonetheless, her champagne flute nearly toppling as a result.

"Let me set this aside," he said.

She had no idea where he put it, only that he was leaning to her again. Her hands caught his arms as his warm, silken mouth whispered over hers. Though the touch was light, Yasmin's breath went ragged.

"These seats are awkward," he murmured. "Should we check out the sleeping car?"

Her eyes widened. Was he suggesting they finally consummate their attraction?

"If this really is the end for us, what do we have to lose?"

He meant what did *he*. Yasmin pressed her lips together. If she spoke the thought aloud, she might stop this from happening. Not wanting that, she got up and held out a hand to him. "Come on then. Let's lose whatever's left together."

He rose, following her down the center aisle. She guessed he was more affected than he let on. His fingers tightened as they went through the connecting door. The sleeping compartments took up most of the carriage's left side. Because the corridor on the right was narrow, the doors slid into pockets rather than swinging out.

"The next door," Joseph said when she stopped.

"Aren't they the same? Or is seven your lucky number?"

"Six has bunks. Seven has a full bed."

"Took note of that, did you?"

His color heightened at her humor. "I never said I didn't want to be . . . completely intimate with you."

"True enough."

She lay one hand on his chest and smiled up at him. She only had a moment to register the brisk pounding of his heart. He drew her palm to his mouth to kiss. His gold eyes burned down at her.

"Don't make me wait," he said. "Even if I've earned it."

"You *have* earned it, but I'd rather not wait either."

The soft growl he uttered made her shiver and go liquid. He squeezed past her, tugging her to the next compartment. There he shoved open the sliding door, stepped inside, and yanked her flush against him. He kissed her with no holds barred, and she cried out against his mouth.

Her arms wrapped him as tightly as his did her.

"God, I want you," he groaned, palming her bottom to pull her higher up.

Her body aligned to his perfectly. Her breasts flattened on his chest, the softness of her pubis conforming to the arch of his erection. Its ridge was hard and thick and dug deliciously into her. Hungrier than she'd known she could get, she wrapped her thighs around him.

Her hands memorized the bunching muscles of his back.

"Yasmin," he breathed. Their tongues drove deeper, their pelvises grinding in a mutual quest for more and more friction. Yasmin went so wet he must have felt it through their garments.

She guessed he liked that. A second later, he slammed her into a wall.

Trapping her with his weight, his mouth plundered hers until she thought she'd go mad from wanting him.

She certainly lost her breath. He did too, tearing loose to nuzzle her neck and pant. As if he'd just remembered there were other parts of her to savor, he shoved one hand into her tunic to squeeze her breast. The feel of his bare palm around her nipple stole the last shred of her patience.

"Help me get these clothes off," she gasped.

"I don't think we should use magic. We might need to save it for something else."

"I have no problem with you stripping me by hand."

"Well, then." He pushed back, wrestling the fasteners that were close. He cursed when her sash resisted giving way.

"Careful," she warned, though his eagerness stole her breath. "If you rip that, I can't get new out here."

He found the knot and freed it. "Guess I'd have to keep you naked then."

The sash slithered free and went flying. Yasmin reached for his tunic buttons, which he graciously gave her five whole seconds to undo.

"I'm faster," he said, fingers racing over them.

Watching him twist his shoulders out of the cloth stopped her heart momentarily.

"Your chest . . ." she said, fingertips to her mouth.

He looked down. "What's wrong with it?"

"Not even one little thing." Her hands went out to stroke: up his centerline, out across his broad, sweating shoulders and down his lovely arms.

"Yasmin . . ."

She tiptoed up and pressed her mouth to his, both their tongues driving deep. She kept on kissing until she ached. It was impossible to stop. She'd been waiting too long to hold him in her arms again.

"*Yasmin.*"

"Shh."

She unfastened the waist of his silk trousers. His breath caught, his gaze locking on hers hotly. His anticipation wasn't misplaced. She slid her hand inside to caress his incredibly erect cock.

His focus blurred, a sound of bliss breaking in his throat. She let out a sound herself. All of him felt so wonderful, from the tight sac beneath his cock to his increasingly slippery crown. His veins were swollen along his length, his girth a delicious resister of pressure.

He moaned her name again when she squeezed gently.

Three times was lucky, she decided.

"Should I stop?" she teased. "Maybe you need a moment to pull yourself together."

He put his hand on hers before she could move it. "Keep fondling me right there. I'm dropping these."

He meant his trousers and underthings.

"Oh," she said once they were puddled around his feet. He was a vision. Despite not wanting to let go, she took a step back to admire him. She was immediately glad she had. She wouldn't have seen his legs where she'd been, and they were spectacular. They had just the combination of grace and muscle she preferred. Even their hairiness appealed. He was very male, her opposite and her match—and never mind how the length of his quadriceps led her gaze to higher things. She should have paid more attention when she'd had her thighs clamped around his narrow hips. His hipbones were strong and competent-looking—designed for sex, she thought. Two grooved muscles dove down to frame his pelvis, giving the impression he'd control each plunge of his hot spear into her soft pussy.

Her core tightened and grew wetter at that idea.

"Am I all right?" he asked as her fascinated study of him drew out.

He actually was unsure.

"You're beautiful," she said. "Exactly everything I like."

"Really?"

She laughed softly. "Really. You're my naked-man ideal."

He smiled and stepped back to her. Two fingertips slid around the back of her final undergarment. "Drop these and we can be skin-to-skin."

She slid them off and grinned at him.

"Oh, boy," he said, his eyes drinking the new view in.

"Oh, girl," she corrected.

Maybe he was too aroused to laugh. His hold tightened on her waist.

"Bed," he said, lifting her.

He laid her gently down on it.

She couldn't breathe as he descended over her. His flattened palms braced his weight on the two-person bed, one bare knee settling on the soft wool blanket while the other stayed on the floor.

"Do you need anything else?" he paused long enough to ask.

She stroked her hands up his hard torso. "Just you. Just your body inside mine."

He kissed her in response, deep and sweet and noticeably hungry. His movements were more aggressive now, the yearning sounds he made noisier. He pulled back before she'd had her fill of enjoying them.

"Show me," he said, his voice gone gruff. His kiss-reddened lips brushed shivery sensations into her ear. "I want to . . . control this, but you show me what you want."

He moved his head to lock eyes again. His glowed, gold and molten and serious. She hadn't forgotten this was his first time. It might as well have been hers too.

"Whatever happens will be all right," she promised. "This won't be the last time we do this."

"Good," he said with the tiniest smile. "As badly as I want you, I don't think one time will be enough."

He drew his second leg onto the bed, centering his knees between her legs. The heat that poured off him amazed her. She touched his breastbone, loving how his heart thudded behind it.

The jerky in-and-out of his ribs wasn't bad either.

"Take yourself in hand," she said. "If you steady your angle, going in will be easier."

He balanced on one arm to obey her.

"Now I'll touch myself. To open myself for you. You can slide between my fingers. No need to worry about missing the target."

He laughed at this. "I'm not *that* clueless."

"You never know," she teased, hitching up her knees for access. "Djinn have gotten lost on the road to Paradise before."

Since he'd bent his head to look between them, she stroked herself. She didn't skip her clitoris. She thought he'd like seeing her fondle its engorged state.

He licked his lips. "You're all glossed up."

"I'm excited." She smiled. "But I know you're not clueless about that either."

"I'm nervous," he blurted.

"It's not a test. You don't have to be perfect."

"I *want* to be. I—"

She pressed his wet tip with her thumb's pad, lightly circling *his* glossiness around the swollen head. The unexpected stimulation silenced him. He shut his mouth and swallowed.

"I'm not perfect either," she said. "We'll bumble through this together."

"Together," he repeated as if he wasn't completely sure.

She wanted to smile but mostly held it back. "Now, if you please."

"Right," he agreed, his eyes on hers again. He shifted his knees a fraction, and then he was against her. A little gasp exploded from him as he began to push.

"Yes," she praised, arching toward the intrusion. "That's the . . . exact spot."

His crown squeezed in and he gasped again. Placed now, he stopped steadying his shaft and clutched her hip instead. His palm was sweating, his heart beating double-time. The muscles of his rear tightened against her bent-up legs.

"Jesus," he breathed and broke through her barrier.

The sting was brief, no more than a pinch and a bit of burn. She breathed through the discomfort until it faded, replaced by the hot, thick ache of wanting him deeper. To her surprise, that ache wasn't being gratified.

Joseph had stopped moving.

"Yasmin," he said. "Were you— Am I—"

His eyes were as wide as saucers.

"You're the first," she said, "to take me this precise way."

"But—"

"Do you really want to discuss this now? Wouldn't you prefer to do what we're both craving?"

"I don't want to hurt you."

She feathered his side with the back of her fingers. "Go slow, and I'm pretty sure we'll both enjoy everything."

He studied her a moment longer. What was going on in his head? Something big, she thought, but what exactly she couldn't say. Possibly, he didn't know himself.

"I'll go slow," he said. "Please feel free to offer suggestions."

He began to thrust, so she didn't have to offer one right then. Actually, she wasn't sure she still had the power to speak. The slow, thick glide of him in her pussy instantly beguiled her.

He seemed equally stupefied by the feel of her engulfing him.

"God," he breathed, dropping to his elbow. "Could I—?"

He gripped her right knee and yanked it higher up his side. She spared him having to ask if that was okay by gripping his shoulders and moaning. She hadn't known how good this would feel: his weight, his muscles, the pressure of his cock pushing in and drawing back inside her.

They moaned at each other, rocking incrementally faster as hunger and pleasure rose. His neck arched as her sheath contracted and pulled at him. Instinct made her do it, and a longing to draw his cock as deep as possible. Sensation spiked higher for both of them.

When he recovered, the look on his face was excitingly determined.

"Can I go harder?" he asked. "Can I take control?"

She wanted him to, and couldn't care if a modern woman shouldn't. She released her clutch on his back, reaching upward to grip the enameled metal rail that served as the bed's headboard.

She hoped its MILION – EXPRESS logo would inspire him to speed ahead.

"I'm braced," she said. "Go at me how you like."

His eyes blazed hot an instant before he did. His hips drove into her, his cock a thick, oiled piston that pounded pleasure into her nerve centers. She was right about his body being designed for this. As steady as any train that ran on a track, he had aim and coordination and, apparently, stamina. Her palms shifted on the rail, her fingers tingling with sheer delight. She almost let go to hold him, but just then he groaned unintelligibly and pushed higher on his arms.

Not only did this show off his muscles, but the angle was excellent, forcing him against a spot on her upper wall that felt so sweet she never wanted his cock to stop massaging it. His crown was sleek and hard, everything she needed in that moment. Lost in her lust for more, her heel dug into the mattress to push her pelvis forcefully back at him. Her neck was arching, her body wild. He gripped her hip to guide her motions.

"I've got you," he panted, one thumb stretching to rub her clitoris.

She moaned with pleasure. *Yes,* she tried to say. *Do that. Do* ***that.***

She guessed her body spoke well enough for her.

He did it and did it and then drove so deep both of them cried out. He felt bigger suddenly, as if his shaft were swelling another bit. The further stretch of her sheath was bliss. She could barely stand her excitement as he pumped ever more urgently in and out. The ache inside her was heaven and torment. As he went faster, fiercer, their energy felt connected by unbreakable fiery chains. This was what intercourse should be: this helpless abandon they each trusted their partner with. No one could be dignified having sex like this. No one could even want to try. Her breasts bounced crazily at his thrusts, her nipples drawn into hard points. Joseph grunted with animal longing. The sound aroused her. She hitched the leg that crooked his hard buttocks higher . . .

He cried out, his thumb working her most intense pleasure spot. His cock jammed inside her at the same time, his spine going rigid as his orgasm thundered past the point of no return. Heat flooded from him, rush after searing rush. His cock was throbbing, shooting. Yasmin caught one glimpse of his sweat-sheened, ecstasy-tightened face before her own climax blinded her. When his body dropped down onto her and shoved deep, she couldn't imagine a single action that would have felt better.

For a long minute afterward, she lay pleasure-shocked. Her arms wrapped his back in a loose but undeniably affectionate embrace. She didn't remember letting the bed rail go.

She must have wanted to hold onto him at the end.

How could their lovemaking be that good? Yes, she had a long-standing tendre for him. Her climax being intense was understandable. This, however, didn't explain the perfect-storm releases they both seemed to have experienced. They were neophytes, not erotic experts. She shouldn't be lying here like a toppled tree, her skin buzzing from head to toe, her soul practically quaking at what it had been through.

Because it was there and she wanted to, she stroked Joseph's short, damp hair.

He made a puppyish, pleasured sound and dragged his cheek over hers.

"Should I move?" he asked, his voice slowed and lowered by lassitude.

He was still inside her but softening.

"If you want," she said throatily.

He pulled out of her carefully. She wasn't as messy as she might have been. He must have remembered to turn his seed to smoke. Though she sensed him looking at her, she didn't turn. She wasn't ready to face him or her feelings that directly.

He wanted to face something. He went up on his elbow and stroked her profile with one finger.

"Maybe I shouldn't ask. It's your business and Iksander's. I am wondering, however, how I came to be your first lover."

"Iksander met Najat soon after I joined the harem. He committed to her and never initiated me. The only night he spent with me was after he banished her for allegedly cheating with Philip. His broken heart drove him mad, I think. He didn't take me the usual way."

"He took you in his smoke form."

"Yes," she said, glad he'd already guessed.

Joseph appeared to ponder this. "I can't account for the satisfaction that makes me feel. It seems primitive."

Naturally, he wouldn't associate that word with himself. Amused, and less insecure because of it, she rolled toward him on the rumpled bed. "I believe it's a common male reaction. The first to plant his flag on a mountain enjoys the victory."

One side of his mouth twitched. "You don't feel similarly gratified at having deflowered me?"

"Maybe a little. It certainly was fun."

"Yes." He smiled back at her. "I'll never forget it."

Considering the fix they were in, he was unlikely to get the chance. The reminder sobered her. "We should work on a possible escape plan."

Joseph sighed and sat up. His eyes widened as he noticed the condition of the efficiently fitted sleeping car. Despite neither of them using magic, it looked like a whirlwind had blown through. Two of the wall sconces were now crooked, and they'd flung their clothes everywhere. Joseph's trousers draped a small trash bin. He fished them out and shook them.

Because it seemed their erotic interlude was over, Yasmin sat up as well. Her attention snagged on the porthole-style window. Gray mist obscured the glass, whorling and licking against it. The color was darker than before. She guessed the In-Between version of night was approaching.

When she looked back at Joseph, he'd returned to sit on the bed again. He wore no shirt, and his trousers were pulled up but not fastened. His casual, half-dressed state was disconcertingly appealing.

"You're right, of course," he said, his forearms wrapping his bent-up knees. "And I might have an idea or two. I realize you know more about the mists than I do, but I've crossed a gulf before."

"On a carpet," Yasmin said, sensing she knew what was coming.

"I was thinking there might be something on the train we could rig up as one . . ." He stopped speaking. "Your face is telling me that's a bad idea."

"Not a bad idea, but—" Not wanting to discourage him from being creative, she chose her words carefully. "Carpets fly *over* the In-Betweens. Once you dip into the mists as we have, traveling to and from specific points is nearly impossible."

"Truly?" he asked. "We know this train doesn't stray too far from the Edgeward coast. Milioners have been hearing it for years."

"We know it *approaches* the coast sometimes. Where it drifts the rest of the time is anybody's guess. The In-Betweens don't have geography as we understand it. Not east and west. Not up and down. Theoretically, we could fly a year to progress an inch."

"We can't just stay here. I don't know about you, but I'd rather not end up mummified."

Seeing his distaste for this idea, Yasmin gave his knee a squeeze. "We can try your carpet plan as a last resort. Before we reach that level of desperation, we should see if we can get a message out."

"Won't it be even harder to send one from in here?"

"Yes," she admitted, trying to sound simply honest and not morose. "On the bright side, it's less likely to kill us than leaving the train's shelter." Joseph choked out a laugh, but she pressed on. "My father owns equipment that has a chance of reaching us. Maybe more than a chance. When people ask what his transport containers can accomplish, he tends to be cagey."

Joseph sat straighter as another idea occurred to him. "Maybe Iksander could send a ship— Oh, but that has the same trouble as a carpet. They sail above the mists. Maybe it's just as well. Gulf-worthy vessels are magic hogs. Coming after us would be obscenely expensive—not that I don't think you're worth it. Okay, then." He nodded to himself. "Your father seems our best option. We should focus on getting through to him."

Though it was pleasant to be agreed with, this would still be a challenge.

"It's too bad my human phone won't call anyone," Joseph said.

"I have my scroll with me. I tucked it into my sash this morning."

"A million years ago," he murmured, which echoed her own thoughts.

Irrationally buoyed by them being in synch, she hopped up to retrieve the length of cloth. Half forgetting she was naked, she sat back on the bed cross-legged.

"Oh," she said as she removed the scroll from its concealed pocket. "My Milion postcard is in here too. I forgot I had that. The clerk said I didn't need to come back to mail it because it was pre-charged. He said just write the address and say a prayer."

Joseph held out his hand to examine the colorful square. Yasmin refused to blush at the silly image the clerk had inserted of her waving.

"Hm," he said. "This is sprinkled with wild magic. I wonder if that helps it get where it's going."

"On land, I expect it does."

"It may help here too."

"You know," Yasmin said. "My scroll and my brother's are secure-linked. I know my dad is the mist expert, but maybe we should try to reach Balu."

"Are you closer to him than your father?"

"I love them both, but . . . maybe. Our older brother turning dark especially bonded us. Other kids looked at us askance even after my parents disowned Ramis."

Sympathy furrowed Joseph's brow, but he shook himself and turned businesslike. "All right. Let's say we have three main goals. One: Inform an ally we need rescue. Two: Make sure the evidence we've collected concerning Dimitriou, LaBass and Co. gets to appropriate parties. Three: Do our best not to die in here. Though I don't relish it, I feel obliged to mention Goal Two is the most important. If LaBass succeeds in ousting Iksander, the damage our citizens would suffer could be as bad as any Luna inflicted."

"I can't disagree with that," Yasmin said.

Joseph's thumb stroking her cheek briefly. "I didn't think you would."

The reluctance in his expression made her think he had more slippers to drop on her.

"You have an idea," she deduced.

"I do. I propose we record an explanatory message on my phone—including video of the dining car and Dimitriou's mummified parents. Then I embed the phone in your scroll. That done, we wrap both in the spelled postcard. That card is specifically designed—by a local—to propel messages *out* of Edgeward Province successfully. We can address the card to your brother, thereby augmenting your scroll's link to him. We say the activating prayer, add as much of our personal magic as we dare for an extra boost, and send the whole package winging off. I know it's a risk, but—"

"It uses up two options in one go!" she exclaimed, unable to contain her dismay. "Three if you count the chance we might find a way to get your phone to work."

"That's an extreme longshot."

"It's better than trying to cross the mists on an improvised flying carpet! We barely survived the trip from the cliff to here."

"You may be right about that, but I believe I'm right about the best way to contact the outside world."

"You *believe,*" she repeated bitterly.

He chafed her wrists to soothe her. "I know I'm not the sorcerer I used to be, but I haven't lost my ability to weigh competing strategies. In this instance, if we use half measures, I fear we'll fail twice as badly."

Was he right? He'd been the sultan's advisor for many years. He'd helped make any number of difficult decisions that eventually paid off.

Her hands were fisted atop her thighs. Finger by finger, she forced them to unclench. "I know you have more experience than me," she admitted.

"Your say matters, Yasmin. Not simply because that's fair but because it's practical. I wish I could wave my hand and accomplish this by myself. I wish it for your sake as well as mine. I can't, though. I *need* you to contribute, preferably without begrudging it. We both know sharing power works best when it comes from an open heart."

She wished his heart were as open to her as hers was to him.

"If you genuinely think I'm wrong, I'm willing to hear you out," he said.

Sincerity sheened his eyes—and regret. He felt the loss of his original body, the personal weakness he thought had led to it. Knowing he was anything but weak, Yasmin gave in and shook her head. "I don't like how right I think you are."

Joseph rubbed her arms before delivering the final blow. "If we're going to do this, better now than later . . ."

~

Presenting their accounts with an eye toward helping the Justice Ministry press charges exhausted the next two hours.

"Iksander will be warned at least," Joseph said. "That's the important thing."

"Right," Yasmin agreed, rubbing her weary face. "That's the important thing."

"Are you too tired to try sending the packet now? We could wait until tomorrow."

"I could use a break, but it's not like I'll sleep tonight anyway."

"Lie down," he suggested. "I want to stretch my legs. You can pray or nap or meditate as you please."

She didn't argue. A bit of space and quiet appealed right then. Joseph shut the sleep compartment's lights off before he left. The windows were nearly but not-quite black. Occasional flickers of wild magic—sometimes near, sometimes far—illuminated the clouds outside. Though eerie, the light show wasn't without beauty.

This is what the world is made of, she thought unexpectedly. *This stormy soup of unformed stuff.*

Maybe the thought was true, or maybe the In-Betweens were trying to seduce her by suggesting she was akin to them.

Are you out there? she asked the goddess she'd grown up with. She'd felt more confident of Her presence when she reassured Joseph earlier.

But faith wasn't about sureness. Or Yasmin didn't think it was. Faith was asking for help and letting the results turn out as they would. Their Creator and Creatoress existed. As djinn, they believed this innately. The Goddess must be here, because She was everywhere. She'd help Yasmin as She thought best, however suited the Divine Plan.

Yasmin lay back and closed her eyes.

"Thank you, Goddess," she murmured. "Thank you, Creator and benevolent wise spirits. Joseph and I appreciate your guidance. We want to help our people, and we'd like to get out of this fix safely. Any support you can give us, we're heartily grateful for."

As prayers went, it was pretty simple. Since nothing further came to her, she said "Amen" and relaxed.

She must have slept. When she opened her eyes, the lights were on again and Joseph perched on the mattress edge. His phone and her scroll rested in his lap.

"I've readied these," he said. "Give the word, and I'll bond them together."

Yasmin sat up and shoveled her long hair back. She felt surprisingly refreshed. "I haven't changed my mind. We should stick to your idea."

Joseph smiled at her sleep softened face. "Very well."

Taking the scroll in one hand and his shiny phone in the other, he turned his attention to joining them.

"Be one," he instructed with quiet assertiveness. "Until you reach a djinni who'll put you to the use we intend, be one and indivisible."

Joseph really was something when it came to sorcery. The phone melted smoothly into the parchment, turning into an exact two-dimensional replica. Its 'screen' was portrayed as on, its little 'apps' as colorful as candy.

"Balu will love that."

"Will he know what it is?"

"Absolutely. He adores human artifacts."

"Luckily for us." He rolled the scroll and stood up. "Do you have the postcard?"

She pulled it out.

"All right. I've sketched a ward in the vestibule where the second class and dining cars connect. The outside doors are shut, but we can crack one to let the packet out. I thought we'd perform our ritual there."

He'd been busy while she napped.

"I couldn't settle," he explained. "I felt better preparing a few things."

When they reached the vestibule, she saw he'd understated how much he'd done. Glyphs drawn in glowing white covered every wall, plus the ceiling and metal floor. After a moment's gawking, she recognized the pattern. "That's Sabin's Multi-Directional Sacrament Protector. I've only seen it in old books."

"I've used it before," Joseph said with a hint of defensiveness. "I know it's complicated, but it produces good results."

"I'm not doubting you. I'm impressed." She toed one symbol carefully with her slipper, noting it didn't smudge. "Where did you find enchanted paint?"

"Behind some pans in the restaurant galley. The chef must have used it to prevent cooking fires."

That was lucky too. Maybe they weren't doomed, after all.

He gestured for her to sit. As she did, the jointed steel plate that allowed the cars to roll along separate grades lurched up and rattled.

"Turbulence," he said, like this was nothing.

Her jumping nerves begged to differ. Ignoring them, she waited for him to sit opposite. Their knees bumped in the confined space. Though she didn't say so, she found this comforting. Joseph produced a pair of scissors.

"Could I cut a lock of your hair? For tying the postcard around the scroll. Because you and Balu are related, using part of you to bind it should help the thing reach him."

She leaned forward to let him snip.

"Sorry," he apologized after. "It's not *too* noticeable."

She laughed. "You could shear me bald, and it wouldn't be my biggest worry. Shall I write Balu's address now?"

Joseph nodded. She jotted it in the proper spot, adding 'C/O AYDIN & VINCA BAYKAL,' in case either of them were home when it arrived. Her parents and her brother did live under the same roof. She didn't think she'd confuse the magic that powered the postcard.

By the time she'd finished, Joseph had spelled the hair he'd taken into a twine-like cord. The little rope was long enough to wind a few times around the bundle and double knot.

"Okay," he said. "We'll add a boost and we'll send it off."

She knew to take his hands without being told.

"Don't give too much," Joseph cautioned.

"I can't give too little," she countered.

"You need to save some reserves. We don't know how long recharging takes in the In-Betweens."

"Whatever you give, I'll match."

He lowered his brows at her.

"I mean it," she said stubbornly. "You're the one who warned against half measures."

He muttered something rude in the human tongue.

"Whatever you said, I can tell it's not nice," she snipped primly.

He rolled his eyes, but her scold amused him. Calmer then, they recited the standard formula for offering up magic. They both must have wanted it to succeed. Power whooshed from them with dizzying speed, infusing the different parts of the tied bundle. Judging she better hurry, Yasmin called Balu's image into her mind. She had many good memories of her brother: him in their office, gracefully serving tea; grinning at her across the family dinner table, too many times to count. As a kid, she'd loved his throaty baby laugh. Sometimes she'd asked to rock his cradle just so she could tickle him.

Joseph was performing a similar exercise. Connected as they were, she caught a flash of Balu through his eyes. Seeming all knees and elbows, he was hopping crazily to human music in what looked like a human hallway—probably in New York. Their own city's guardians were present, along with their shared fiancée, Elyse. Freed from their world's constraints, Balu looked wild and happy and very young.

Come dance, she heard him urge Joseph. *It's easy and so much fun!*

Easier than the Tiger Tango, she wagered.

"Brace yourself," Joseph said in a voice that was slightly thinned. "The spell should be charged enough. I'm opening the outside door. Pick up the scroll and keep a grip on it."

He reached behind him, tugging the handle manually. The door swung inward, allowing dark gray mist to heave at the opening. Yasmin's throat threatened to close with fear, but

Joseph's protections held the dangerous stuff at bay. The bundled scroll had the opposite reaction. The instant the mist attempted to intrude, the thing jerked within her hold and tried to fly toward it.

The address she'd written was glowing.

Seeing she needed help controlling it, Joseph added his hand to hers.

"May He who smooths all paths shepherd you," he intoned. "May He lend you wings to achieve your intended purpose in the best and most timely way. The Glorious City thanks you for service, and so do we. If it please the Creator, let our vision be accomplished."

As he spoke, their package bucked harder within their grip.

"Amen," Yasmin said breathlessly.

The address flared brighter and went finger-singeing hot.

"Let go," Joseph instructed.

They let go, and the scroll leaped free, sucked out by the In-Betweens like a scrap of wood pulled into a tornado. Its disappearance seemed to be the cue for the mists to surge in at them. Sparks crackled off the nearest glyphs.

"Shit," Joseph said, jumping up from the spell circle. "The wards are overloading. Help me shove the door shut again."

Despite his strength, he strained to close it without success. Rather than do the same, Yasmin took the short running start the vestibule allowed and threw her whole weight at it. Her shoulder hit, and the door slammed shut. The mist that had slipped in yanked back out with a disconcertingly annoyed sound.

"Jesus," Joseph panted, facing her irately. "What if the door swung out? You'd have ended up in that soup."

"I remembered the hinges only worked one way."

"You remembered."

"I did," she insisted.

She pushed back, trembling and sweating all over. Her shoulder hurt but—out of pride—she refused to massage it. Joseph didn't look much better than she felt. Like her, he'd braced on a wall to stand. When it came to boosting the scroll with their magic, they'd erred on the side of overdoing it.

He glanced around the vestibule in dismay.

"The shield," he said.

They'd burned out the ward completely, nothing but charred outlines remaining.

"The protection did what it was supposed to."

"True." He exhaled in resignation then looked at her sheepishly. "Sorry I snapped at you."

"You were worried for my safety."

"All the same . . ." He trailed off and grimaced. "Don't laugh when I wobble to our room."

"I'd be glad to laugh. It would mean I had strength to spare."

He smiled faintly and pushed through the door to second class seating.

Yasmin followed, feeling hollowed out in more ways than one. They'd taken their best shot—with no way to know if they'd succeeded. Worst of all, unless some miracle occurred, they wouldn't find another option a tenth as good.

From here on out, they had little to do but wait.

CHAPTER FIFTEEN

Djinn in Waiting

The next day dragged for more reasons than fatigue. Forget being trapped in theoretically romantic surroundings. Sleeping like the dead was the most they accomplished in their shared bed. Though it wasn't much of a change of scene—every window looked out on an identical sea of clouds—they traded Compartment 7 for the second class seating car.

"Damn," Joseph cursed, shoving aside the engineer's handbook he'd discovered in a seat pocket. "Why didn't I think to stick Dimitriou's father's will in our scroll bundle?"

This wasn't a new conversational theme. He'd been second-guessing his actions ever since they crawled out of bed.

"That would have been a bad idea."

"That document was solid evidence!"

"Its vibration doesn't link to Balu or anyone we hope to reach. Who knows what including it might have knocked off balance?"

"Maybe," he conceded.

"Filming it was good enough. You need to let it go."

He heaved a gusty sigh. If he started in on how the 'old him' would have found some genius solution, she was going to break something. At this point, the 'old him' sounded a tad obnoxious.

"I didn't used to question myself like this," he muttered.

Goddess help me, she thought.

"What?" he asked, noticing her exasperated expression.

"Never questioning yourself isn't the same as always being right. Everything considered, you might be a better djinni now."

He gaped in shock.

"I prefer you as you are," she said.

"You're . . ." For a second, she thought he was going to say 'in love with me.' ". . . biased," he finished less heatedly.

Yasmin decided to change the topic. She jerked her head toward the engineer's manual. "Did you find anything in there?"

"Not that helps us." He started to sigh again then stopped. "We could search the other sleeping compartments. We only spot-checked them before. There could be old supplies left behind. It's something to do anyway."

"I'm game," she said.

She pushed to her feet and went. Somewhat to her surprise, he chose to explore the same room as her.

"Best stick close," he said. "We wouldn't want to get separated by a danger we don't expect. I'll check the wardrobe cabinets."

Her throat tightened, but she nodded. She went to her knees to peer beneath the lower bunkbed's skirt.

"Complimentary slippers," she announced, pulling out a pair. "Complete with the Milion – Express logo."

"Empty hangers," Joseph responded. "Plus a bottle of spring water."

"Well, that's not nothing. If you find more crackers, we'll have dinner."

His mood had lightened. Despite the truth of her statement, he cracked a smile. "I'll try the bathroom. Don't tell your Goddess, but I'd kill for a half-charged teeth cleaning disk."

Yasmin was thrusting her arm under the upper mattress, partially blocking his route there. She supposed he'd grown used to her company. Otherwise, he'd have waited for her to step aside. Instead, he squeezed by her without thinking.

Their energy was more connected than she realized—no doubt due to teaming up for the spell and their lovemaking before that. As Joseph's hard front brushed her soft bottom, electric sensations surged into her. Her nipples tightened like they'd been pinched. She became aware of her sex—too aware for comfort. Parts of her pussy swelled while other parts slickened. An immediate, nagging ache reminded her they hadn't been intimate again.

Joseph froze and inhaled sharply.

"Pardon," he said, clearing his throat and pushing past more quickly.

Had there been *movement* behind his garments while he did this?

If there had, he wasn't going to act on it. As her face flamed, she heard him briskly opening and shutting cabinets.

"I suppose," he said with not quite convincing casualness, "concubines are trained to flatter men's egos."

Yasmin's eyebrows screwed together. "What does that have to do with the price of tea?"

He stuck his head out the narrow door. A telltale flush tinted his cheekbones. "You know. Yesterday. When we were together. You were—" he searched for the right phrasing "—complimentary."

"Are you fishing for more praise, or have you convinced yourself I faked my orgasms?"

"Well, I did my best, but it's not as if I have much experience."

"Neither do I! Honestly, Joseph, do you really think I'd—"

Without warning, a violent jolt knocked them off balance. Yasmin gasped and caught herself on a wall as metal crunched and groaned. The awful noise culminated in the sound of glass exploding and tinkling down.

"Christ," Joseph breathed. "I think we collided with something."

She hadn't known there was anything in here to collide with.

Her mind was trying to wrap around this when Joseph staggered up and toward the compartment door.

Don't, she tried to object, but he'd already yanked it open to search the hall.

"Uh," he said, which didn't suggest good developments.

She joined him in the doorway, her hand naturally gripping his shoulder. She'd been thinking of the train as impregnable, but the far end of the sleeping car currently resembled a stomped tin can.

Actually, it resembled a stomped tin can someone had taken a hacksaw to.

Smoke poured in the various rips as if the metal were burning.

Joseph suddenly breathed harder.

"That's not smoke," he said.

Of course it wasn't. It was the stuff of the In-Betweens eagerly coming to swallow them. Yasmin froze like a deer about to be devoured.

Joseph recovered before she did. He grabbed her wrist and pulled.

"Second Class," he barked, heading toward it. "We'll barricade the connecting door between us and it."

Yasmin stumbled after him, praying—perhaps childishly—that they didn't end up chased to the dining car with the dead mummies. Her heart was beating a mile a minute, her feet as awkward as granite blocks.

She tripped and fell when someone called her name. The sound came from behind her.

"Yasmin, stop! You have to run this way!"

She twisted around even as Joseph helped her up. She couldn't see through the increasing cloud, but the voice called her name again.

"That's Balu," she said, yanking back against Joseph's onward pull. "He and my father must have crashed into us."

"Are you sure?" Joseph asked.

He meant the In-Betweens might be playing tricks with their perception.

"Come *on*," Balu called. "We need to get out of here."

The impatient plea certainly sounded like her brother.

"Ninety percent sure," she said.

"All right." Joseph turned to face the cloud with her. "We got through the mists before. We can do it again."

They twined grips and ran into it. By default, Yasmin was in the lead. Her slippers hit solid floor for the first three bounds. After that, whatever lay beneath them turned mushy. The mists, their prize long denied, were making up for lost time by voraciously dissolving the car's structure.

Yasmin's body suddenly floated up weightless.

"Got you," Balu crowed.

Her brother's strong, skinny fingers clamped over her free wrist. The mist didn't rattle him enough to let go. He tugged her through the churning cloud with Joseph trailing behind her.

She couldn't see any part of either djinni except their hands.

Then she saw nothing but pitch black.

"Are you in?" asked another voice she recognized.

"We're in," Balu answered breathlessly.

Hinges squealed and heavy metal clanged—as if the door to a treasure vault had swung shut. Yasmin fell, weighted, the same as she had on first entering the train. Her kneecaps didn't appreciate the impact.

"Ow," she and Joseph complained in unison.

"Dad?" she asked a moment later. "Is it really dark or have we gone blind?"

He chuckled and lifted her, pulling her into the best hug ever. "It's really dark. Let me catch my breath, and I'll turn on the lights again."

"I guess you got our message."

"Your 'message' practically broke down our front door. You might have overdone the boost you gave it."

She didn't want to stop squeezing him. "That's Joseph's fault," she mumbled into his shoulder. "He thought I should give less than him."

"He should have known better. Our Yami never shrinks from a challenge."

He hadn't called her Yami since she was little, when Balu mispronounced her name that way. Now her father kissed her forehead and stroked her hair. "Step back, sweetie. I want to get underway."

"I've got the lights," Balu said.

Lines of them flicked on, illuminating their surroundings in a cold green-white glow. They were inside the hold of a large, cylindrical shipping tank. Forty feet in length and maybe half that in diameter, the walls were thick, bolted steel—so thick the only sign they'd collided with a train was a single shallow dent. Ring stanchions for tying cargo studded the curving floor. One of them anchored a rope Balu was currently unknotting from his waist. She supposed that explained how he'd pulled them in without mishap.

At the far end of the container, a metal ladder led up to a service hatch.

She knew these tanks weren't meant to carry people, having neither sleeping quarters nor a galley. Creature comforts consisted of a couple cushions flung over a crossbeam. A collection of empty wrappers suggested Balu and her father had sustained themselves on their journey with MFPs—miniaturized food packets.

As her eyes adjusted to the dimness, she made out a virtual forest of spell symbols. They were engraved and not painted on the container's surfaces.

The clank of a lever shifting drew her attention to her father. He stood on a rudimentary pilot's platform, performing the combination of mechanical tasks and spellwork necessary to get them going. The process must have been partly automated. After lowering his head for a final prayer, he returned to them.

"Wow," Joseph marveled, busy craning at the walls. "I should have guessed. This hold is a mirror space. That's why the In-Betweens don't affect it. It belongs to a different reality."

"What?" Balu said, his head jerking to their father in surprise.

Yasmin felt rather shocked herself. Her father's face didn't deny the guess. Looking uncomfortable, he rubbed his jaw and hemmed. Apparently, Joseph had deduced his most closely guarded secret in less than two minutes.

"I recognize the feel," he explained. "I've spun a few spaces like this myself."

Mirror spaces were highly complex creations, replicating real world objects in alternate dimensions. Naturally, no one doubted Joseph the Magician was up to it.

"If you could," her father said delicately, "I'd appreciate you keeping that underneath your hat."

"Of course," Joseph said before pausing. "A circumstance *might* arise where I'd need to share the information with the sultan. Other than that, I wouldn't violate your intellectual property."

"Thank you," her father said then pointed at his son. "That goes for you too, blabbermouth."

"I wouldn't blab," Balu said. "I'm not twelve-years-old anymore."

He was all of nineteen—grown up in his own mind but probably not in the mind of anyone else present. Perhaps to take the sting from this, their father patted his shoulder.

"Scold Yasmin," Balu demanded, undermining his claim to maturity.

"Your sister is a born secret keeper. I've known that since she was a girl."

Grinning, Yasmin stuck her tongue out at her brother.

Balu let out a disgusted huff.

"Sir," Joseph said, perhaps to forestall a squabble. "Might I ask: Do you replicate your containers from full-size models or do you scale up from miniatures?"

Her father allowed this was an interesting query. The two walked off deep in technical discussion.

"Talk about blabbering," Balu muttered. "Dad's totally star-struck."

"That's all right. If anyone can be trusted, it's Joseph."

Balu's attention sharpened, though she'd spoken absently. "You've changed your tune about him."

"I never said anything bad about him. You're the one who thought I was prejudiced."

Balu continued to gaze at her. "Something's different. What happened between you two?"

"Nothing," she said, vowing she wouldn't blush. "Or nothing that's your business."

"Uh-huh."

Yasmin pursed her lips stubbornly. "Tell me what's been happening at home. Did you make sure Iksander got Joseph's phone?"

"I'm not an idiot. Once we saw the evidence on it, I flew it to the palace personally. Laid it in the one of the guardian's hands myself. No one who shouldn't know about it will."

"Good," Yasmin said. "Joseph and I went through a lot to get that. —And thank you for rescuing us."

Balu smirked at her remembering this. "You owe me, sis. As I recall, *you* didn't venture into the In-Betweens when you helped rescue me."

"You're reminding me what a brat you are."

He reached out to squeeze her shoulder. "Seriously. I'm glad you're okay. I don't know how I'd have stood losing you."

"Me either," she agreed, touching his face gently. She knew he was thinking about Ramis. If any good came out of their brother's downfall, it was learning to value each other. "You're precious to me. And I'm very proud of you."

"Shucks," Balu said, making a joke of the human word.

"Brat," Yasmin repeated with relish.

CHAPTER SIXTEEN

Thieves in the Night

Yasmin and the others took a flying carpet from the Baykal warehouse to their villa. Though her father must have been tired, he handled the pilot rod. Yasmin expected Joseph to make excuses and head off separately. He didn't, and she was glad, though she warned herself not to read too much into it. His gentlemanly nature might have made him feel obliged to see her home safely.

As they landed, sunshine lit the family garden. Yasmin realized she wasn't sure what time or even what day it was.

"You made it!" her mother cried, rushing onto the terrace to greet them.

She hugged Balu and kissed his cheeks, and then it was Yasmin's turn.

"Sweetie," she said, embracing her tightly. "Thank the Goddess. My little Yami is home again in one piece. Oh, but how thin and pale you look! Didn't that terrible man feed you?"

Yasmin assumed the 'terrible man' was Stefan Dimitriou.

Overcome with emotion, her mother pushed back to wipe her own tear-streaked cheeks. Joseph hung a step behind her father, giving them space for their reunion. Vinca glanced at him with a mix of curiosity and caution.

"He looks worse than you," she confided—not quite quietly enough.

Joseph had the good manners to pretend he hadn't heard.

"Missus Baykal," he said, offering her a respectful bow. "I'm very pleased to make your acquaintance. Your daughter is a fine woman."

"Well," her mother said, taken aback by the solemnity with which he delivered the compliment. "We've always thought so. And we're extremely grateful to you for helping her escape that awful man's clutches."

"Yasmin helped me as much as I helped her."

This disconcerted her mother too.

"That is . . . gracious of you to say. Do come in. I'm planning a special evening meal."

It was Joseph's turn to look startled. He scratched his jaw awkwardly. "You're kind to invite me, but I really ought to return to the capital. People at the palace will be waiting on my report."

"No, they won't," Balu said.

Joseph stared at him.

"The guardians gave me strict instructions. You and Yasmin aren't to go anywhere. Arcadius and Cade want Dimitriou to believe he succeeded in killing you. The sultan's putting together an operation to arrest him. Knowing you're alive and that you've delivered evidence could drive him and his co-conspirators underground."

"It's true," Vinca said. "Just in case, we've sent the servants on vacation."

"Does that mean *you're* making dinner?" Balu asked.

Yasmin laughed at his hopeful tone. Joseph looked at her questioningly.

"My mother's an excellent cook," she explained.

"I am," her mother agreed. "And your father hasn't spoiled me so badly that I've forgotten my old talents."

Convinced everything was settled, Vinca turned to lead them into the house. Aydin fell in beside her, his arm slinging fondly around his wife's slim shoulders.

"Do you want a hand in the kitchen?" Yasmin asked, aware that a meal for five—especially the sort of meals her mother liked to make—wouldn't be a small matter.

"No, no," her mother demurred. "You need to recharge. Your father will serve as my aide de camp."

Her father bumped her hip playfully with his. "I didn't exert energy today?"

"Please. You took your man-toy out for a ride. How is that difficult?"

Yasmin hadn't seen her parents joke like this in a while. She knew they loved each other, but this was different.

They're like sweethearts today, she mused.

"Joseph," her mother said over her shoulder. "I've put you in the room next to Balu's in the men's wing. If you like, you can wash up and lie down there."

Yasmin laughed at Joseph's expression. Clearly, he wasn't accustomed to having his every move organized. Deciding he wouldn't mind, she nudged his shoulder companionably.

"There's no point fighting her. Getting her way is my mother's special gift."

"I'm not— Your mother is being generous. I simply hoped I might have a room near you." He'd lowered his voice for her ears only. The fact that he wanted to stay close by did wonders for her ego.

"Not a chance in hell," she responded cheerfully.

~

She was less cheerful when she realized she'd be stuck by herself till dinner. Her batteries *were* drained, but resting up alone was boring. Evidently, even former concubines grew accustomed to having things to do.

Deciding to treat recharging like a job, she changed into sunning clothes. Modest enough to suit her mother, the robes nonetheless allowed her to lie out by the pool and soak up healing radiance.

Despite an intent to read, her magazine-loaded scroll didn't hold her attention. Balu's room overlooked the walled garden area. His and Joseph's voices drifted out the window, which—unlike the women's wing—was below head height. The men were 'hanging out' as humans said, having a friendly argument over what they'd appreciated most in New York.

"Times Square," her brother said. "Talking to people there was the best."

"The snow in Central Park was pretty, though I never could like the cold."

"Club music," her brother countered. "And watching humans dance."

"I preferred the opera."

"The opera! Joseph, that's for old men."

"I admired the museums too. What human artists do with humble materials is as good as sorcery."

Her brother laughed full out. Yasmin told herself she didn't begrudge him. Balu was enjoying teasing his idol, and Joseph seemed to relish the exchange too. He fit her family without much effort. The realization stirred uneasiness, the same as she'd felt over him accompanying her home.

She couldn't help the thought that slipped into her mind: Really, it would be nice if she and Joseph were destined for each other.

~

Dinner gave her opportunities for similar musings. Her mother had outdone herself with the meal. Joseph's admiration for her talent was as unfeigned as his compliments were polished.

"Those are good manners," her mother said, wagging her finger at Balu. "If you want to get on in life, you'll learn from his example."

"My manners are fine," Balu objected laughingly. "I just don't always waste them on family."

"They are fine," Yasmin agreed. "I've seen him dust them off at work."

Joseph laughed, pleasing her with his appreciation of her humor.

"*Work,*" her mother repeated darkly. "*Trouble* is what your detecting business leads to." She passed a dish to her new favorite. "I'm sure you agree after this weekend."

"Perhaps," he said diplomatically. "Then again, husband-hunting hasn't turned out so well for Lady Toraman."

"Good one!" Balu crowed.

Joseph's mouth quirked but he controlled it. "Forgive me, Missus Baykal. You're so gracious. I should have kept my opinion to myself."

"I'm sure you're entitled to it," her mother replied stiffly. "Though if you ever do take a wife, you may find you'd rather yours stay home."

Joseph's amusement disappeared in a blink, replaced by nearly blank-faced surprise. Her mother's tone implied a man like him was unlikely to marry. Yasmin supposed eunuchs didn't often. Even so, the way Vinca put it had been insulting. Given her previous warmth, the sudden change was all the more startling.

"Mom," Balu scolded quietly. "Joseph is a good man . . . and our guest."

"Of course," her mother said, rising from her cushion. "Forgive me. I'll see to brewing the coffee now."

Her 'forgive me' wasn't quite an apology to Joseph. Yasmin looked at him. Though he wasn't blushing, she suspected this required will. He met her gaze and shook his head slightly. She understood the message. Even now, he didn't want her to correct her mother's assumption. His role as the sultan's supposedly unbeatable magician was too important to undercut—certainly too important to care about a prick to his pride.

Respect made her smile at him.

"I hadn't planned to," she said.

"Hadn't planned to what?" Balu asked.

"Have coffee," she said nonsensically. "But maybe I'll help with tea."

Her father squeezed her hand as she passed. "She's sorry she hurt his feelings," he murmured. "She just can't make herself say the words."

Yasmin knew that too. She smiled at her father and continued to the kitchen.

~

Predictably, considering the awkwardness that preceded it, their post-dinner tea and coffee lasted the minimum time that counted as polite. Yasmin tried to speak to Joseph after the cups were cleared but wasn't quick enough. Her father invited him for brandy and a hookah in his study.

Yasmin opened her mouth to say she'd join them.

"Just boring business talk," Aydin said, heading that off too. "Plus, you know how you are about the smell of tobacco."

She'd have put up with it this once. No way was her father planning a 'boring' conversation. The pair was going to discuss magic—a topic she could have contributed to!

"Not tonight," he said when she scowled at him.

Joseph shrugged and looked apologetic. She concluded no help was coming from that quarter.

"Well, I can't come," her brother volunteered with annoying good spirits. "I have plans. I'm flying out to meet friends. —No gossiping," he promised before their father could warn him.

Even if she weren't currently playing dead, Yasmin couldn't follow his example. Nice females weren't supposed to smoke out at night, a rule her mother always insisted she follow.

She hadn't finished seething over that as she lay, arms folded and jaw set, in her bed later. If anyone had business to discuss with Joseph, it was her!

Actually, her father had interrupted her last conversation with Joseph too. They'd been arguing over her supposedly flattering him in bed when the shipping container smashed the train. Admittedly, her father hadn't planned that. Also admittedly, he wouldn't have minded curtailing that line of talk. While not as hidebound as his wife, he wouldn't relish thinking of his daughter as a sexual free agent.

Was it any wonder Yasmin couldn't wait to return to her own apartment, where she could live like a real adult?

Overcome with annoyance, she sat up, tugged her hair, and growled.

The action calmed her. Home or not, she didn't absolutely have to follow her parents' rules. She *could* visit Joseph, the same as he'd visited her at Dimitriou's.

Thanks to her afternoon resting up, she blurred into vapor form easily. Even better, the servants being on 'vacation,' her chance of being caught in the villa's male wing was low. She solidified cautiously outside the guest room door.

Joseph opened it before she tapped.

"Oh," he said. "Come in. I was checking if the coast was clear before I vaped to you."

She went in, pleased that he'd had the same idea.

The guest room was pleasantly masculine, with elegant ceiling coving and rich navy upholstery. Though she hadn't been here before, she only glanced at her surroundings. Joseph's face drew her attention magnetically. She felt as if she hadn't seen him in days and needed to remind herself of his charms. There was his lean jawline, here his smooth toasty skin and fine eyebrows. His gold eyes were tired but stunning, his lashes no less dark and thick than before. He was staring back at her the same way. Whatever he saw curved his perfectly incised mouth upward.

"Why am I so relieved to be alone with you?" he wondered. "We were just stuck together on that damned train."

"Family life can feel claustrophobic if you're not used to it."

"I don't think it's that," he said.

His answer could have been more informative. "Did you want to speak to me?" she asked.

"I'm not sure I can think straight until I do this."

He took her face between his hands and kissed her, deep and gentle and intimate. Instantly enchanted, Yasmin's toes curled inside her slippers. Her hands drifted to his waist, where she ordered them not to grip tighter than his were. Despite the vow, by the time he pulled back, her fingers had dug in.

He must not have minded. His gorgeous eyes glowed with arousal. They flared brighter when Yasmin licked the taste of him from her lips.

"No," he said with a hint of teasing. "That didn't help at all."

It hadn't helped her either.

"Maybe we need to do more than kiss."

Her voice was husky. He stroked her cheek, tilted his head, and delved into her mouth.

This time, his carnal intent was clear. Her reasons for holding back dissolved. She wrapped him in her arms, delighting when his body reacted. His arms went around her too, pulling her fully against him.

"I need you," he said. "I'm so hard I hurt."

"Take me," she urged, and magicked his clothes away.

Hers flew off a moment later.

He groaned her name, his palm dragging down her spine and over her bare bottom. She could tell he liked touching her this way. His skin was sweating already, his cock pulsing forcefully where their combined embrace trapped it between them. Though she enjoyed these sensations, she was ready for more. She wriggled in his hold until her heels found the floor again.

"Come on," she said, tugging him by the wrist.

She intended to lead him to the bed.

"Next time," he panted. "I want to take you in a new way against the wall."

He didn't hesitate to turn her by the shoulders, guiding her forward until her palms pressed the smooth plaster. Her heart jumped into a gallop.

She liked when he got masterful.

"Here," he said, moving her hands higher. "This is a good spot to brace."

"You've been planning this."

"Oh, yes," he agreed throatily. "Planning, imagining, and just plain sexually obsessing."

He crowded into her as he spoke, his huge erection rubbing her up and down. He caressed himself with her and her with him, seeming reluctant to miss a single curve of her bottom cheeks. She groaned to feel him grow hotter, thicker, harder with every pass. His thighs were against her, their muscles another form of masculine assertion pressing her. With one hand to squeeze and massage her breasts, he caught her pelvis in the other's enclosing grip.

"Are you ready?" he asked even as her cream overflowed his fingers. "Can I thrust inside you now?"

He rubbed her clit with two fingers, pushing down the swelling and up again. Yasmin gasped at the sharp pleasure. The bone beneath intensified the pressure he could exert.

Right that second, the pressure was perfect.

"You make it hard for me to answer when you do that."

He nipped her earlobe and rasped out a hot whisper. "You make me hard as granite when you go wet."

He shifted angles, the crown of his cock suddenly strafing her pussy lips. She mewled at the satiny skin teasing over her.

"Yes," he breathed as she arched. "Push your ass back at me."

His foot slid between hers to coax her leg outward. She moved her second leg on her own. His fingers shifted, searching out the place they both wanted his cock to go. A second later, it was there, the tip round and sleek as it glided in. Her hands curled tensely on the wall.

She couldn't think of a single thing that felt as good as him slowly filling her.

"God," he gasped as he reached her end.

She moaned his name, a broken sound of longing. He echoed it as he drew back and surged in again. His protracted motion was agony: delicious but tormenting. He kept it up, wave after wave, thrust after thrust, until they both shuddered.

"It's hard to go this slow," he confessed.

"Don't go slow anymore. I want to be overwhelmed."

He mouthed her shoulder. "You overwhelm me," he whispered.

She braced as he pulled back again. She suspected she was going to get his full effort. She wasn't wrong. As if he'd reached into her mind, he gave her everything she wanted—speed and strength, heat and size, panting breaths and groans of uncontrolled shared delight. His fingers found just the right spots to pinch and rub. Sensations pummeled her inside and out. She came like a lever flipping, instantly jumping onto an orgasmic track.

He gasped, gunshot-style, as her pussy clamped around him. He must have been close. His pace intensified, the sound of his abdomen smacking skin impossibly exciting. She spiked a second time, and heat shot into her lengthily.

To her shock, he pulled out all the way after.

"Bed," he explained, lifting her even as she turned to object.

Bed seemed like a wonderful idea. "Yes," she agreed, arms twining behind his neck.

He laid her down and came into her in almost the same motion.

She moaned with pleasure. As he thrust, carefully at first and then picking up speed and force, her hands took their turn roaming him. Oh, she loved his shoulders, and his back, and his spine, and the tight muscles of his rear. His ribs and diaphragm were wonders, the way they moved so vigorously for his breaths. He gasped when she pinched his nipples, as if she'd hurt him a little bit.

"Too much?"

He shook his head, drops of perspiration flinging from him with the motion. "Do it again."

She was at the lower end of the mattress, her legs bent up to match his thrusts. Neither of them was doing this very smoothly. Power was what mattered. Power and friction and driving him into her as deeply as possible. The flush that stained his cheeks was blotchy, the sweat that beaded them glittering. She had no doubt she looked just as disheveled.

"When you go, I'll do it," she said.

He growled, deep and menacing in his throat. Suddenly, his hips churned into her even faster. His chest dropped closer. She couldn't see his face anymore. His body felt like it was everywhere, as if every part of her were surrounded and affected by his desire. Her blood roared in her ears. The rush should have deafened her, but she seemed to hear two heartbeats.

Both were thudding like engines.

They were almost there. Joseph gripped her hip and slung in. Her insides jolted, and she couldn't believe how good it felt. His shaft swelled, preparing to release again.

Yasmin remembered her promise.

She found his nipples and twisted hard. All the muscles in his body tightened, his breath exploding as his excitement hit an even higher crest. He jerked up, jamming in from his pelvis. The sight and feel of his abandonment flipped another switch for her. Ecstasy wrenched outward from her sex. She came so hard she had to gulp for air.

Minutes passed before she could move beyond breathing.

"Mm," Joseph said sleepily.

He was still on her, in her, his forehead resting on the covers next to her.

"Need air," she said.

He rolled so that she was on top of him. That was fine. She liked staying connected the way they were. He patted her bottom as if testing the gesture out.

"I thought that might be pleasurable," he said. "The wall thing, that is. I didn't realize we'd want to do the bed thing too."

Yasmin had just enough strength to laugh. "I hope this means you've given up your belief that I've been faking my enjoyment to flatter you."

"Your responses did strike me as genuine."

She pushed up on her forearms to smile at him.

"You *seem* sophisticated," he said defensively. "And you're very alluring. Whatever you lack in practical experience, you were a concubine. I couldn't help thinking you had expectations I might not live up to."

"You lived up to them. In any case, I wasn't dwelling on who I used to be. Tonight I was just a woman who wanted a man she cares about."

She didn't mean to pressure him about his feelings, but perhaps it came out that way. Joseph's face went quiet and serious.

"Yasmin, how can I put a name to my emotions when, until recently, I didn't think I had a right to them? What did I have to offer any woman, especially one who belonged to a djinni I'd sworn allegiance to. —No, don't squirm away. I want you to know I care. I want you to know you can count on me. I'm not going anywhere. Please give me time to get used to this."

Yasmin felt like she'd known forever he was the man for her. Her throat was tight. If she answered, she knew she'd cry.

Joseph's expression twisted with sympathy. "Please don't look like that."

She swallowed hard and controlled herself. "I can't pretend not to feel what I do. No more than you can pretend to feel what you don't."

"You're right. I shouldn't ask that of you. In truth, I'm in awe of your honesty."

His words weren't nothing. They simply weren't the ones she wanted to hear from him.

CHAPTER SEVENTEEN

Entertaining Angels

Opening her eyes in her childhood bedroom was disconcerting. She'd slept well at least. Judging by the angle of the sun, noon was approaching. Deciding to behave as she would if she'd been in her own apartment, she got up to prepare a meal. The servants being gone, and her parents not out of bed, she had the kitchen to herself. That presented another choice. Cooking manually was harder but more nourishing for their race. Naturally, she knew what her mother would advise.

"Food is love," she quoted humorously.

Thus motivated, she had eggs sizzling in a pan by the time Balu joined her to perch sleepily on the agate topped prep table.

"Orange juice," he mumbled. "Please, if you love me."

Yasmin smiled. Her brother was even less sociable in the morning than she was.

A shuffling noise and a yawn told her Joseph had arrived too.

"Want help?" he asked politely.

"You could make orange juice for my brother."

"Magic-squeezed is fine," Balu added, more considerate of a guest than a mere sister. He rubbed his face with both palms. "I guess I could heat up leftovers from last night if anyone wants them."

Joseph allowed he would enjoy that.

They sat at the good dining table, eating quietly, when a knock sounded on one of the high windows.

"Hello," someone called, nose pressed against the glass. "Sorry to interrupt. No one answered the front door."

"It's Connor," Joseph said, clearly surprised to see him hovering there.

Connor was the male member of the sultan's love triangle. He wasn't in smoke form, just levitating in the air.

"He must have news," Yasmin said, immediately feeling more alert. "Maybe they've arrested Dimitriou."

Realizing someone ought to do it, she magicked the aperture open.

"Thank you!" Connor exclaimed, beaming at all of them as he floated in and down onto his feet. Yasmin didn't know the consort well, but he had to be the happiest djinni she'd ever met. "I'm so glad to see you and Joseph safe! We heard you've been having big adventures. You're Balu, aren't you? How nice to meet you! You're as beautiful as your brave sister."

Connor was rather beautiful himself. Also tall and well built. He had an unusual energy about him, as if his power were of a simpler and purer nature than most djinn's. His eyes were a soft, swimming blue. Once seen, it was difficult to look away from them.

"Uh," her brother said. "Would you like some food? And a chair?"

"Yes and yes," Connor accepted delightedly.

Her brother laughed; it really was impossible not to. The dining chairs were low but had tall backs—a compromise between East and West. Balu rose and pulled one out for their visitor. "I expect you're here to speak to Joseph and my sister. Why don't I fill a plate for you and come back?"

"You can listen if you like," Connor said. "Arcadius and Cade say you're quite reliable for your age."

The testimonial pleased her brother, who bounced from the room grinning.

"Is there news?" Joseph asked.

Connor's good-natured face pulled into lines that were almost serious. "The news is a little challenging, though I do think we should have hope."

"What happened?" Yasmin asked.

Connor smiled at her. His gaze was so sweet and gentle it made her a bit dizzy. "I'll start at the beginning, the way our fiancée Georgie advises . . ."

* * *

Connor's Tale

First, know Iksander was grateful to get your evidence concerning the treacherous plot. The Justice Minister believes it establishes a basis for prosecution, plus the guardians observe the scroll in particular is nicely organized. I don't which of you that's thanks to, but congrats! The necessary folks consulted, the guardians organized a mission for taking Dimitriou into custody. The plan was to bring him and any other fish they could hook for trial in the capital.

Because they didn't want word to get out prematurely, the team they assigned was small. A dozen guards would accompany them, plus a sorcerer to handle magical containment for transport. Arcadius didn't want Iksander along but, considering the political aspect of the threat, the sultan thought he needed to be seen confronting Dimitriou.

They *were* going to leave me behind. I'm not a fighter, I admit. I am, however, useful for seeing things that will happen before they do. Sometimes, anyway. I didn't foresee what happened in Milion.

Initially, our arrival went smoothly. We set down at Dimitriou's gate and, though his household troops challenged our right to enter, Dimitriou instructed them not to fight. He had nothing to hide, he said. Therefore, they had no cause to resist.

"My sole request," he proclaimed for all to hear, "is that the charges be made clear before you haul me away in chains. I am a lord . . . and the elected speaker for this province. That much respect doesn't seem too much to ask."

His confidence was our first warning that he might have a backup plan.

The guardians wanted to take him without delay. We did have a proper arrest order. Iksander said other lords wouldn't like the precedent this set. A leader who ignored their privileges was a leader they wouldn't mind seeing overthrown.

"Our case is strong," he argued. "Whatever evidence Dimitriou suspects we have, he can't know the half of it. Why not present some of it here and now? When his supporters learn the depth of his depravity, they'll beg us to remove him."

They debated a little longer, but Iksander's mind was set.

The sorcerer—a man named Celik, in case you're curious—fitted Dimitriou with a special ankle shackle to prevent him magically escaping.

Dimitriou accepted the restraint. An ally of his, an older man named LaBass, proposed we present our case in the square, where all Milion's citizens could watch. Even I saw this meant more loyalists, some of whom were trained fighters, would have time to congregate. We'd be outnumbered, no matter how much right we had on our side.

Iksander accepted this suggestion too . . . on the condition that LaBass also be shackled.

The man didn't like that, I tell you! His aura went very dark, as if a storm of anger were roiling his energy.

"Let them have their way," Dimitriou advised. "The sooner they present their little 'case,' the sooner everyone will know it's preposterous."

He was so dismissive it made me uneasy.

Sadly, I couldn't think how to speak against it, and the plan was agreed to.

While this was going on, the females of the house had been hanging back inside. Probably, they didn't want to leave the shadows with so many rough males around. The sight of Dimitriou being led away was too much for one. She ran out, full speed, and jumped on Iksander's back.

"Bastard!" she cried—if you'll pardon me repeating the insult. "Wasn't it enough that you betrayed your wives? You have to smear Stefan too? He's ten times the djinni you are, you snake-eating ifrit spawn!"

She called the sultan plenty more besides as she beat him wildly about the head.

I suppose the soldiers weren't sure how to restrain a maddened female aristocrat. Arcadius moved while they were still gawking.

"Enough," he said, pulling her firmly but gently off. "Recall your dignity, Lady Toraman."

She didn't appear to care about dignity. She wept and railed as Arcadius held her, thrashing very much as if she wanted another go at him. Iksander's face bled from her scratches, though he wasn't more harmed than that. His expression as he looked at the djinniya might have been the saddest I've ever seen.

"Safiye," he said. "I know I've earned your anger but not for this. I hope, in time, you understand I'm trying to protect you too today."

She spat at the grass and sobbed.

"Safiye," Lord Dimitriou said. His voice succeeded in quieting her. "Be strong, darling. This is nothing to worry over. If I need you, I'll send someone."

I think he shocked her by suggesting she stay behind. If he felt sorry for that, it didn't show. She hadn't picked up her jaw when he turned to go.

Some of Dimitriou's staff flew ahead to alert his allies in town. As we arrived, the square was full and growing fuller by the moment. It looked like all of Minion was turning out. I hoped this was a good thing. Apparently, a few of the townspeople had spelled a large white cloth to drape the town hall's facade. I learned the sorcerer Celik intended to project the video from Joseph's phone onto it.

Before he did, Iksander climbed the steps beneath. He wanted to prepare the djinn who'd gathered for what they'd see. Despite my anxiety, hearing how calm he was settled me. Well, you know how Iksander is when he speaks from the heart. Anyone can tell he cares about being as good a ruler as he can. He assured the audience he had no personal grudge against Dimitriou or LaBass. This wasn't about shocking them with salacious material. This was about justice for crimes past and preventing crimes future.

I sensed most of the Milioners were willing to reserve judgment.

You two, of course, are familiar with the contents of Joseph's phone. Celik played portions of both your video testimony. The conspiracy's friends heckled the show at points, but not so much that you were drowned out. The claim that Lord Dimitriou had arranged to have people killed, including his own parents, met with louder objections. Many in the crowd cried 'shame' at the footage of their desiccated bodies. Some seemed to think Dimitriou incapable of the deed. Others objected to the remains being displayed disrespectfully. Another group sounded as if they'd begun to fear the charges might be true.

That, at least, was how it seemed to me.

Perhaps Dimitriou also sensed sentiment shifting. He made his own assertion.

"These scenes are pure fantasy!" he argued. "Everyone knows you can't trust human technology—or humans, for that matter. Not one but two magically savvy members of that race fill privileged roles in Iksander's court. In our realm, humans have the advantage in enchantment. Either or both could have cooked up this so-called evidence. Given the trouble the sultan has led us into, he can't afford to be challenged by someone more popular. I don't say I have ambitions of that nature, but *he* may believe I do."

The crowd exploded in hot debate.

"Patience," Iksander said, calming them again. "There is more to watch. You shall see how these threads connect."

The footage of Dimitriou's zombie love nest shocked everyone.

People groaned and called out things like 'blasphemy' and 'degenerate.'

"The blasphemy is theirs," Dimitriou countered with fiery anger. "Theirs, who invent these disgusting lies. Milion, I'm one of you. You've known me all my life. Whatever flaws I've demonstrated, none approached this atrocity. I *protect* the vulnerable. I do not prey on them."

"We can settle this," LaBass interjected, his cool voice rising above the others. He'd been standing toward the rear of the crowd, observing its reactions. "At least, I believe we can. Presumably, the sultan knows the location where these unnatural acts allegedly occurred. Why don't we go and see for ourselves?"

Iksander wasn't the only djinni surprised by this suggestion. Dimitriou, as well, seemed taken aback by it.

He caught his breath and recovered. "Yes," he said smoothly. "Why don't we go and see?"

Iksander couldn't refuse even if he wished. "I'm certain Lord Dimitriou doesn't need directions. For the rest of you, the spot is beneath a ruin west of the Temple of Demeter, on a cliff by the In-Betweens."

"The abandoned flour mill," someone said, recognizing the description. "In the old days, they used wild magic to turn the grindstone . . . until the cliff face sheared unexpectedly and made the area too dangerous."

I didn't like the sound of cliff faces shearing, but none of the locals seemed especially alarmed. As if it were decided, djinn began summoning carpets for traveling there.

After a brief consultation with Cade and Arcadius, Celik the Sorcerer took the two shackled men with him. If they had it in mind to run before the charges could be proven, he had the best chance of stopping them.

"They're too calm," Iksander observed in an undertone. "LaBass seems to think Dimitriou has a trick up his sleeve. He's counting on it to save him too."

"We have to play this out," Cade advised. "I'll warn the guards to prepare for circumstances going pear-shaped. If they do, we'll fly our prisoners out of here as quickly as we're able."

"We'll face resistance," Iksander said. "And from a larger force."

"I'm not worried," Arcadius put in. "I'd match any of our men against ten of theirs."

"You may have to. I had a view of the crowd from the steps. I counted uniforms." Iksander's tone was wry. He glanced at me as we moved toward the carpets.

"Ride with me," he said.

I saw he was feeling serious, so I tried not to smile too much. Still, as always, I was happy to simply be with him. Georgie would have wanted him to have my support, and knowing I'd be pleasing her made me happy twice over. Though the guards could see and weren't a hundred percent accustomed to our relationship, I took his hand as we lifted off.

Iksander wagged his head at me. "You'd think this was a picnic, the way you act."

"You can let go, if you want."

He returned my clasp instead. "Georgie will kick my ass if you're harmed here because of me."

"She won't. Anyway, I think you made the right choice, letting Dimitriou have a bit of a hearing here. You're not all powerful. You rule because the different strata of your people allow it, because they have faith you'll be mostly competent and fair."

"*Mostly.*" Iksander rolled his eyes like he was amused.

"Mostly is the best any incarnated being can do."

Once we landed, the guardians led the way down the long staircase you described. Because the steps were narrow, only a portion of the crowd could follow. Determined to see, I squeezed into the line. Quite a lot of wild magic washed upward from below. I didn't mind it, but I could see people shuddering. They gritted their teeth and kept going. So close to the mists, the discomfort seemed to be expected.

Our next sign of trouble was that no welcome mat lay at the bottom. More troubling, there also was no door. An irregular stone gap opened into darkness.

With a grim expression, Arcadius went in.

The glow he called up revealed an old dugout chamber with nothing inside it. No furniture. No Fifties kitchen. Certainly no dead-alive love slaves. Curious, Cade crouched and touched the floor. The surface of the stone was glassy, as if it a flame hotter than a blowtorch had melted it.

"This place has been scoured clean magically," he said. "Lord Dimitriou must have guessed we'd investigate. He had plenty of time to remote-trigger a self-destruct."

Others studied the room's surfaces. At first, they seemed to agree with Cade's assessment—and to find the bunker's condition suspicious.

"This could have happened anytime," someone scoffed, a safe claim to make, given how the proximity of the mist confused normal perceptions. "It could even have been done when the mill was operational. Perhaps this space was smoothed out for storage."

"Bootlegging, more likely," someone else suggested. "Who builds plain old storage this far underground?"

Neither theory helped our cause. I closed my eyes to find out what I could sense. I thought I saw djinn-shaped figures screaming as unworldly heat ignited their flesh and bone. They had a *kind* of life in them, though not the sort I was used to. A half-life, I mused. They hadn't been conscious as we understand it, but they were still sentient.

"Dimitriou burned his playthings," I said aloud. "To destroy the evidence of his crimes. They died a second time in terrible agony. They knew he'd betrayed them."

A few djinn glanced at me and looked unnerved.

"You're making that up," scoffed the one who'd claimed the bunker could have been destroyed any time. "There's too much wild magic hereabouts for anyone to tell."

"I can tell," I said. "I have more Sight than most."

This was true, but, "You're the sultan's consort," the ornery djinni insisted. "You'd say anything to please him."

He made it sound like being Iksander's consort wasn't an honor but instead a cause for shame.

"I wouldn't lie about something this important," I said. "I'm 98 percent honest . . . 95 if I'm having a tricky day."

Cade laughed softly and gave my arm a pat. "You aren't going to convince these djinn. We'll have to leave it for the courts to settle. Perhaps a committee of impartial experts can determine what happened here."

His words made the best of the disheartening development. Probably, that was by design. The djinn around us were calm as we tramped back up the stairs and into the ruin.

"I'll take my apology now," was how Dimitriou greeted us. "Since your so-called evidence has been disproven."

"And how would you know that?" Arcadius asked. He, I've observed, does supercilious even better than his double.

Dimitriou smiled at him. I noticed a larger crowd of townsfolk than before around him. They and the local guards had drawn nearer in support. I don't know if they felt the same loyalty toward LaBass, but since he stood next to the younger man, he shared the benefit.

"Remove these cuffs," he demanded. "As you've seen, we are innocent."

"Hardly that," Arcadius said. "As you yourself have asserted, evidence can be tampered with."

"Slander," LaBass blustered.

"Never mind," Dimitriou said, touching his arm to cut short the rant. "My friend and I will be leaving now. If you wish to stop us, your men need to use those weapons they're carrying."

He seemed to know the guardians wouldn't order that. If at all possible, Iksander wanted to avoid armed conflict. Whatever their affiliation, Milioners were his people too. To our sides' dismay, the accused turned their backs on us and walked. Their escort followed their example. Muttering things like *we showed them* and *capital elites think they can bully us*, they ushered their leaders safely across the now-trampled wild grasses.

"Don't worry," Celik said quietly. "They won't get far. The minute Dimitriou and

LaBass try to cross the boundary to leave town, their cuffs will turn into boots."

"Boots?" Iksander asked.

The magician nodded. "Two-inch thick. They'll cover each man from toe to knee. Better yet, the metal I used to form them is iron-laced. They won't be able to smoke free. Provided they don't amputate their legs, we can track them anywhere."

"Their legs wouldn't grow back?"

"Severing them while booted would count as a magical injury. I'm no Joseph the Magician, but I assure you there's not much chance they could override my spell."

Not much chance wasn't the same as none. Iksander seemed to know this but didn't challenge the sorcerer. "If that's the case, they'll likely stay in Milion. We need more troops to separate them from their protectors. I'd like an intimidating number in order to discourage bloodshed . . . preferably *before* they figure out how to wriggle loose. Damn the scroll net not working in this place."

Cade had a suggestion. "Connor could take a message. He's a fast flier, and we weren't counting on him to fight."

"I'd be happy to," I agreed.

"I know you mean that literally," Iksander said with a slanting smile. "Very well. We'll go that route."

The guardians composed quick instructions while Iksander and I hugged goodbye. He did the backslap thing he would have for any soldier, but his eyes told me I meant more. I *might* have teased him by mouthing, 'I love you.' I wanted to be sure I left him in a positive mood.

Flying as fast as I could *was* exhilarating. I gave the guardians' contact their note, answered his questions, then sat in the palace gardens to cogitate. I wanted to tell Georgie everything, but looping you two in seemed like it ought to take priority. I flew here, and you know the rest.

The End until what happens next!

* * *

Connor finished his story triumphantly. In spite of the seriousness of the situation, Yasmin was tempted to giggle. You'd think the consort had never recounted a tale before. That didn't seem possible. Most djinn had told too many to count while they were still little.

"I should go out there," Joseph said, his plate cold and shoved aside.

"To testify?" Yasmin asked. "I know we witnessed the events directly, but shouldn't we share our account in court, properly? Iksander's lawyers might not want Dimitriou knowing every detail of the case against him. Plus, we can't assume Milioners will believe us any better in person."

"I mean I should go out there to bolster Celik. He's good, but he doesn't have my experience. I'm sure Iksander would rather restrain that pair with enchantment than force of arms."

"If that's why you're going, I should go too. I'm not saying you can't handle it, but we've already worked together. We're stronger as a team."

Joseph furrowed his brow at her. "You really want to return to Milion? You're safe here. You don't have to face Dimitriou again."

"I hope this doesn't insult you, but I'd want to go even if you weren't. I'd like to see this through to the end."

Joseph continued to look perplexed. "Iksander didn't ask for you."

"He didn't ask for you, either."

"Give it up," Balu laughed from what was usually their father's seat. "Yami only gets that look when she's really determined."

Joseph turned his head to him. "You'd let your sister fly into danger."

"Have you seen her run from it yet? Anyway, she's right. You two make a good couple. —Magically," he added when Joseph shot him a sharper look.

Her brother squirmed, probably believing he'd accidentally insulted his idol.

Joseph considered him a moment longer, then sighed resignedly.

"All right. We'll return together. I trust you," he said, holding Yasmin's gaze firmly. "You *will* exercise good judgment, you *are* an asset, and I'm grateful for your help."

He sounded like he was trying to make the words true by saying them. In that moment, she didn't care. They rang as sweet to her as if he hadn't a single doubt.

"From your mouth to the Goddess's ear," she joked.

CHAPTER EIGHTEEN

Instruments of the Goddess

Balu flew them back to Milion on the family's fastest Persian. Ostensibly, he did this so Yasmin and Joseph would arrive fresh. In reality, Yasmin knew her brother didn't want to miss what happened next.

They circled town until they found Iksander and his men. Circumstances had changed since Connor left. Evidently, the guardians' reinforcements beat them there. A cluster of tents—festive in appearance but in actuality a temporary headquarters—dotted a fallow field near the Temple of Demeter. The largest tent flew a light blue pennant on which the white Nummius leopard reared.

"Shall I land there?" Balu asked, knowing the leopard was Iksander's family emblem.

"Wait till the guards wave us down," Joseph said. "When they do, I want you to find Celik. Tell him I sent you and offer your services as a skilled amateur. If he accepts them, fine. If he doesn't, fly back to town and wait. I don't want you in the way any more than I want you hurt."

"I can't stick with you two?" Balu asked.

"No," Joseph said.

"No," Yasmin confirmed, when her brother turned pleadingly to her. Once Iksander knew his best magician had arrived, he'd move Celik off the frontline and Joseph on. Wherever Celik ended up, Balu would be safer there.

"But—"

"Joseph is being generous. I'd send you home if it were up to me."

"That's mean."

"Do you want Mother and Father to think Joseph *isn't* a good influence on you?"

That shut him up. He muttered when they landed but did as Joseph said.

"That was sneaky," Joseph complimented. "You really do have a strategic mind."

Side by side, they entered the royal tent.

Iksander and his guardians stood at a light camp desk, studying a local map. Yasmin hadn't seen the sultan since their divorce, the details of which his lawyers had handled. Her former master was as beautiful as ever with his thick golden hair and his noble warrior face. Interestingly—at least to her—she felt perfectly calm to see him. Not resentful or regretful to have lost his favor. Not even shy to be in the presence of her social superior. She remembered a childhood lesson from temple school.

In the eyes of the Goddess, all djinn are equal.

She smiled at Iksander when he looked up.

"You're here," he said, including her and Joseph in the greeting. "Good. We sent Connor off so fast, I didn't think to ask him to speak to you. Recovered from your ordeal, it looks like?"

"We are," Joseph said. "Where are LaBass and Dimitriou?"

"Camped out on the other side of Demeter's house trying to pry off their new footwear."

"Celik's boots worked then?"

"Yes. He's done well, but I'm happy you've arrived. As you can see, we don't have the conspirators in hand. Dimitriou has announced a self-styled public hearing to prove his innocence, scheduled for this evening at sunset. His allies barricaded the post office and got word out with the booster there. Djinn have been arriving from neighboring towns ever since."

"Loyalists, I presume?"

"He hasn't been shy about stacking the audience in his favor. This movement LaBass is building is looking more and more organized."

"Even loyalists can be made to see the truth," Yasmin said. "Connor said he thought we should have hope."

Iksander seemed a little startled that she'd spoken.

"That's a direct quote," she added.

"Well, sometimes he knows things the rest of us don't." Though he didn't exactly overflow with optimism, he smiled slightly. "You've reminded me I have something I want to return to you."

He pulled a little carry tin from his pocket and handed it to her. Curious, Yasmin unscrewed it.

"My braided lock!" she exclaimed, identifying the coil inside. "The one we used to tie the scroll and postcard together."

"It seemed best to return such a personal object to its owner."

Yasmin definitely wouldn't want anyone using this to do attack magic against her. Joseph, either. The lock was infused with his essence too.

"Thank you," she said sincerely.

"Least I could do," he said. "Now why don't we four talk strategy."

Joseph opened his mouth to say it ought to be 'we five.' That was nice, but Yasmin shook her head. The sultan was their sovereign, and she—ironically—wasn't someone he knew well. He was entitled to choose whoever he trusted to consult. She squeezed Joseph's arm to reassure him it was all right.

"I'll be outside," she said. "I'm sure you'll find me if you need me for anything."

~

She didn't have far to walk before finding a craggy boulder to sit against. Djinn in uniform seemed to be everywhere. Some guarded tents others ducked into. Some strode about the camp on errands, while still more patrolled the perimeter. No one seemed agitated. The atmosphere was calm and professional.

And male. As far as she could tell, she was the sole djinniya in the vicinity.

Somewhat to her surprise, no one challenged her presence.

Maybe she was learning to look like she had a right to be anywhere.

She turned her gaze toward the Temple of Demeter. Perhaps a mile from Iksander's camp, the building drew many eyes. Though a haze blurred the horizon, the sky was clear. The edifice stood out distinctly, being near no other structures on flat terrain. Yasmin easily made out its triangular pediment and white columns. She wondered if Demeter were aware of events unfolding around her house. Did divinities pay that much attention? Supposedly, named gods had their being nearer to people. The goddess Yasmin followed was simply 'She' or 'the Creatoress.'

She clasped her hands together before her mouth but wasn't sure what to pray. The idea of Dimitriou and LaBass winning tonight's standoff both frightened and angered her. Dimitriou in particular had demonstrated his base nature. Yasmin wanted passionately for this conflict to resolve in Iksander's favor but couldn't be sure it would. How could any djinniya know what the Creators had in mind? What if corrupt, power-mad murderers ruling the Glorious City *was* a thread in the Divine plan? Deities were by nature ineffable.

Guide me, Goddess, she thought. *You teach that the humblest djinni matters. If the essence of what I wish can be, please help me be a part of bringing it about. If it cannot be, please give me the strength and wisdom to work toward a happier future for our city.*

She wiped her cheek where a tear spilled over. She had prayed. Now she would be quiet.

~

She was as calm as she was getting when Joseph came for her at dusk.

"It's time," he said, extending a hand to help her rise. "Dimitriou's side is illuminating the temple steps. He'll be well lit for his rally."

"LaBass and he know their theater, I guess."

He lifted her knuckles to his mouth. "I told Iksander we'd take a spot near the front. I'm not sure what we'll be up against. We may have to act on the fly."

She nodded. This was her impression too. "Iksander didn't object to me taking part?"

"He asked me to thank you. Your willingness to support his leadership surprised him." Joseph laughed. "I suspect he underestimates how much you enjoy your newfound freedom . . . and how much help you can offer."

They were walking among a crowd—and not only a crowd of guards. Civilians joined the moving mass: Milioners and djinn from other towns, pushing closer together as they approached their goal.

A large, gently fluttering banner hung down from the temple's pediment. The magic-powered spotlights were trained on it. Their light revealed a white sailing ship on a blood red ground.

"What do you suppose that's about?" she asked.

"Perhaps it's their pirate flag," Joseph quipped, making her laugh unexpectedly. "Seriously, I don't know. Something LaBass masterminded, I wager. He's more of a planner than Lord Dimitriou."

The crowd had grown dense, hampering them from moving closer. Joseph didn't try to push more aggressively.

"This ought to be near enough," he said.

Yasmin supposed it was. They could have lobbed a javelin up the marble steps, assuming their arms were fit. A sturdy brass chain on posts barred the audience from going higher than ground level. She and Joseph were ten or so bodies back from the front. Thankfully, the audience space was dark, and Joseph didn't wear livery. The throng had no way of knowing which side they supported.

Assuming her eyes weren't playing tricks, she *thought* she saw LaBass lurking in the lee of one of the tall columns. If it were him, was it good news or bad that he was sticking close to his accomplice?

"Dimitriou," someone near them shouted. "Dimitriou, speak to us."

The chant spread, soon joined by rhythmically stamping feet. So many took up the petition that the ground vibrated. The stamping caused silvery wisps to issue around their feet, probably the dusty remnant of old wild magic dews. Whatever the source, the wisps made the grass look as if it were smoking.

Speak to us. Speak to us. Lord Dimitriou, speak to us.

Joseph shook his head in horrified disbelief. Unnerved as well, Yasmin wrapped her hand tighter around his.

"He's coming," someone nearer the front announced.

He was . . . and he didn't come alone. Dimitriou led Safiye onto the high platform. She was robed in white—modest, lovely, with rainbow glints here and there to mark her outfit's lavish diamond embellishment. Though she seemed to come voluntarily, her face was nearly as white as her garments. As foil to her, Dimitriou wore velvet so deeply blue it read black. When he reached the center of the stage, he lifted Safiye's arm as if claiming victory.

The djinn around them let out a cheer.

Stefan and Safiye looked as fine as any sultan and his kadin.

"His boot is gone," Joseph said. "And the cuff. Damn it. I was hoping Celik's restraint would stick."

"Friends," Dimitriou began, lifting his hands for quiet.

The crowd fell silent within a breath.

He smiled in recognition of their respect. "Friends," he repeated. "Thank you for giving me this chance to prove my innocence. I promise you won't regret it." He turned slightly to gesture behind him. "I expect you see this flag and wonder what it means. It is our flag, friends: symbol of our ships coming in. Symbol of the good fortune that should and, I believe, *will* be shared by all of us."

"Shared by some a lot more than others," Joseph muttered cynically. "And so much for *not* harboring ambitions of rulership."

Dimitriou couldn't hear him. Joseph had pitched his comment for Yasmin's ears alone. Up on the temple step's, the murderer's expression increased in seriousness. "You've heard lies about me this day, accusing me of terrible, depraved things. Some of you may believe them. Others may speculate. Before we move into the future we all deserve, I must set your minds at ease."

"Show us you aren't dark!" someone's voice lifted to demand.

A plant, Yasmin thought. The person's timing was too perfect.

"Yes," Dimitriou nodded soberly. "That's the core question, isn't it? If any djinni had done what our current sultan claims . . . if he'd murdered and raped the dead . . . if he'd committed parricide, and theft, and who knows *what* atrocities our current sultan wants to ascribe to me . . . if any djinni had done these things, he'd have turned ifrit a thousand times over. His soul would be black as pitch. He couldn't hide what he'd become if he were the greatest sorcerer our dimension had ever known.

"Even the Empress Luna, who—on our current sultan's watch—wreaked havoc on all of us . . . even she revealed her ugliness to those who knew how to look for it."

"Well, that isn't true," Joseph said. "Luna looked completely normal until the end. I can vouch for that personally."

Yasmin didn't think Dimitriou cared about sticking to the facts . . . or what could be proved in any court but public opinion. On the other hand, when it came to magic, Luna had been massively more adept than Dimitriou. He *should* have turned dark. And it *ought* to be visible. Yet there he stood, on a goddess's very doorstep, without lightning striking him.

He had to know how virtuous the setting would make him look.

"The steps," she said slowly.

Joseph turned to her. "The steps?"

"My brother Ramis hid that he'd turned. It took a lot of energy, but he could conceal the signs for hours at a time. What if, along with putting cutouts between himself and his dirty deeds, Dimitriou is using magic to prevent the change from manifesting in the first place."

"I don't think that's possible."

"Maybe it is with those wild magic cakes."

Joseph glanced back at Dimitriou. "You think he's got some stashed underfoot up there?"

"He might consider it insurance. In case Demeter takes offense at him trumpeting his virtue in front of her." She wasn't joking. The uneasy, magic-stuffed atmosphere made her feel anything might happen.

"We could scan the steps and see," Joseph said. "If the cakes are there, possibly you and I could remove them. Iksander is willing to give this poseur a bit of rope, but there's no reason to let him have that kind of advantage."

Joseph's suggestion seemed good to her. They blew out their breaths and centered. As she scanned, she had a sense of displacement. She wasn't sure if she were seeing through her inner eye or his. Maybe both. That was a little odd. She'd had no sense of breaching his personal barriers. Maybe he'd dropped them? She supposed Joseph was getting used to them working in unison. In any case, her guess had been correct. She discerned a cavity beneath the thick marble paver supporting Dimitriou. The heap of disks within it glowed. Yasmin counted six—no, seven of the things. Trying to move them telekinetically was no use, though she and Joseph broke into a sweat with the fierceness of their effort.

"Damn," he said, giving up. "Those things are as slippery as greased pigs."

"He's set protections around them. We could try spelling a hole in the marble. See if we can get some of the magic to leak away."

They had slightly better luck with this, though the opening they created was miniscule.

"That's not going to help much," she sighed.

"We can't spend more energy on it. We might need the power for later."

They'd forgotten to speak as quietly as they should.

"Shush, you two," complained the person in front of them.

Yasmin and Joseph shushed. As they'd worked, she'd listened with half an ear to Dimitriou nattering about Safiye, reminding everyone she'd been Iksander's until he cast her off. Would such a worthy, highborn djinniya, who could have any man she wished, consent to marry an ifrit? Of course, she wouldn't! Consequently, she too confirmed his virtue.

Moreover—here his voice became impassioned—if they needed further proof that the evidence against him was fabricated, could any man with so comely a marital partner dream of stooping to the acts he'd been accused of? The mere idea was laughable.

Wait a second, Yasmin thought. Did Dimitriou say he and Safiye were *married?*

"Darling," he crooned, kissing the hand of his maybe-wife. "Please forgive the display I'm obliged to make. It isn't fair to you that your devoted spouse thus expose himself. Regrettably, I owe it to our people not to leave a shred of doubt."

Crap. Him calling himself Safiye's spouse confirmed it. They must have rushed a ceremony this afternoon. She noted that—in Dimitriou's mouth—'our people' sounded a lot like 'all people, everywhere.' Most definitely, he wasn't referring to Milioners alone.

By this point, only an idiot would believe he didn't covet Iksander's throne.

Safiye inclined her head, indicating she gave permission for the display Dimitriou had in mind. Would anyone but Yasmin see her elegant stiffness as discomfort? As to that, was Yasmin reading more into her manner than was there? *Did* the former concubine approve of Dimitriou's intentions? As far as she could tell, Lady Toraman wasn't being forced to go along with this.

"Good Lord," Joseph murmured. "I think he's about to strip.

This appeared to be the case. Dimitriou began unfastening his waist sash. Before he'd finished, a servant hastened onto the floodlit platform to take the removed item. Dimitriou's man-of-the-people line must not extend to letting expensive garments lie on a dusty floor. His valet in place, he didn't hesitate. One by one, he handed off his clothes until he was naked.

The djinn who watched sucked in a concerted breath.

Seeming unself-conscious, Dimitriou lifted both arms and turned. He didn't do this hurriedly. He gave the crowd time to survey him.

Yasmin couldn't deny the show was good. Dimitriou was exceedingly well formed. Though his face was ordinary, his Creator had compensated by blessing his physique. On top of that, his fondness for carpet polo had sculpted him. His shoulders were impressive, his torso tapered, his legs long and muscular. His skin was flawless—without a single sign of spiritual infirmity. His relaxed genitals were likewise unobjectionable. Smooth. Regular. Decent in size but not outrageous. In truth, they resembled pictures from her concubine training manuals.

Immaturely perhaps, she decided they were a teensy bit boring.

When he'd completed his rotation, Dimitriou dropped his arms and stood serenely. "Would your sultan bare himself to you like this? Considering some of his recent habits, do you think *he'd* be this unblemished?"

Yasmin thought he might but doubted Dimitriou cared. He had to know Iksander was unlikely to accept this particular dare. At the least, the sultan would think it undignified. Asking the question was what mattered. Putting suspicions into people's heads.

In this and other things, Safiye's new husband was successful.

"That's no ifrit!" someone called. This time, she thought the pronouncement might be spontaneous. Others seconded the opinion. *He's no murderer. Look how perfect he is, how healthy and fit.*

"He's light," someone cried, and this too was taken up.

"He's light djinn. He's light! Lord Dimitriou is light!"

"Uh, boy," Joseph sighed.

Without warning, the illumination that blazed onstage dimmed to a blue flicker.

The acclamations petered out, replaced by murmurs of confusion.

What's happening? people asked. *Get those spotlights back on!*

An icy shiver crawled across Yasmin's shoulders. Joseph must have felt it too, because his hand clutched hers.

"Someone's doing a spell." He turned this way and that to find the perpetrator. "A big one."

Yasmin wasn't sure this was true. The rising power felt organic rather than organized. Was Demeter stirring? She shuddered at that idea. Praying to deities was one thing. Directly encountering them didn't strike her as comfortable.

Joseph grabbed her hand and pointed. "Look at the mist."

In the diminished light, she spied a thin, steam-like spout of power issuing from the hole they'd made earlier. A glance with her inner sight suggested they'd nicked a wild magic cake.

"Not that," Joseph said. "Check the wings. See the silvery fog creeping onto the stage?"

She saw it then, swirling ever thicker across the marble floor. "I think the leak is attracting it."

What 'it' was, she didn't know. Something that liked raw magic. Something that didn't read like a regular djinni in vapor form.

Soon the crowd saw it too. "What's that?" someone cried fearfully.

The gathering mist swirled like a dust devil. Sparkling, it grew taller and denser, ultimately coalescing into a blurred female form. Veiled in smoke that resembled modest clothes, it glided to the place where Dimitriou's hidden cache spouted.

Safiye and the valet retreated. Dimitriou held his ground, scornfully staring down the figure, though it wasn't more than an arm's length off. Perhaps the specter hoped to drive him back as well. It seemed to consider him, to hesitate as if gauging the threat he posed.

Temptation overcame it. It bent into the power stream and inhaled. Dimitriou's eyes widened. Yasmin concluded he hadn't noticed the magic leak before.

The specter's pleasured sigh as it drank was clearly audible.

When it straightened, it was nearly solid, nearly alive-looking. Replenished, it threw back its veil and smiled—not nicely—at the male facing it.

"*Tara*," Yasmin gasped softly.

Dimitriou must have recognized her too. He tossed his head haughtily. "You're nothing but a cheap illusion, another of the sultan's cooked-up attempts to malign my good character."

"*Is* Celik doing that?" Yasmin asked Joseph.

"I don't think so. I think that's a genuine hungry ghost." He cracked a fleeting grin. "That would make this Tara's second afterlife. I guess LaBass's old mistress isn't easy to get rid of."

At the moment, Tara wasn't interested in the businessman. Her focus stayed on Dimitriou. "You shouldn't have married her," she said, her zombie form's petulance replaced by a warning tone. "You said I was the one you loved."

For just a breath, Dimitriou seemed shaken. Tara's words implied real knowledge of him and her. "Lies!" he declared a moment later. "Everyone knows the beautiful Safiye is my soul mate."

"Hm," Tara said. "I think maybe you prefer me to look like this."

Her traditional gray robes transformed in an eyeblink. Now she wore the poufy skirted human dress from the love nest beneath the ruin. Djinn gasped as they recognized the outfit from Joseph's phone video. If they hadn't known who Tara was before, they did then.

"Tricks!" Dimitriou said, his voice rasping the slightest bit.

He didn't realize Tara wasn't done.

"Not good enough?" she taunted. "I guess you prefer this."

Her appearance changed yet again. Color drained from her lifelike skin. She went white and then slightly green. She was once more a living corpse, her eyes without spark, her skin beginning to mottle with decay.

"I love you, Master," she said in her dizzy-sweet zombie voice. "Would you like a martini?"

She held one out to him, the glass having materialized at her naming it. Dimitriou gasped and shrank back—as anyone might have. Then, definitely *not* as anyone might have, he began to breathe faster.

"My God," the djinni beside Yasmin murmured. "He's getting an erection."

Naked as he was, his body's reaction was unmistakable.

"More tricks!" Dimitriou said, slapping both hands over the unwelcome development. "My enemies create this illusion. They're desperate to smear me."

Illusions didn't require two-handed coverups.

Tara threw back her head on a full throated laugh. "Don't be shy, Master. I know how much you enjoy fucking my cold pussy. Shall we make Ivy watch from the other bed? Remember how you magicked her eyelids open? Even when she was dead, she didn't want to look. Forcing her was fun, wasn't it? Being able to. You'd made it so she didn't have the mental wherewithal to refuse."

Tara circled him, her icy green-white fingers trailing across his skin. Her victim shuddered in reaction, but within what should have been undiluted horror was a frisson of arousal.

"Maybe you'd rather your 'soul mate' watched," Tara stage-whispered in his ear. "Of course, you'd have to kill her first, wouldn't you? Then you wouldn't have to work so hard to get excited."

Tara knew her target. Dimitriou's erection jerked violently enough that he had trouble holding it. He moaned, the sound as obvious a betrayer as his sex organ.

No longer front and center but still within earshot, Safiye covered her face and sobbed. Someone took her by the shoulders to comfort her. The djinni wasn't LaBass or the valet.

"Stop this," Iksander said quietly.

"I said *stop it*," he repeated when Tara's ghost continued her caresses.

Iksander didn't command the sort of magic Joseph and Celik could. He did, however, exude authority. The ghost stopped and looked at him.

"This is beneath you," he said. "Vengeance belongs to God. It's past time for you to cross over. —Don't be afraid," he added. "Whatever sins you've committed can be forgiven. Mercy is His province too."

He spoke as if he had personal knowledge. Whether Tara believed or not, she ceased resisting him.

"You are right. This—" she paused to curl her lip "—degenerate isn't worth my time.

I will go to whatever fate awaits me."

The sultan's speech seemed to have decided her. With startling swiftness, her form snapped down to a glowing spark and vanished.

Her disappearance allowed Dimitriou to regroup. One hand—all he could currently spare—gestured at Iksander.

"You arranged these tricks. You wanted to parade your dubious virtue in front of everyone." In response to this, the sultan raised a cool eyebrow. His eloquence temporarily failing him, Dimitriou turned to the crowd again. "He won't do what I have. He remains concealed. The Goddess is my witness: I am the honest one!"

Perhaps this was the final straw for Demeter. The first law of being light—the most important one, some said—was that djinn honor their Creators. Then again, maybe Tara had eaten too great a portion of Dimitriou's magic protection. Yasmin wasn't sure it mattered. Whether the goddess or his own poor choices called the punishment down upon him, the results were horrible.

His feet turned gray first—not corpse-gray but more the hue of smoke. No one but Yasmin noticed until the tide reached his bare kneecaps. Dimitriou must have felt something then. He stiffened and look down.

A tide of scales joined the gray creeping up his limbs.

"Stop that," he ordered Iksander, his eyes fiery.

The sultan lifted his palms in a silent declaration of innocence.

The tide swept upward fast. The murderer's torso was gray now too. His feet experienced a spasm that sent him tumbling onto his hands and knees.

"Who's doing this?" he demanded in a strange nasal tone.

Yasmin gasped. His nose was lengthening—four inches, eight—until it flopped like a small elephant's.

"He's grown a tail!" someone cried.

He had. The thing lashed angrily from the fulcrum of his tailbone.

"Look at his feet! Good Goddess, are those hooves?"

"It's a trhhh—" Dimitriou seemed to be trying to say this also was a trick. As he did, his tongue flicked out like a snake's, garbling the final word.

Someone in the crowd threw a clod of dirt at him.

"Liar!"

"Think you can fool us all?"

"You're ifrit!"

"You're a damned dark djinni!"

Dimitriou wasn't so changed he couldn't flush with shame and anger. He staggered back onto his hooved feet, struggling to hold himself upright on legs that no longer bent like a djinni's should.

"I am your lord," he protested thickly through his changed mouth.

The next clod of dirt hit his scaly chest.

"Arrest him!" the flinger said.

The crowd took up this chant with the same enthusiasm as they'd previously yelled accolades.

Arrest the ifrit. Arrest him. Murderers belong in jail!

The djinni's nerve finally failed.

"He's going to run," Joseph said. "Shit. Without that boot, I don't know if we can stop him."

A vivid picture of what to do flashed into Yasmin's mind—as if a supernatural arrow had shot it there.

Was the goddess inspiring her?

"The lock," she said, digging for the tin she'd stuck in her sash pocket. "It's still carrying a charge. And we already know it can work around wild magic."

She unscrewed the tin, fumbling a bit to get the coiled braid out.

"Cup your hand," she said.

Joseph complied as easily as if it were his own idea. *He trusts me,* some part of her took a twinkling to exult. Ignoring it, she dropped the braid into his palm.

She'd cupped her hands under his when an uproar among the crowd announced Dimitriou was indeed fleeing. Turning dark hadn't weakened him—the opposite, actually. Bellows of dismay broke out as he bulled past his would-be captors. Yasmin blocked out the furor to collect her faculties.

"You're a net," she firmly informed the lock, "an instrument of Demeter, divine and unbreakable. If it pleases Her, do my bidding. Seek and catch the djinni, Stefan Dimitriou. Carry him back alive and do not for any reason allow him to escape."

Joseph murmured his own enchantment, separate but compatible. Glowing glyphs sprang to life in the air, swiftly circling their cupped hands. One by one, the braid sucked in the symbols. Joseph nodded, satisfied.

"Seek, catch, hold, and return," he intoned.

As he reinforced Yasmin's order, the lock flamed bright and transformed. A large butterfly-style net hovered above their heads. Eager to fulfill its mission, the net zoomed off in the same direction as its quarry.

Because the top of the temple steps seemed the best viewing spot, Yasmin and Joseph swung over the restraining chain at the base and jogged up. No one stopped them. Everyone was focused the other way. From Yasmin's hours sitting out and Joseph's studying maps, the terrain was familiar.

They saw their creation hadn't succeeded yet. Dimitriou was uncaught and on the run. He didn't spy his supernatural shadow until he'd sped through the enraged crowd. They weren't quick enough to keep up, but his spelled pursuer was relentless. The net was meters behind and closing when he twisted to check his lead. Alarmed, he veered right, even faster, across the countryside.

"I'm not worried," Yasmin said to Joseph, her nail jammed between her teeth.

"Me either," he responded. "He's hellish fast, but I don't think he can change form."

"He's dropped to four legs! He's heading for the ruin. Do you think he's got more magic cakes stashed there?"

"No," Joseph said. "I think that bunker is the place he feels safest. I think he's hoping to barricade himself."

"The net won't let him," Yasmin said hopefully.

"It won't," he agreed, surer than she was. The net surged closer, shrinking the gap between.

"Oh!" Joseph cried, grabbing her with excitement. "He's tripped. It's got him. It's pinning him to the ground!"

After that, as the adage goes, the only job was to say 'Amen.'

CHAPTER NINETEEN

Independent Souls

The two guardians, Cade and Arcadius, took charge of transporting the humiliated Dimitriou—still enmeshed in the magic net—to the cell that would house him while he awaited trial. Yasmin was glad to hear the new ifrit hadn't been able to smoke free. She liked thinking that she and Joseph—and of course Demeter—were no one to trifle with.

The task of tracking LaBass fell to Iksander, Joseph, and herself.

They found him in a storage room, down a stairway under the temple floor. The businessman had tried to run when Dimitriou did but hadn't gotten far. A handful of ritual candles lit the space in which he sat slumped on a wooden chair. His right leg necessarily extended in front of him. Rough black metal encased his foot and shin.

Evidently, Dimitriou had spent no magic unshackling his confederate.

"Yes, yes," LaBass said impatiently, one hand sketching a get-on-with-it circle. Though he wasn't dark, or not yet, the flickering light turned his face devilish. "I concede. You've caught me. I thought I'd secure my future raising that djinni up. I never guessed the perverted bastard would ruin me instead."

"You know," Iksander said. "I'm not the enemy of wealth and privilege you and your cronies seem to think."

"No, you're the enemy of tradition. You want to narrow the gulf between high and low. To be a friend to the poor and a liberator of djinniya. You don't even see how intolerable your positions are." LaBass seemed weary but not repentant. His gaze fastened on Yasmin. "You're a loss, I confess. You'd have made a wonderful addition to the cause."

"If you weren't a traitor, I'd say 'thank you.' Oh, wait. No, I wouldn't. You're repulsive for too many reasons on top of that."

LaBass seemed not to register her anger. He snorted morosely. "Humor. I expect I'll miss that for the next little while. By the by—" Now he pinned Iksander with his dark eyes. "I know things you'll want me to confess. Prepare to bargain hard before I cooperate."

"We'll see," Iksander said, no stranger to bargaining himself. "Thanks to Joseph, we know quite a lot already. You might be interested to hear we have Eamon Pappus in custody. You know, the charming fellow who recruited Joseph for your cabal." Iksander clucked his tongue. "He's not exactly stoic, is he? My guards tell me he was singing like a canary before the cuffs were on."

Though LaBass tried to hide it, this, at last, caused him to look alarmed.

~

Yasmin wasn't sure how it happened, but a short while later she and Joseph found themselves alone on the temple grounds. The mist had retreated, and a bright half-moon rode the starry sky. The grassy plateau was abandoned but for a few locals. They moved in the distance as shadowed silhouettes, magically extinguishing the torches that had helped light tonight's drama.

It's done then, she thought. *For now anyway.*

Her breath washed out on a sigh.

"Are you well?" Joseph asked.

"Actually, I'm so relieved I'm exhausted. Dimitriou had that crowd ensorcelled. I was afraid Iksander wouldn't come out victorious."

She felt him consider her. "You respect him."

"He's shown me who he is when he has no need or desire to charm."

"And who is that?"

"A good man. Very nearly the same man as when he plays sultan. You're like him that way. You don't change. You're who you are, through and through." She laughed softly. "I'm more of a chameleon. Suit my face to my company."

"I see your true face, I think. Through and through." She didn't have a chance to pick apart what he meant, because he shook himself. "It's cool out here, and we've very much lost our bed and board. Where do you do wish to go?"

"Home," she said longingly.

"To your parents' villa?"

"I meant my apartment, but of course you're right. My parents will want to hear what happened and see that I'm unharmed."

"We could stop by their house, and then I'll fly you to your apartment."

When she looked at him, his expression was careful. "You're not too tired?"

"No. Besides, I could pilot a carpet in my sleep."

"I accept then. And thank you for your kindness."

He seemed pleased by this, which in turn pleased her.

"This way then," he said. "I nabbed a carpet from the soldiers and stashed it not far from here."

They walked to it side by side. When their shoulders bumped from closeness, it was almost like holding hands.

~

As expected, Yasmin's parents were glad to see her. Balu was home already, and the servants had been called back. They also seemed excited to hear about recent happenings. Hopefully, having fresh news to share made up for the curtailment of their surprise holiday.

Yasmin's father seemed to have decided Joseph could be treated familiarly. They gathered for hot mint tea in the informal parlor, where the floor cushions were designed for comfort and not impressing guests. Balu definitely wasn't over his big adventure. Despite their parents' presence, he recounted Dimitriou's downfall with great relish.

"He went gray," he explained excitedly. "And scaly like a reptile, and then his nose got longer and all droopy. Actually, his nose looked like a limp man part. Which is funny, when you think about it. If his actual man part had stayed that limp, he might not have lost his followers."

"Balu," their mother scolded predictably.

"We've all seen man parts," Balu said.

"Son." Her father looked like he was struggling not to laugh. "That isn't polite tea talk."

"I'm just saying he got his. Life comes at you fast, I guess."

This was human phrasing, but Yasmin caught the gist.

"Speaking of life coming at you," Joseph said. "I wonder what will become of Lady Toraman."

Yasmin had wondered that as well. Safiye might no longer be at Stefan's mercy, but people wouldn't soon forget she'd stood by him. The image of her robed in white like a vestal virgin atop those temple steps, providing cover for a homicidal necrophiliac, would be burned into many brains.

"Don't we know a cousin of the Toramans?" her father asked.

"Oh, yes," her mother answered. "Adelaide Japore, who married the glassmaker. That's two bad matches Safiye has entered into now. I expect the Toramans will have to ship her off to another territory until her reputation recovers."

Joseph sat straighter in alarm. "She can't go into exile. She might need to be questioned!"

Her mother's eyes widened. "But Lady Toraman didn't know about the plot, or so Yasmin claims. I suppose she wouldn't have hated landing in a throne, if it turned out that way. The Toramans always were ambitious."

She was singing a different tune now that Yasmin's association with her former colleague seemed unlikely to do her good.

"Once news spreads, *your* reputation will be fantastic," her brother crowed. "Your first time out as a detective, and look what you accomplished!"

"Helped accomplish," Yasmin corrected.

"Your contribution was essential," Joseph said. "And that's not me flattering you. Iksander will probably give you a medal."

"You see." Balu shoved her shoulder. "You're medal material. Clients will line up around the block."

Yasmin stopped blushing and brightened. "I hadn't thought of that. Lots of clients would be nice, wouldn't it?"

"It'd be extra nice if I could get a raise."

Yasmin laughed. "You've barely worked a week. Despite which, because I'm such a nice boss, you can sleep in tomorrow. We'll start bright if not early at eleven."

A glimpse of her mother's downturned mouth warned she was, yet again, about to protest Yasmin's insistence on earning her livelihood.

"My, look at the time," Yasmin exclaimed, setting down her tea and rising. "Joseph and I should get going."

~

As promised, Joseph flew her to her apartment near the harbor. He landed on the roof, which she planned—as soon as she got a minute—to find lounge chairs and planters for. String lights might be pleasant too. Some of her neighbors had them, and she thought they looked festive. She was still a stranger here. A female curiosity. If she made this a little garden, then sat out here some evenings, she bet the locals would relax enough to make friends with her.

Though he could have lifted off again right away, Joseph swung off the carpet to contemplate the view. "You could put seats up here. It looks like your neighbors do."

"I was just thinking that."

He turned to face her smile. His expression was somber. "I suppose I should let you rest."

"You could come in," she offered. "If you aren't too tired. I've got tea, and I believe I left the place tidy."

He hesitated, thoughts she couldn't read going through his head. "I . . . would like that. Though I think I've had tea enough."

She cursed herself for feeling awkward after everything they'd shared.

You'll sit and chat a bit, she counseled herself as she unspelled the lock on the rooftop door. *Whatever else you and Joseph are to each other, you're friends by now.*

They trooped down the stairs together.

She was hit by a stronger pleasure than she expected as they entered the apartment. Small it might be, but this was her place: her furniture that she'd chosen, her closet-sized kitchen. Because the sitting room felt stale, she went to one of the deep-set windows and opened it. She could do that if she wanted—with or without a shielding screen.

"You know," she said, leaning out to savor the late-night breeze, "the air around here is fine after the market's closed. There's hardly any fish smell left."

"You're settling in."

"I guess I am." Her right to choose asserted, she shut the pierced wooden privacy shutters. They'd come with the place, and the cutout patterns were pretty.

Calmer now, she turned to Joseph. He was perched on a cushioned chair arm, watching her intently.

"I'm not sure anyone but I would notice," she said, "but you look a bit nervous."

She meant to set him at his ease. After all, if she ought to be comfortable with him, the reverse was true as well.

Joseph shifted on his perch. "I planned to do this tomorrow, after I'd composed my thoughts. Perhaps it's just as well you invited me in tonight. I suspect more time to think would just make me more nervous."

"More nervous about what?"

He blew out his breath. "First, I'd like to thank you."

"That's not necessary. Everything I did was my own choosing."

"Yasmin."

Though she didn't know where he was heading, she laughed at his suffering tone. "All right. Go ahead. I'll try not to interrupt."

"What I want to thank you for, especially anyway, is helping me feel like myself again. I'm not even sure how it happened. I haven't changed from a week ago. Certainly, I didn't accomplish the magic we did alone. I've noticed, however, that I feel ready to face whatever I have to next. I'm not overconfident, I don't think. Simply . . . steady inside myself."

"I'm glad," she said, and bit back a joke about sex being good for men's self-esteem.

He must have noticed her amusement. "It wasn't the sex. Or not just that. You believe in me, and you're definitely no one's fool. I suppose I needed to share my secrets and still be respected more than I realized."

"Everyone needs that," she said.

He rose and took her hands. Yasmin's pulse jumped inside her wrists. This was more than a thank you.

"I needed it from you," he said in a husky voice. "I wanted you from the start. You're so beautiful even I couldn't mistake that physical reaction. Looking back, though, I also admired you. Your skill. Your spirit. Your willingness to stick your neck out for other djinn. You're brave and smart and, well, pretty much the definition of worthy. If what's inside me isn't more than caring, I don't know what the word 'love' means."

His eyes were gleaming, their golden depths taking on a glow.

Never in her life had anyone looked at her like he was.

"What are you saying?" she asked, terrified to jump to the wrong conclusion.

He squeezed her fingers and filled his lungs. "I'm saying I love you. I was an idiot not to recognize it before. Now that I do, the feeling is so big I think I might burst from it. I want you to marry me, Yasmin. I want you to do me the honor of being my wife."

He was saying everything she'd dreamed of. Her blood surged with happiness. She opened her mouth to accept.

"I can't," she burst out unexpectedly. "I want to," she added as Joseph widened his eyes in shock. "So much I can hardly believe I'm saying this. I love you too, with my whole heart and soul."

"But—?" he said.

He'd pulled her hands to his chest. To her relief, he didn't let her go but continued to caress them. She took courage from that and went on.

"Until I moved here to start my business, I'd never been on my own. I'd never budgeted expenses or cooked myself breakfast. I'd never been the boss of me. I think I needed that as much as you needed someone to know your secrets and accept them."

"I hope you know I wouldn't boss you," Joseph said. "Or expect you to stop working. I hope we can collaborate together again some time."

"I'm gratified to hear you say that."

"I'm still hearing a 'but.'"

"I haven't had *enough* of this," she said in a worried rush. "Of standing on my own two feet. Of answering to no one but myself. I still want to be with you. Really, truly, I do. I hope you won't throw me over because of this."

A smile curved his mouth. "So . . . you want me to be a part of your independent life."

"Yes," she said in relief.

"And if I expressed a preference for being your only lover, you would consider that?"

"More than consider it," she assured. "And, um, naturally I'd prefer to be your only too."

"I'd be honored to pledge that."

"You could stay over here sometimes," she added hopefully. "You know, if that was convenient. I'm aware the sultan has the right to make demands on you."

"Your mother will go bonkers if she finds out."

He was grinning now. Yasmin was pretty sure 'bonkers' wasn't good.

"Do we have to tell her?" she inquired.

He pulled her into a laughing hug. "I see you *do* need more practice being your own woman. I'll leave deciding what to tell your mother to you. I should warn you, I was somewhat forthcoming with your father."

"My father?" She pushed back to look at him.

"The other night, when he invited me for brandy in his study. He saw you had feelings for me. I thought he'd worry less if I explained my changed circumstances regarding my doubled form."

"You told him *that?"* Yasmin had trouble finding breath. "I thought you considered not being a eunuch a state secret."

Joseph colored the slightest bit. "I didn't want him thinking his daughter had lost her mind—falling for half a man, as it were."

"You never were half a man, though I appreciate the consideration." She frowned as a new thing occurred to her. "He'll tell my mother. The first time she wistfully mentions grandchildren."

"Won't she keep it between her and him?"

"Possibly," Yasmin said. "She doesn't tell her friends everything. Still, you shouldn't count on it."

"Maybe it doesn't have to be such a secret anymore. Magically speaking, you and I together are nearly the equal of what I was before. If Iksander were to put you on retainer, as a royal consultant, he'd seem just as defended as before."

"You wouldn't mind telling him the truth?"

Joseph stroked a loose lock behind her ear. "I should have told him already. I think, perhaps, I underestimated his capacity to value me as I am."

"He won't mind that we're together," she said surely.

"No," Joseph agreed. "I think he'll be happy for both of us."

"I'm happy for us too. And for Balu! He'd hate if you felt awkward continuing as his friend."

"I'd have tried not to disappoint him, no matter what happened between us. I like your brother. He's a genuinely good-hearted, intelligent young man."

Affection welled up inside her. That was Joseph to the core. He didn't form connections lightly, but when he did he stuck to them.

She took his face gently between her hands. "You, Joseph the Magician, are the best man I've ever met."

"Well, that can't be true. What about—"

She kissed him to silence.

"Hm," he said after a few enjoyable minutes. His hands slid over her in way that inspired impatience. "I suppose it would be rude to contradict you."

"Very." She squeezed his bottom as he was squeezing hers.

"There is, however, always room for improvement. You know, by way of practice."

"What would you like to practice?"

Smiling, he whispered in her ear.

"All right," she said, unable to repress an anticipatory shiver. "Let's see how tidy I left my bed . . ."

She doubted he cared. He pulled off her clothes between kisses on their short, stumbling journey to her bedroom.

"No lights," he said when she would have spelled on the overheads. "You're lovely by moonlight."

That was hard to object to, especially when he magicked his robes away. Slats of brightness from the shuttered window played over him beautifully.

She purred as she rubbed his fabulous, muscled chest.

He jerked when her thumbs stroked around his navel, and again when she pulled both hands up his rigid cock. It seemed natural to go to her knees before him, to tip him toward her mouth, to sheath her teeth with her lips, and suck him adoringly.

"Yasmin," he moaned as she bobbed slowly up and down.

His fingers kneaded her scalp. His hold was light, but he couldn't quite help directing her. The muscles of his thighs bunched tighter, his hips beginning to thrust in age-old motions. She loved the power she had to bring him pleasure, to wind him closer to the crucial point where he would lose control. When his breath broke at a well-aimed caress from her pointed tongue, she drew back to look up his lean body.

She wasn't sure she'd ever been so happy.

"Ready to practice now?" she teased.

He laughed, plenty of humor but little sound in it. "Showing me how it's done, are you?"

"I'm sure you can show me a thing or two. If you put your mind to it."

He could. He levitated her off the floor and dropped her onto the bed.

She gasped in surprise at the sudden landing. The power he'd used to lift her tingled on her skin.

He laughed and crawled over her. "I'm done in now," he warned. "I'll have to do the rest manually."

"Believe me, I'm not worried about your perf— Why are you turning around like that?"

"Oh, go on, a fine former concubine like you? Surely you've seen pictures."

She had, but: "You don't think that's too advanced for us?"

He put his mouth on her and chuckled.

My, she thought, squirming irresistibly closer to his face. He was good at this! The pull he put into his cheeks as he tongued her clitoris sent voluptuous streaks of feeling into her sex and spine. Was she as adept as him? But maybe it didn't matter. She knew he liked what she did. Besides, since he'd positioned them head to toe, his beautiful, throbbing cock was delightfully convenient.

She took the hint and petted it full length.

His wriggle and hum encouraged her to resume her previous activities.

As soon as she surrounded him with her mouth, a current of desire and pleasure, an infinity loop for lovers, sprang up between their bodies.

"*God,*" Joseph moaned against her. He took her in again a moment later, his efforts even more intense, even more effective than before.

She worked to focus on what she did to him: pulling him in, sliding him out, laving him wet and warm. His veins rose to greater firmness against her tongue, his gasps coming as raggedly as hers. She pushed up his upper leg to massage his testicles. His spine tensed for that—as if the sensations were *too* sharply pleasurable.

He reminded her this part of him was new.

"Don't stop," he rasped when she eased up. "I love that. I promise I'll hold on."

A promise to hold on suggested he didn't intend to finish with them in this arrangement. That intrigued her enough to decide she'd hold on too.

They twitched with mini-quakes of almost-peaking before he turned around again.

"Me on top," she panted, nudging him onto his back.

He smiled and breathed hard while she swung on top of him. "I'm all yours, beloved. Use me as you will."

What she willed was to slide him slo-ow-ly inside of her.

"Mmm," he hummed, once his thick, thudding cock was fully embedded.

She was on her knees, wriggling just a little—the better to enjoy her seat on his hard saddle. His glowing eyes crinkled with a smile as he squirmed similarly beneath her. His hands caressed her bare upper arms, spreading excitement throughout her entire body.

"Wouldn't you like to come closer?"

His tone was polite, his expression teasingly suggestive.

Yasmin came down on her elbows. "Closer like this?"

He kissed her in answer, the motions of his tongue tempting and delicate. She shivered with rising pleasure. Her breasts had settled on his chest, and she suspected they both liked that. This time, when her hips wriggled, they seemed to do it by themselves.

"I'd like to thrust in earnest now," she confessed.

His eyes fired, his pelvis lifting as he swelled fuller inside her. "You'd make me happy if you would."

His hands slid around her hips, gripping them just hard enough to share control with her. She pushed upright again to ride him, vigor seeming what they both craved. He moaned at her careful upward draw, and again for her downward push. Her walls clasped his penis in soft tight warmth, the crazy pulse inside her matching the crazy pulse in him. Sensing the time for restraint was over, she planted her palms on his pectorals and gave him everything she had.

Their cries rose together then.

"Yes," he urged, hips shoving up off the bed at her.

She flung her head back and rolled on him harder.

She had no words, only groans and gasps as their mutual urgency rose. He palmed her breasts, her waist, then focused on the apex of her feeling at the top of her pussy lips. Her approaching climax threatened to overwhelm her. He made being on top seem easier than it was. Working herself on him felt distractingly wonderful. As wound up as she was getting, directing her thrusts for both their benefit was difficult. It didn't help that his chest was sweating. She had to dig in to keep her grip.

He must not have minded. He cursed with pleasure through gritted teeth.

"God," he choked out. "I'm going to explode."

They went together, clamping tight, shoving deep. Heat rushed powerfully into her as her body shuddered with ecstasy. The spasms were white-hot sweet. She felt them most in her sex, but the honeyed tingles spread outward too.

She sighed long and low in the aftermath.

When she opened her eyes, he was smiling up at her.

"What?" she asked, because he appeared to be holding back a laugh.

"I think I'm not the only one who's getting more confident."

A blush joined the heat already basting her sweaty cheeks. She tossed her head loftily. "You're an acceptable practice partner."

"Just acceptable?"

"I'd go as far as inspirational."

He gave in to the laugh and rolled her under him. His strong limbs were warm and loose. "As it happens, I find you inspiring too. Give me a minute, and we can practice more."

The lovemaking that ensued was calmer but quite enjoyable.

"I love you," she said, snuggling into him afterward.

He smiled as he kissed her brow. Her long hair spilled across them in lieu of a blanket. "I shall always endeavor to be worthy of your esteem."

"Shall you?" she teased in response to his formality.

Against her temple, his smile broadened. "At the least, I'll make you breakfast in bed tomorrow."

"Good enough." She rubbed his chest before kissing it. "I'm sure I'll enjoy waking up to that."

The assumptions behind their joking pleased both of them.

"Yasmin?" he said a moment later.

Something in his voice made her go up on one elbow. The bedroom was dim, but a soft gold glow burned behind his eyes. When he didn't speak, she ran one fingertip down the side of his somber face. Was his expression a little shy?

"Tell me," she said reassuringly.

He swallowed before he did. "You make me feel like I finally have a home . . . a connection rather than just a room whose door I shut behind me at the end of the day. Everyone I know seems to have those ties, or if not, the hope of them. You make me believe I can belong somewhere."

Her eyes stung as she stroked his cheek. "You belong," she said huskily. "I hope you'll belong with me even if I haven't said 'yes' yet."

"*Yet*," he repeated, his mouth curving. He was a man, all right. The smug triumph in his tone left no doubt of it.

"You can count on me," she said, rather than roll her eyes. "I'm not going anywhere."

He heard her seriousness—and the echo of his own words. When she lay down again, he rested his head against her breast. She hugged him lightly, and his hand caressed her hip. The comfort the gestures brought was new.

This is love too, she thought. *This desire to soothe each other.*

"Excellent," he said sleepily, his lashes tickling her skin as his eyelids shut. "Someone has to eat that breakfast I'll be cooking . . ."

CHAPTER TWENTY

The Detective

As promised, Joseph served her in bed the next morning. Because he didn't only serve her breakfast, her smile wouldn't leave her mouth as she bounced down the building stairs to work.

Though she was a few minutes early, Balu sat bright-eyed and smoky-tailed at his station in the reception area.

"Tea," he said, handing her a steaming glass in a pretty brass holder.

She took it by the handle and patted his shoulder.

"Yes," he agreed, though she hadn't said a word. "I *am* the best co-detective ever."

"Secretary," she corrected dryly, already turning toward her office.

"Don't disappear yet. Someone from Justice messaged as I arrived. They want you to come in for a deposition as soon as possible."

She paused and looked at him. "Scroll them back. See if I can do it this afternoon. I'll answer questions better if I review my case notes first."

Her ordinance manuals could use a review as well. This was a serious legal matter, involving threats against the state. She wasn't certain how much of Safiye's business she was required—or allowed—to share. Did her father know a good lawyer? Maybe she needed advice from a professional.

Her nerves had tightened by the time she shut her door.

That's all right, she calmed herself. *You'll figure this out just like you have other things.*

No one knew everything about a job the first week they were on it.

She laughed softly and headed for her desk. Most people didn't have a first week like her.

Her hot mint tea tasted especially sweet as she blew on it and sipped.

It ought to taste sweet, of course. Being here, running her own agency, was precious. If men like LaBass and Dimitriou had succeeded in stealing Iksander's throne, the simple act of sitting in this office could have been forbidden her. Thankfully, the criminals were locked up in tiny, escape-proof cells. When she'd asked, Joseph had assured her they wouldn't be at all comfortable. No fancy food. No servants. No compliant mistresses.

Their lawyers will dread visiting, he'd promised.

Yasmin wouldn't apologize for being glad of that.

As long as I'm being interrogated, I should mention Ubba Halfdan, she thought a sip later. Considering the previous day's turmoil, the folks at Justice might forget Dimitriou stole his estate from its rightful heir. Though the mists would have swallowed the altered will by now, Joseph had filmed the document. Assuming the rest of the footage held up in court, it should count as valid. With luck, the ifrit's murderously acquired wealth could be yanked from his scaly hands.

That possibility inspired an outright grin.

On top of everything else, Dimitriou would hate losing his title.

She'd finished her tea and was paging through an ordinance manual when Balu tapped on the door. Rather than get up, she spelled it open a few inches. Balu stuck his head in.

"We've got a client," he said, low and confidential. "She's crying, and she looks rich."

Okay, maybe—as Balu's boss—she needed to train him in sensitivity.

"Send her in," she said. "And ask if she'd like water."

She rose to greet the woman, who was indeed weeping. She startled Yasmin by immediately gripping both her hands. This wasn't a common greeting between strangers.

"*Thank you*," the djinniya said, squeezing her fingers fervently. "My sister has gone missing. It's been two weeks since anyone heard from her. The authorities think she's run away with a man, but I don't believe it. I thought I'd go mad until my seamstress told me about your agency. Just knowing you exist has given me hope again."

"Well," Yasmin said, gently rubbing the woman's arm. "I'm happy to have done so. I'll do my best to find the truth for you."

Modest as it was, her promise caused the djinniya to break into renewed sobs. Supplied for the situation, Yasmin offered her a clean handkerchief. Protectiveness rose inside her as the woman tried to compose herself. Pride rose too, partly for the services she could offer but also for her visitor. Whatever had happened to this woman's sister, she wasn't going to sit around waiting for someone else to act.

Djinniya like her are why I'm doing this, Yasmin thought.

"Please make yourself comfortable," she said, gesturing to the guest cushion. "Tell me everything you know about your sister, and we can get started."

Though the topic was serious—and engrossing—as they spoke, she was aware that thoughts of Joseph were warming her. He was right. Being believed in by someone worthy was steadying. Gratifying as it was to stand on her own two feet, it was also good to find a partner who made her feel stronger.

Please enjoy this excerpt from *Hidden Talents*,
the book that kicks off my Hidden series!

Hidden Talents

Werewolf cop Adam swears to protect and serve all the supernatural creatures in Resurrection, but he also watches out for unsuspecting human Talents who wander in from Outside.

Telekinetic Ari is just such a wanderer. She's tracking a crime boss who wants to exploit her gift for his own evil ends—a mission that puts her on a collision course with the hottest cop in the RPD.

Adam wants the crime boss too, but mostly he wants Ari. She's the mate he's yearned for all his life. Problem is, getting a former street kid into bed with the Law could be his toughest case to date.

"*Hidden Talents* is the perfect package of supes, romance, mystery and HEA!"
—paperbackdolls.com

CHAPTER ONE

Dusk settled over the city of Resurrection like a blanket of bad news.

That's me, Ari thought, flexing her right fist beside her hip. *Bad news with a capital B.*

This wasn't just whistling in the dark. Ari had been bad news to some people in her life. To her parents. To every teacher she'd had in high school. *You'll come to no good*, they'd threatened, and she couldn't swear they'd been wrong. Certainly, she hadn't turned out to be a blessing to Maxwell or Sarah. Because of her, Max was in the hospital with too many broken bones in his arms to count, and Sarah was God knew where. But at least Ari was trying to change that. At least she was trying to be bad news to people who deserved it.

To her dismay, Resurrection, NY wasn't what she'd been led to believe when she'd looked it up on the internet.

She stood on the crest of a weedy hill outside the metropolis, her presence hidden by the deeper shadow of a highway overpass. She'd been expecting a down-on-its-luck backwater. Storefronts stuck in the seventies. Maybe a real town square and a civil war battlefield. Instead, she found an actual cityscape. The skyline wasn't Manhattan tall, more like Kansas City. Few buildings looked brand new, but many were substantial. They formed a grid of streets and parkland whose core had to encompass at least five miles. This was definitely more than a backwater. Resurrection reminded her of city photos from the early decades of the last century, when *skyscraper* meant something exciting. What could have been a twin to the Chrysler Building stuck up from the center of downtown, reigning over its brethren.

Finding the Eunuch among all that was going to take some doing.

You have to find him, she told her sinking stomach. If she didn't, she and her very small gang of peeps would be looking over their shoulders for the rest of their lives. At twenty-six and thankfully still counting, Ari had endured more than enough hiding. She was stronger now. She'd been *practicing*. Henry Blackwater, aka, the Eunuch, wouldn't know what hit him.

"Right," she said sarcastically to herself. She'd be lucky if she got out of here alive.

But faint heart never vanquished fair villain. Ari knew she'd been born the way she was for a reason. Maybe here, maybe soon, she'd find out what that reason was.

CHAPTER TWO

No one messed with people who belonged to Adam Santini. Unless, of course, the person messing with the person was also Adam's relative.

"You. Ate. My. Beignets." To emphasize his point, Adam's irate cousin, Tony Lupone, was bashing his brother's head against the squad room floor.

Since Rick's skull was made of sterner stuff than the linoleum, he laughed between winces. "What sort of cop—*ow*—eats beignets anyway?"

"Your faggot brother cop, that's who. Your pink-shirted faggot brother cop who's whupping your butt right now."

Amused by their exchange, Adam leaned back against Tony's cluttered desk. The precinct's squad room was a semi-bunker in the basement. A mix of ancient file cabinets and desks were balanced by some very revved-up technology. Grimy electrum grates on the windows protected them, more or less, from things that went bump in the night outside. The hodgepodge suited the men who manned it better than most workplaces could. Rough-edged but smart was the werewolf way. At the moment, Tony was so rough-edged his eyes glowed amber in his flushed face. His big brother could have defended himself better than he was, if it weren't for his rule against hitting his siblings.

"Ow! Lou!" he complained to Adam. "You're supposed to be my best friend. Aren't you going to call off this squirt?"

"You're the one who ate his fancy donuts."

"All dozen of them!" Tony snarled, his grievance renewed. "I brought them in to share."

"Shit," said longhaired Nate Rivera, Adam's other cousin, once removed. "Now *I* want to whup you."

Considering even-tempered Nate was growling, Adam judged it time to end the wrestling match. "All right, you two. Enough. Rick, I'm docking your next paycheck for the price of his beignets. Dana, if you'd be so kind, raid the coffee fund and pick up another batch for tomorrow night."

"None of which you're going to enjoy, Mister Pig!" Panting from the exertion of trying to give his brother a concussion, Tony rose and pointed angrily down at him. "You can choke on your damned donuts."

Wisely, Rick remained where he was while his little brother stalked back to the break room, where his heinous crime had been discovered. The dress code for the detectives was casual. Rick's gray RPD T-shirt was rucked way up his six-pack abs. His concave stomach didn't betray his gluttony. His fast werewolf metabolism saw to that.

"My head," Rick moaned, still laughing. "Come on, cuz. Give your beta a hand up."

Adam sighed and obliged. None of his wolves were small, but Rick was six four and all muscle. Even with supe strength, Adam grunted to haul him up. "Some second you are. You had to know this would cause trouble."

"I couldn't help myself. The box smelled so good. Plus, he was totally obnoxious about bringing them in for everyone."

"So you knew you were stealing food from my mouth?" Nate interjected, not looking up from his paperwork. "Not cool."

"He's sucking up. Ever since he came out, he's been—" Rick snapped his muzzle shut, but it was too late.

"Uh-huh," Nate said in his dry laid-back way. He'd spun around in his squeaky rolling chair to face Rick. "Ever since he came out, your brother stopped being a butch-ass prick. In fact, ever since he came out, he's been the nicest wolf around here. You don't like that 'cause you're used to being everyone's favorite."

"Crap." The way Rick rubbed the back of his neck said he knew he was in the wrong. Being Rick, he couldn't stay dejected long. A grin flashed across his handsome olive-skinned face. "Can't I still be everyone's favorite? Do I have to turn gay too?"

"I don't know," Nate said, returning to his work. "So far only gay boys bring us good breakfasts."

Seeing Rick's private wince, Adam patted his back and rubbed. Touchy-feely creatures that werewolves were, the contact calmed both of them. He knew Rick was still working on accepting his little brother's big announcement. Werewolves were some of the most macho supes in Resurrection, a city that had plenty to choose from. Adam knew Rick loved his brother just as much as before. He suspected Rick was mostly worried Tony would end up hurt. Being responsible for policing America's only supernatural-friendly town made the wolves enough of a target. Turning out to be gay on top of that was as good as taping a target onto your back.

"Tony will be all right," Adam assured his friend. "Everyone here is adjusting to the new him."

Rick rubbed his neck once more and let his hand drop. Worry pinched his dark gold eyes when they met Adam's. "They're pack. They have to love him."

Adam didn't believe this but wasn't in the mood to argue. Plenty of folks endowed being pack with mystical benefits. Some were real of course, but as alpha, Adam wasn't comfortable relying on magic to cement his authority. He thought it best to actually *be* a competent leader.

"Boss," Dana their dispatcher said. The young woman had her own corner of the squad room. Apart from its cubby walls, it was open. Banks of sleek computers surrounded her, each one monitoring different sectors of the city. The sole member of the squad who wasn't a relative, Dana was the most superstitious wolf Adam had ever met. Anti-hex graffiti scrawled across her work surfaces, the warding so thick he couldn't tell one symbol from another. How they worked like that was beyond him. Despite the quirk, Adam took her instincts seriously. Right then, she didn't look happy. Her silver dreamcatcher earrings were trembling.

"Boss, we've got a suspected M without L in the abandoned tire store on Twenty-Fourth."

M without L referred to the use of magic without a license. Adam's hackles rose. Jesus, he hated those. "Who's reporting the incident?"

"Gargoyle on the Hampton House Hotel." She touched her headset and listened. "He says it's a Level Four."

Adrenaline surged inside him, making his palms tingle. Gargoyles were rarely wrong about magical infractions. While the strength levels went up to eight, four was nothing to sneeze at. Thumb and finger to his mouth, Adam blew a piercing whistle to get his men's attention.

"Suit up," he said. "We've got a probable ML on Twenty-Fourth."

"Don't forget your earpieces," Dana added. "I'll help coordinate from here."

Adam's men were already loping to the weapons room. "Load for bear," he said as he followed them. "We don't know what we're in for."

~

Resurrection, New York couldn't have existed without the fae. For nearly two hundred years, it had sat on an outfolded pocket of the fae's other-dimensional homeland, *in* the human world but only visible to a special few.

Those who wandered in from Outside found it less alien than might be expected. The founding faeries had used the Manhattan of the 1800s as their architectural crib sheet. Since then, the bigger apple had continued to provide inspiration. Immigrants especially liked to recreate pieces of their native land. Resurrection had its own Fifth Avenue and Macy's, its own subway and museums. Little Italy still flourished here, though—sadly—its theater district was as moribund as its role model. Adam was familiar with the theories that Resurrection was an experiment, created to see if human and fae could live peaceably as in days of old. Whether this was the reason for its existence, he couldn't say.

The only fae he knew were exceptionally tight-lipped.

Whatever their motives, Resurrection had become a haven for humans with a trait or two extra. Shapechangers of every ilk thrived here. Vamps were tolerated as long as they behaved themselves. The same was true of demons and other Dims: visitors from alternate dimensions who entered through the portals. If a being could get along, it could stay. If it couldn't, it had to go. And if the visitors didn't want to go, Adam and the rest of the RPD were just the folks to make sure they went anyway.

The job fit Adam better than his combat boots, and those boots fit him pretty good. He loved keeping order, protecting the vulnerable, kicking butt and cracking skulls as required. The only duty he didn't like was apprehending rogue Talents. Sorcerers were trained at least, and demons who went dark side were generally predictable. Talents were the wild cards in an already dangerous deck. Their power was raw, depending not on spells but on how much energy they could channel. That amount could be a trickle or a mother-effing hell of a lot.

The previous year, a Level Seven Talent who'd gotten stoned on faerie-laced angel dust had taken down the six-lane Washington Street Bridge. Just popped it off its piers and let it drop in the North River. If the bridge's gargoyles hadn't swooped in to save what cars they could, the loss of life would have been astronomical. Adam still had nightmares about talking the tripping Talent into surrendering. If tonight's incident ran along similar lines, he might need a vacation.

Along with the rest of his team, Adam clutched the leather sway-strap above his head. Nate was driving the black response van because no one else dared claim the wheel from the ponytailed Latino. They all wore body armor and helmets, plus an assortment of protective charms. Their rifles leaned against the long side benches between their knees. The guns could fire a range of ammo, both conventional and spelled. Rick, who had a knack for effective prayer, was quietly calling on the precinct's personal guardian angel. Sometimes this worked and sometimes it didn't, but even the atheists among them figured better safe than sorry.

"God," Tony said, tapping the back of his head against the van's rattling wall. "I hope this isn't another thing like the bridge."

"Amen," Carmine agreed. The stocky were was the oldest member of their squad, the only one who was married, and—yes—another of Adam's cousins.

Before he could smile, Adam's earpiece beeped.

"You're four blocks out," Dana said. "The gargoyle is reporting another series of power flares. Still nothing higher than a Four."

That was good news. Unless, of course, the Talent was warming up.

"Okay, people," Adam said. "Watch your tempers once we get inside. Be safe but no killing unless you have no choice."

He didn't warn them against hesitating. Given their inbred hair-trigger werewolf nature, hesitating wasn't an issue.

~

The defunct tire store sat on a small parking lot between a very well locked print shop and a transient hotel. Apart from the hotel, which wasn't exactly bustling, the area wasn't residential. A cheap liquor outlet on the corner drew a few customers, but the main business done here after dark was drugs. Most of the product filtered in from the human world. Since this was Resurrection, some was also exotic. If you knew who to ask, you could score adulterated vamp blood or coke cut with faerie dust. Demon manufactured Get-Hard was popular, though it tended to cause more harmful side effects than Viagra. Every EMT Adam knew had asked why they couldn't get GH off the street. All Adam could answer was that they were doing the best they could.

Policing Resurrection couldn't be about stamping out Evil. It had to be about making sure Good didn't get swallowed.

The reminder braced him as he and his team ran soundlessly from the van onto the buckled and trash-strewn asphalt of the parking lot. His scalp prickled half a second before a soft gold light flared around the edges of the boarded-up back windows.

Adam had answered previous calls to this location. The rear section of the tire store was where vehicles had been cranked up on lifts for servicing. Fortunately, there was plenty of cover for slipping in. Unfortunately, lots of flammables were inside. Adam took the anti-burn charm that hung around his neck and whispered a word to it. That precaution seen to, he hand-signaled Rick and Tony to split off and block escape from the front exit.

This left Adam, Carmine and Nate to ghost in the back.

The flimsy combination lock on the door to the service bay had been snapped—probably magically. Adam and his two detectives ducked under the low opening. Inside, the scent and feel of magic was much stronger, the air thicker and hotter than it should have been in autumn. A male voice moaned in pain farther in, standing Adam's hair on end. Without needing to be told, Nate peeled off to the right. Adam and Carmine took the left.

Scattered heaps of tires allowed them to creep up on their goal without being seen. One bare bulb dangled from a wire, lighting the far end of the garage. In the dim circle beneath it, the Talent had her moaning victim tied to a plastic chair. The sight of her stopped Adam in his tracks. Christ, she was little. Five foot nothing and probably a hundred and small change. She looked to be in her twenties and wore the kind of clothes street kids did. Ripped up black jeans. Ancient T-shirts that didn't fit. Her oversized Yankees jacket had its sleeves torn out and was decorated with unidentifiable small objects. Her hair was a shade of platinum not found in nature, standing in white spikes around her head. A swirling red pattern was dyed it, as if her coiffure were her personal art project. What really got him though, what had his breath catching in his throat, was the clean-cut innocence of her face. Outfit and hair aside, she looked like a tiny Iowa farm girl.

It made his chest hurt to look at her. The part of him that needed to protect others wanted to protect her.

Knowing better than to trust in appearances, Adam shook the inclination off. He tapped the speaker fixed into his vest with the signal for everyone to hold. The victim was still alive. They could afford to take a minute to discover what they were up against.

As they watched, the girl lifted her right hand. Pale blue fire outlined her curled fingers. Her already bloodied victim shrank back within his ropes. He was some kind of elf-human mixblood with long gray hair. He was a lot bigger than the Talent, but that didn't mean their fight had been fair. Despite the elf blood, he didn't give off much of a magic vibe. A near null was Adam's guess. His run-in with the Talent had left damage. He looked bad: eyes swollen, bruises, shallow cuts bleeding all over. Though he seemed familiar, as injured as he was, he was hard to identify. Even his smell was distorted by blood and fear.

"I can do this all night," the Talent said in a voice that was way too sweet for a torturer. "Or you can tell me where to find the Eunuch."

Carmine and Adam came alert at that. This was a name they knew too damn well.

"Lady," said her bloodied victim. "I have no idea who you mean."

The girl closed her glowing hand gently. The man she was interrogating arched so violently he and the plastic chair fell over. He screamed as blood sprayed from a brand-new cut on his chest. Carmine started forward, but Adam gripped his shoulder.

"Wait," he murmured. "That cut was shallow. He's not in immediate danger."

Carmine shook his head but obeyed. When the man stopped writhing, the girl drew a deep slow breath. With no more effort than gesturing upward with one finger, she set man and chair upright. Despite the situation's danger, something inside Adam let out an admiring *whoa.*

"Clearly," she said, "you think you ought to be more afraid of your boss than me."

"Lady," panted the injured man, "*everyone's* more afraid of him."

The girl's lips curved in a smile that had Carmine shivering beside him. Admittedly, the expression was a little scary. For no good reason Adam could think of, it made his cock twitch in his jockstrap.

The Talent spoke silkily. "I'm glad we've established you know who I'm looking for."

Adam expected her to cut him again. Instead, discovering her victim did know the Eunuch inspired her to up the ante on her torture. The blue fire she'd called to her hand now began gleaming around her feet. She was drawing energy from the earth—and no piddling amount either. Her glowing hand contracted into a fist, and her victim's face went chalky. Adam was pretty sure she was telekinetically squeezing his beating heart. Unless she was really good at medical manipulation, she was going to kill him.

"*Go*," he said sharply into his vest microphone.

Even in human form, werewolves weren't slowpokes. What went down next was textbook perfect. Adam and his men were on the Talent so fast she didn't have a chance to shift her attack to them. Nate got her nose squashed down on the oil-stained floor, then snapped electrum plated cuffs snug around her wrists. The cuffs were charmed so she couldn't break them, no matter how powerful she was. The Talent struggled, then cried out as Nate yanked her roughly onto her feet.

He dropped a depowering charm around her neck for good measure. Immediately, the energy-charged air settled back to normal. The girl gaped at the enchanted medal, then straight up at Adam. Adam's heart stuttered in his chest. Her eyes were a breathtaking corn-fed blue, her lashes a thick dark brown. The twitch she'd sent through his cock morphed into a throb. Carmine shot him a look of surprise. Adam fought an embarrassed flush. The smell of his arousal must have gotten strong enough to seep through his clothes.

"'bout time you showed up," the girl's victim huffed. "This bitch needs to be locked up."

Carmine flipped up his face shield and turned to consider him. The man flinched back, obviously wishing he'd refrained from complaining.

"Aren't you Donnie West?" Carmine asked. "'Cause I know we've got a handful of outstandings on your drug dealing ass."

"Uh," said Donnie, abruptly recognizable under his bruises.

"That's what I thought," said Carmine, and let out his belly laugh.

Through all of this, the Talent's eyes moved from one of them to the other, taking in their gear and their guns and getting wider by the second. When Rick and Tony caught up to them from the front, Tony's upper canines had run out and his amber eyes were glowing. The girl sucked in a breath like this shocked her, though a partial change when younger wolves got excited wasn't uncommon.

"What the—" she said before having to swallow. "What the hell kind of cops are you?"

Still holding her from behind, Nate's slash of a mouth slanted up in a devilish grin. "Well, what do you know," he drawled. "Looks like we've got ourselves an Accidental Tourist."

~

The entire Hidden series is available now.

ABOUT THE AUTHOR

Emma Holly is the award winning, *USA Today* bestselling author of more than forty romantic books featuring billionaires, genies, faeries and just plain extraordinary folks. She loves the hot stuff, both to read and to write!

If you'd like to discover what else she's written, please visit her website at www.emmaholly.com.

Emma runs monthly contests and sends out newsletters that sometimes include notice of special sales. To receive them, go to her contest page.

Thanks so much for reading this book. If you enjoyed it, please consider leaving a review. That kind of support is very helpful!

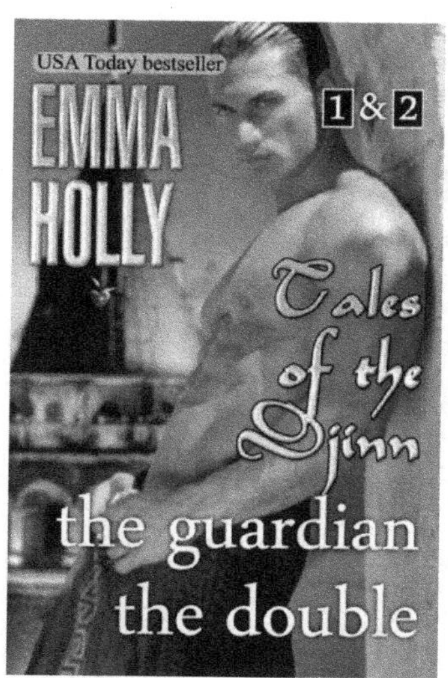

When a mysterious stranger with a briefcase full of cash moves into Elyse's brownstone, she never imagines he's a genie. Cade is gorgeous and sophisticated, but nothing about him adds up . . . that is, until she learns he's a magical being desperate to break a curse on his home city.

Teaming up with a human female isn't the only challenge Elyse's tenant will have to face. His trip to Elyse's world created a duplicate of himself, a not-quite carbon copy who believes *he's* Cade's superior.

Commander Arcadius should be easy for Elyse to resist. He's arrogant, insensitive, and a chauvinist—making it obvious he doesn't think much of her. Then, bit-by-bit, she sees past his prickly exterior. Arcadius is who Cade used to be before they met. If she fell for one man, chances are she'll fall for the other.

Two full-length novels of the Djinn

"FANTASTIC! [T]his may be the best thing she has written to date . . . an epic tale of romantic fantasy."—**In My Humble Opinion**

"Addictive . . . should not be missed!"—**Long and Short Reviews**

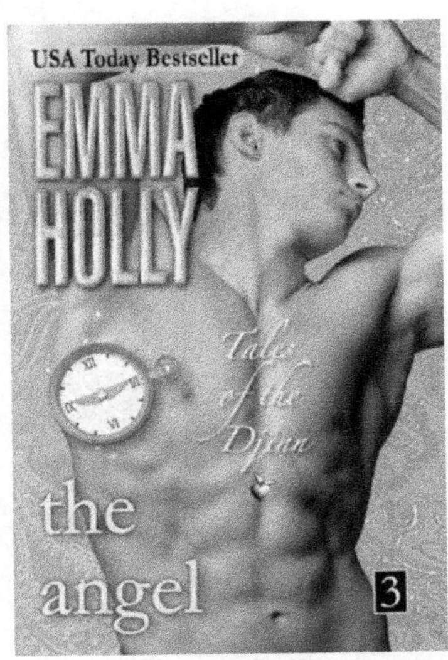

Georgie thinks her life is perfect. She's got an angel for a boyfriend, a library imp to teach her magic, and a mysterious wealthy guardian who funded a childhood most girls only dream about. When sexy genie Iksander claims this life isn't hers, she tells him to screw himself. When he proves it—then asks her to help the endangered citizens of his home, she has a choice to make . . .

Book 3 in The Tales of the Djinn

"Well thought out and surprising! I thoroughly enjoyed this one! A great continuation of the Djinn series."—amazon reviewer, **texas girl makes good**

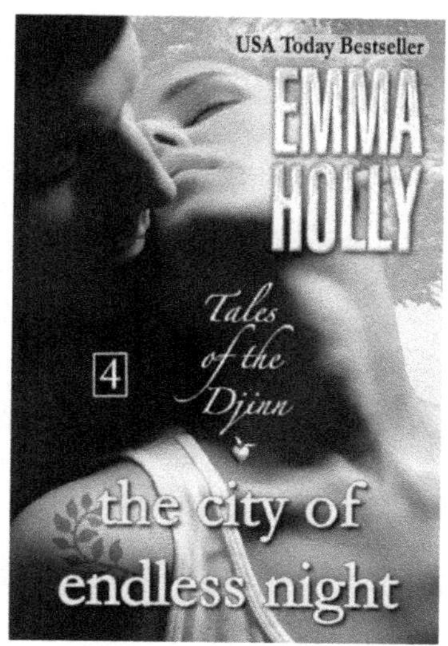

When your boyfriend is a real live angel other men can't compete.

Amateur magician Georgie swears this is true . . . until she and Connor leave everything they know to help the genie world. That's where she discovers angels don't have a monopoly on sex appeal.

Sultan Iksander would rather lose his smoke than fall for Georgie, no matter how smart and brave she is. The human race are rivals to genie kind—and angels are just traitors! His mission to save his people is what's important, not getting tangled up in love triangles.

Only Connor believes in their chances for happiness. This angel knows love is worth fighting for, whatever form it takes.

Book 4 in the Tales of the Djinn

"Emma Holly transports you into a fantastic world of magic, mystery, and erotic delights . . . absolutely wonderful."—D. Antonio, **In My Humble Opinion**

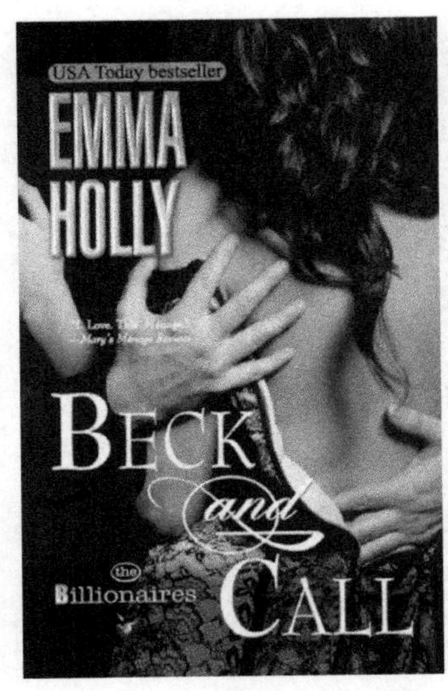

The man everybody wants

Women can't keep their hands off billionaire Damien. The mysterious mogul has it all: fast cars, killer looks, and a brain that just might be his best asset.

Mia loves her job at a PI firm. Her coworker Jake stars in most of her daydreams, so seeing him every day is no hardship.

Jake hasn't believed in human goodness since he worked black ops for the CIA. Romancing innocent Mia is unthinkable, no matter how enticingly submissive she seems to be. Then a case of corporate espionage forces them to pose as dom/sub duo, to catch the eye of accused wrongdoer Damien. No fantasy is off limits for this voyeur—until the attraction the pair exerts lures him to go hands on . . .

"I. love. this. ménage. I am still smiling about these characters.
Another outstanding story."
—Mary's Ménage Reviews

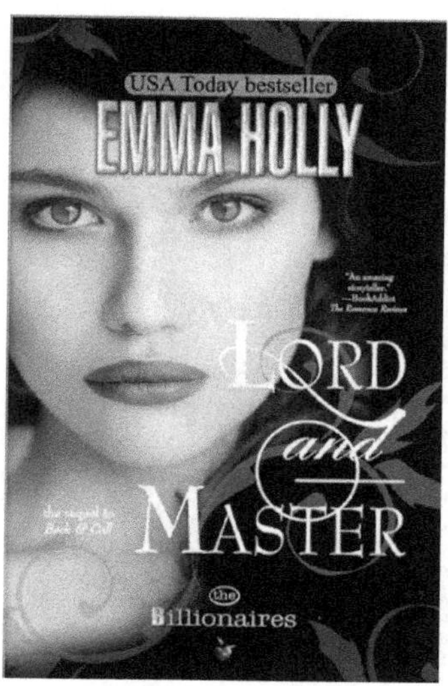

My name is Mia and I'm a lucky girl.

Billionaire Damien didn't stop being moody just because Jake and I moved in with him. Fortunately, I've devised a strategy. I inherited a share in an exclusive erotic club, and they're beta testing a role-play game. Surrounded by period perfect detail, members pretend to be Edwardian lords and ladies . . . or stable masters, if they prefer.

By switching up our dynamic, I'm hoping to smooth the snags in our otherwise fabulous ménage. Neither of my lovers has trouble opening his heart to me, but Damien would benefit from exploring his dominant side, and he and Jake could be easier with each other.

That's my goal anyway. My plan might go up in smoke when Jake and Damien concoct their own scheme for me!

The sequel to *Beck & Call*

"So good it defies description . . .The entire premise of the book was fantastic . . . [L]ives up to and exceeds expectations."—Jean Smith, **x-treme-delusions**

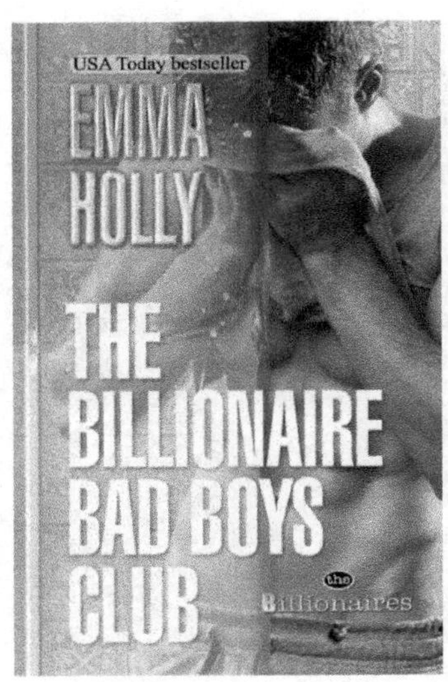

Self-made billionaires Zane and Trey have been a club of two since they were eighteen. They've done everything together: play football, fall in love, even get smacked around by their dads. The only thing they haven't tried is seducing the same woman. When they set their sights on sexy chef Rebecca, these bad boys meet their match!

"This book is a mesmerizing, beautiful and oh-my-gods-hot work of art!"
—**BittenByLove** 5-hearts review

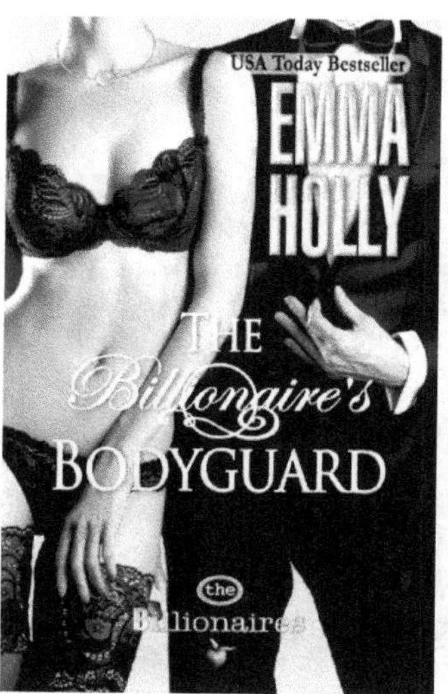

A.J. is as cynical as she is badass, a former cop turned bodyguard. A lifetime of hard knocks taught her not to trust—a handy trait in her line of work. Given the right motivation, she knows anyone will betray their near and dear. Rather than let them betray her, A.J. keeps her shields nailed up.

On the surface, Luke's life seems charmed. He's a Hollywood action hero whose looks inspire fantasies. Known for being easygoing and kind to fans, his latest film made him a billionaire producer. Problem is his high profile is attracting a dangerous class of admirer.

Threats like the one Luke faces aren't new. A.J. saved his life once already. Now he doesn't trust anyone but her to guard him. With a deadly enemy lurking in the shadows, this star-crossed pair better pray A.J.'s skills are sharp!

"A romance story fans of *The Bodyguard* will appreciate ... a great read and an easy recommend."—Xeranthemum, **Long and Short Reviews**

(formerly published as *Star Crossed*)

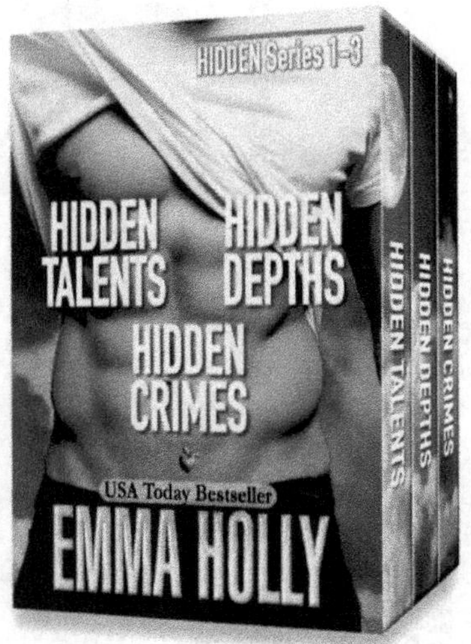

Three full-length paranormal romances: *Hidden Talents, Hidden Depths* and *Hidden Crimes.* Whether they're irresistible werewolf cops, sexy wereseal kings, or sassy firefighting tigresses, these supernatural heroes turn up the heat!

"The perfect package of supes, romance, mystery and HEA!"
—**Paperback Dolls** on *Hidden Talents*

"You will fall head over heels [with] the amazingly sensuous and intensely graphic world . . . One of the best erotic romances I have ever read."
—**BittenByLove** on *Hidden Depths*

"If you are looking for suspense, passion and a touch of the paranormal, don't look any farther than *Hidden Crimes.*"—**Joyfully Reviewed**

CPSIA information can be obtained
at www.ICGtesting.com
Printed in the USA
LVHW011316060119
602928LV00017B/633/P